FALSE FICTION FRACTURED FACT ALTERED

by

Marilyn R. Rosenberg

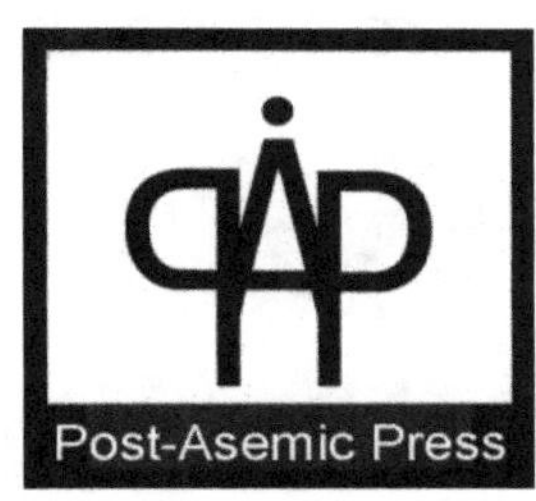

Post-Asemic Press 008

ISBN-13: 978-1-7328788-3-9

Contact: postasemicpress@gmail.com
Postasemicpress.blogspot.com

Cover Art by Marilyn R. Rosenberg

A dynamic and liberating journey that takes us far beyond the neat and disciplined ranks of book typography into the unknown.

—Simon Morley, author of *Seven Keys to Modern Art*

I've known Marilyn R. Rosenberg's work since the mid-80s and have had the honor of publishing her work as an issue of the visual poetry magazine Xerolage. In the era of fact facts and fake fakes these gestures of pen, pencil and brush expose the pre-cognitive gestures of a mind always moving thru a landscape populated by the enigmas of language yet to be understood. We open the notebook to remember, to project, to learn how to think again. The never-ending story never ends, or so we are led to believe. Believe in the marks your hand makes when no one is watching. They will never lie.

—mIEKAL aND, poet and publisher at Xexoxial Editions

FICTION

FALSE FICTION

ALTERED

FICTION

FICTION

FICTION

FICTION

FRACTURED FACT

Marilyn R. Rosenberg

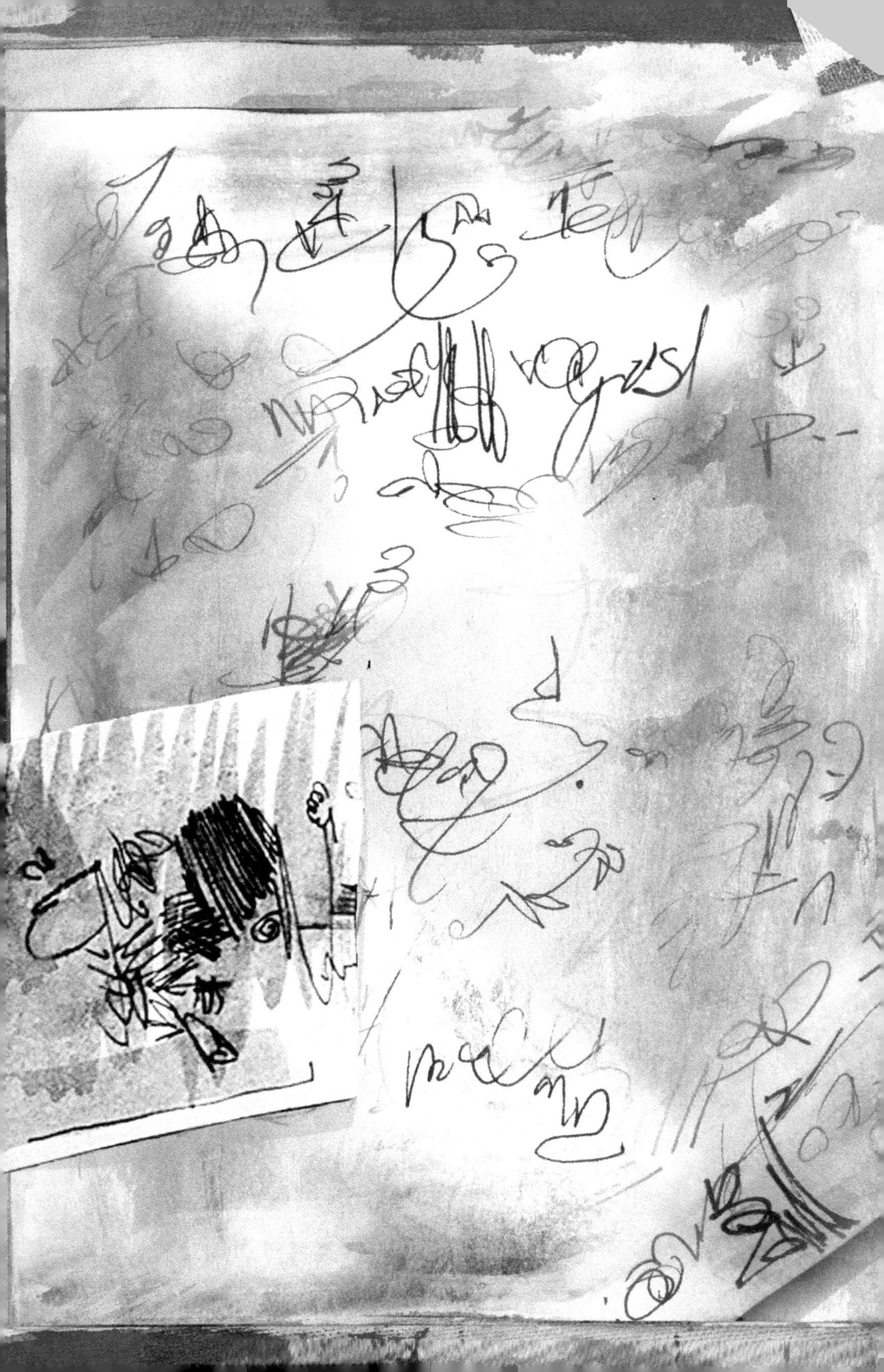

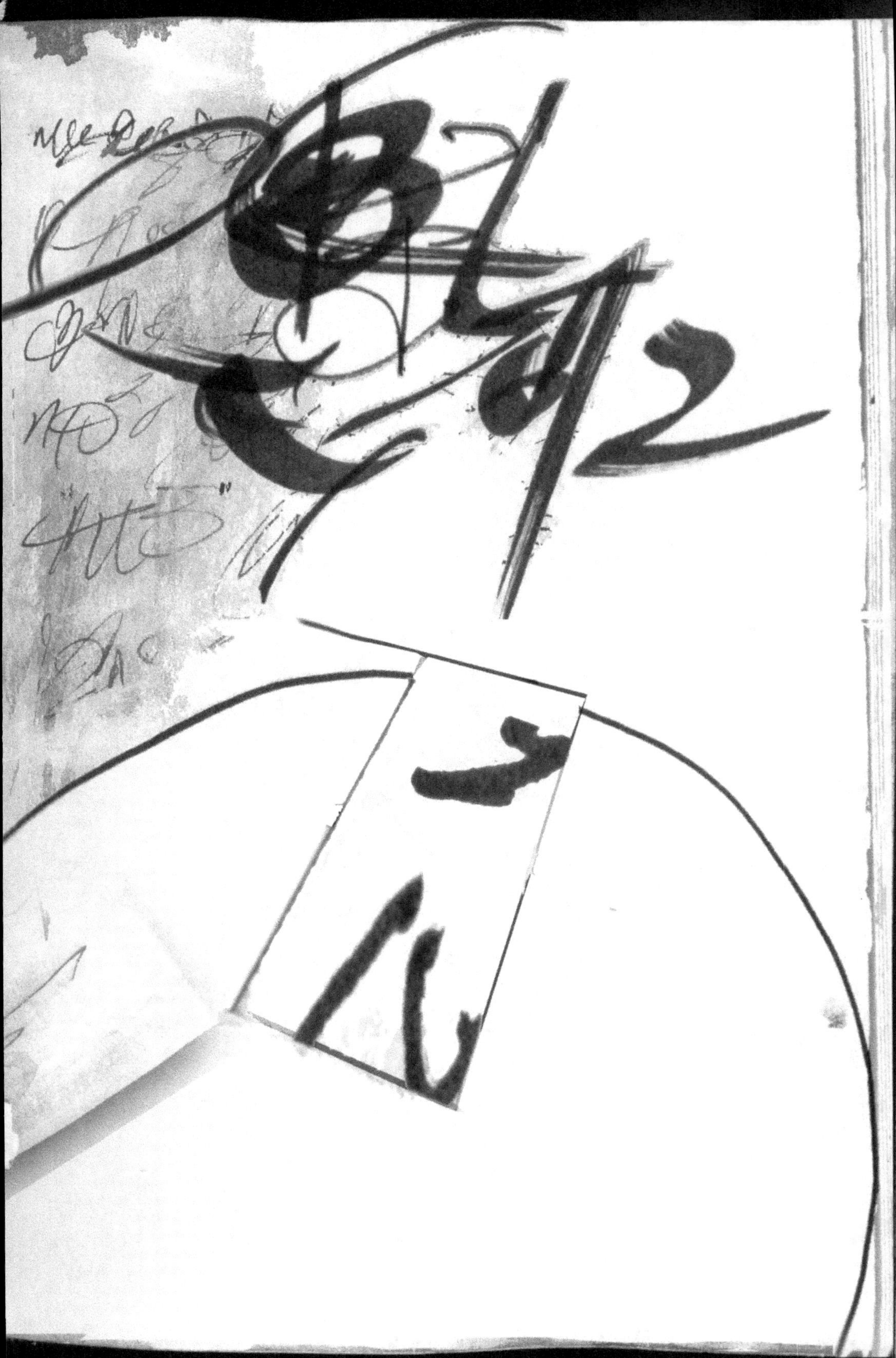

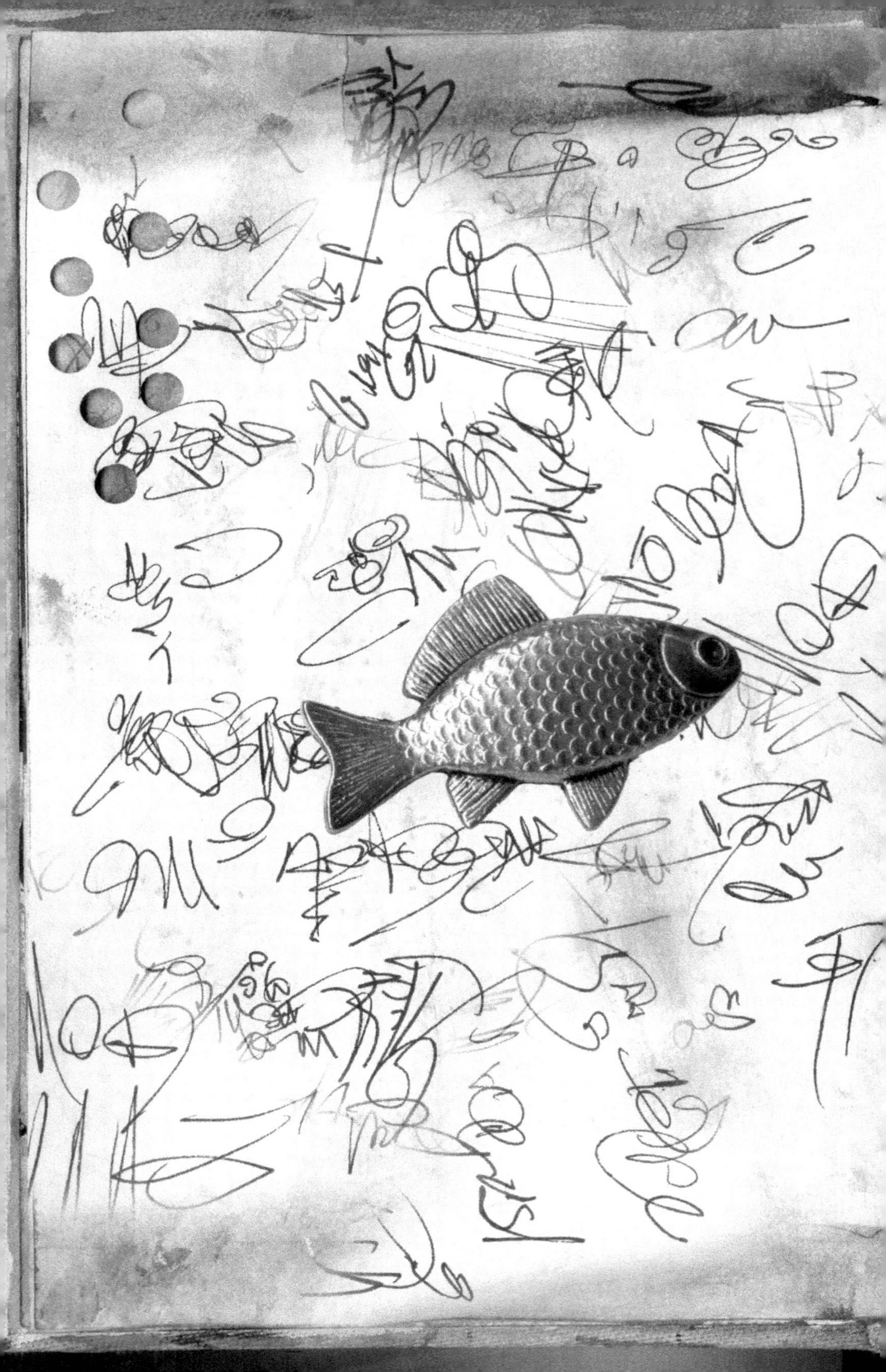

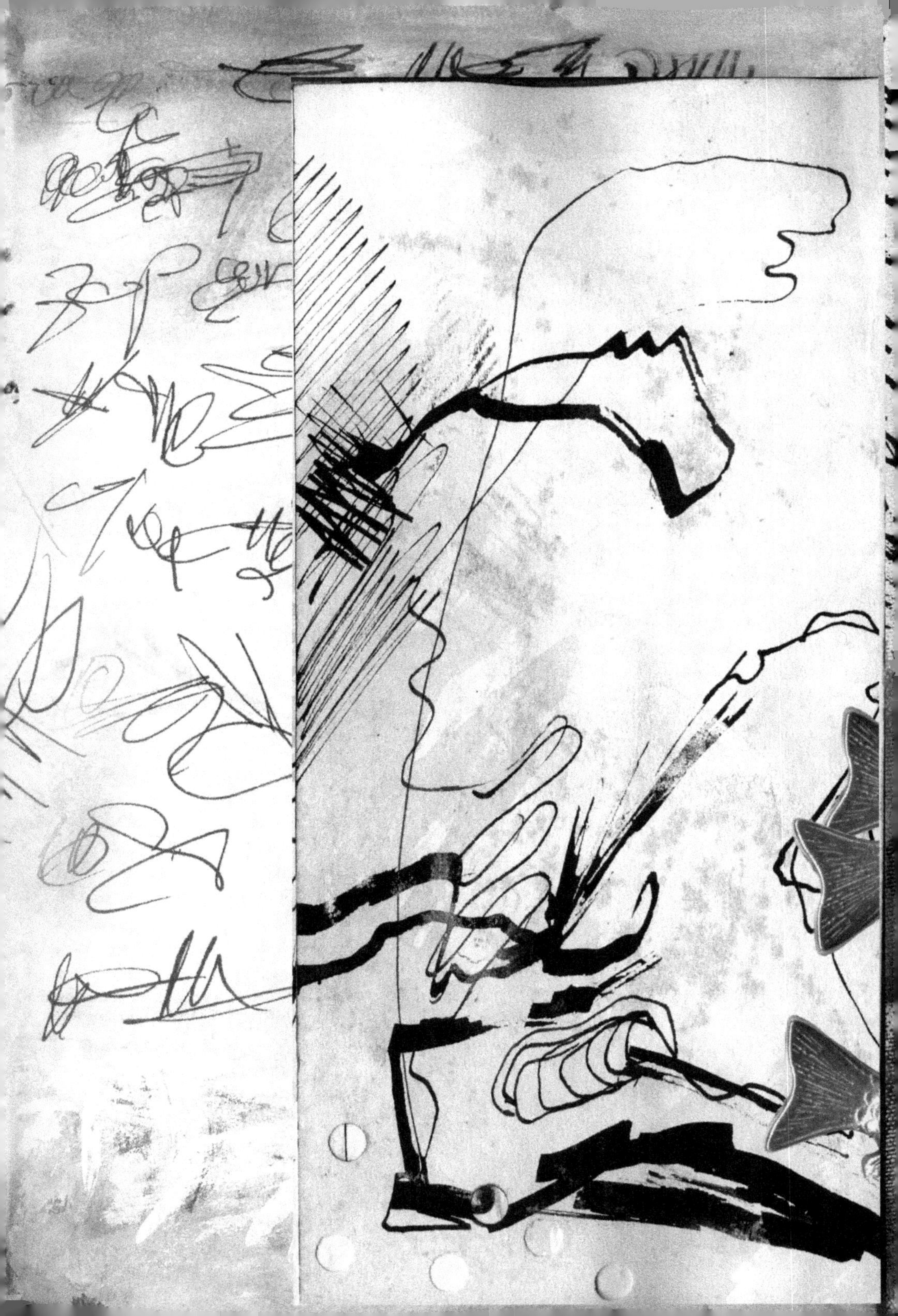

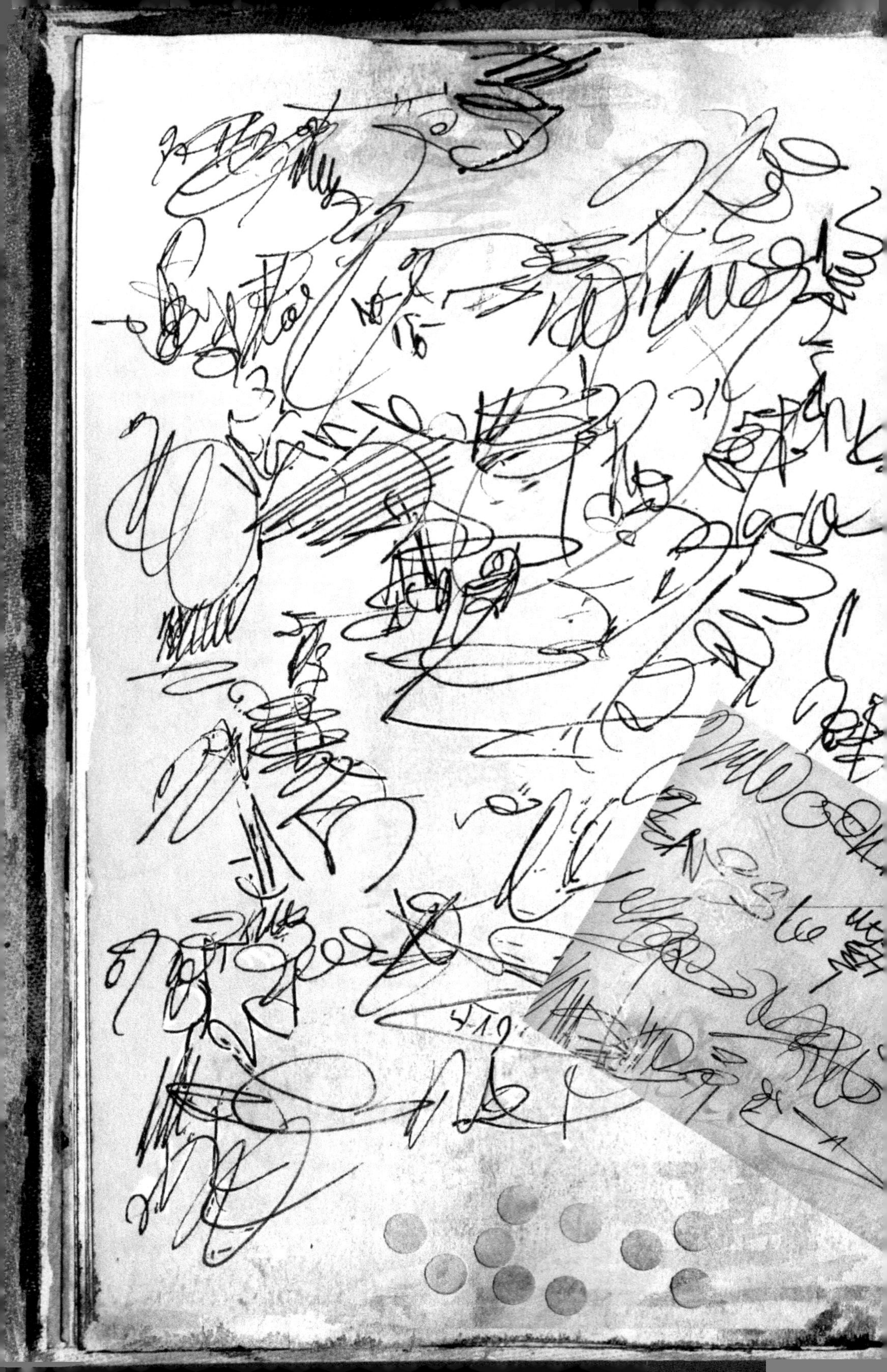

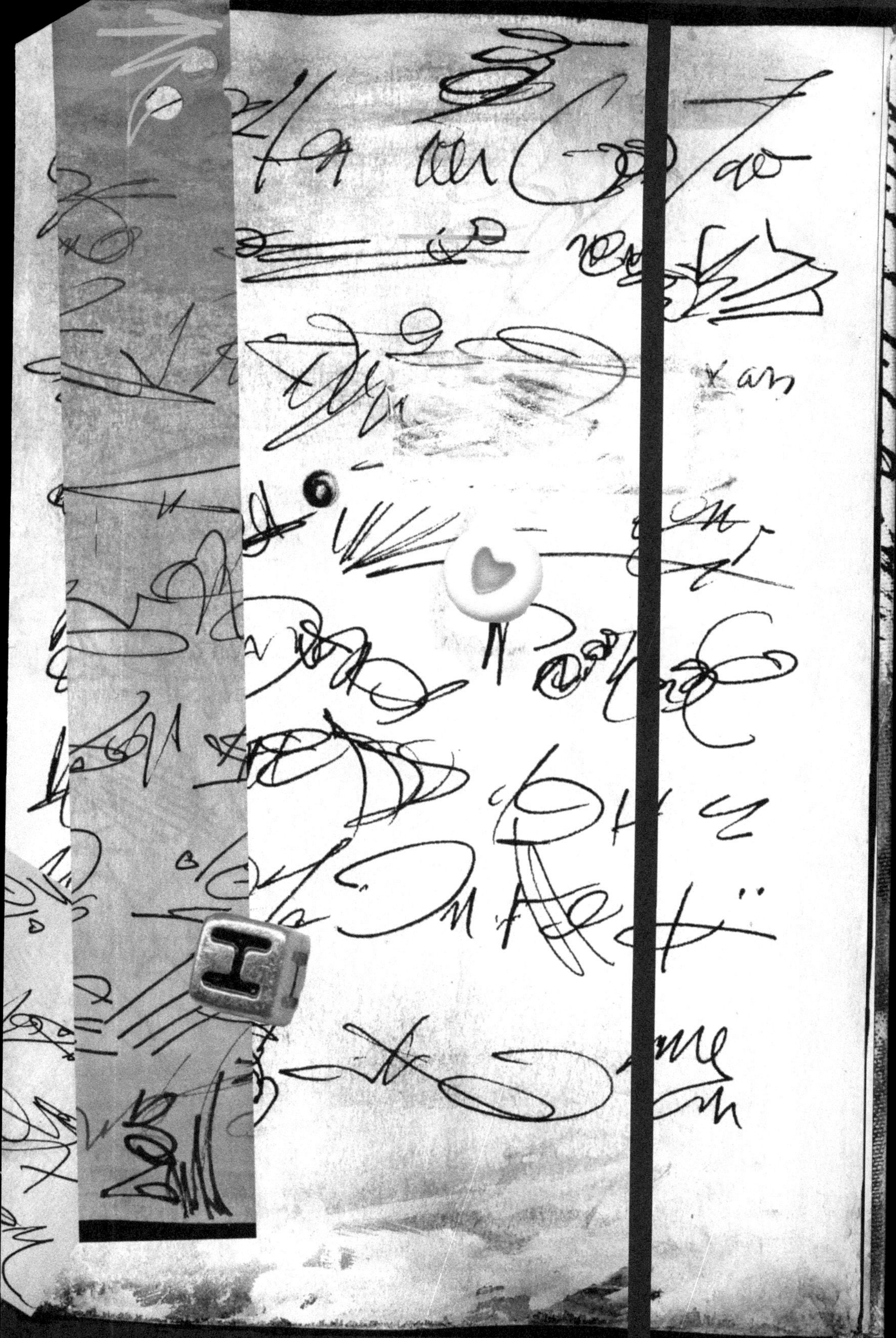

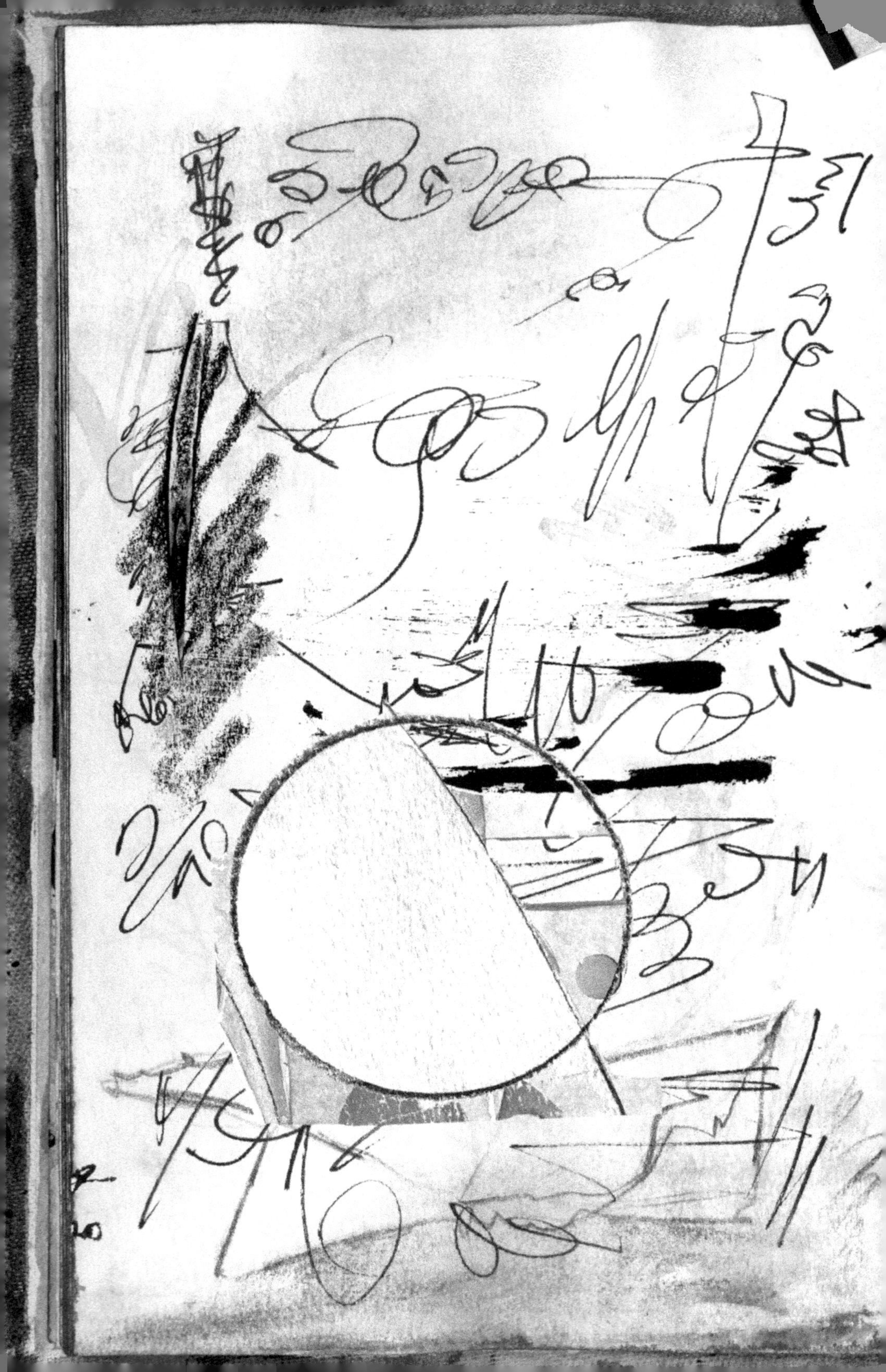

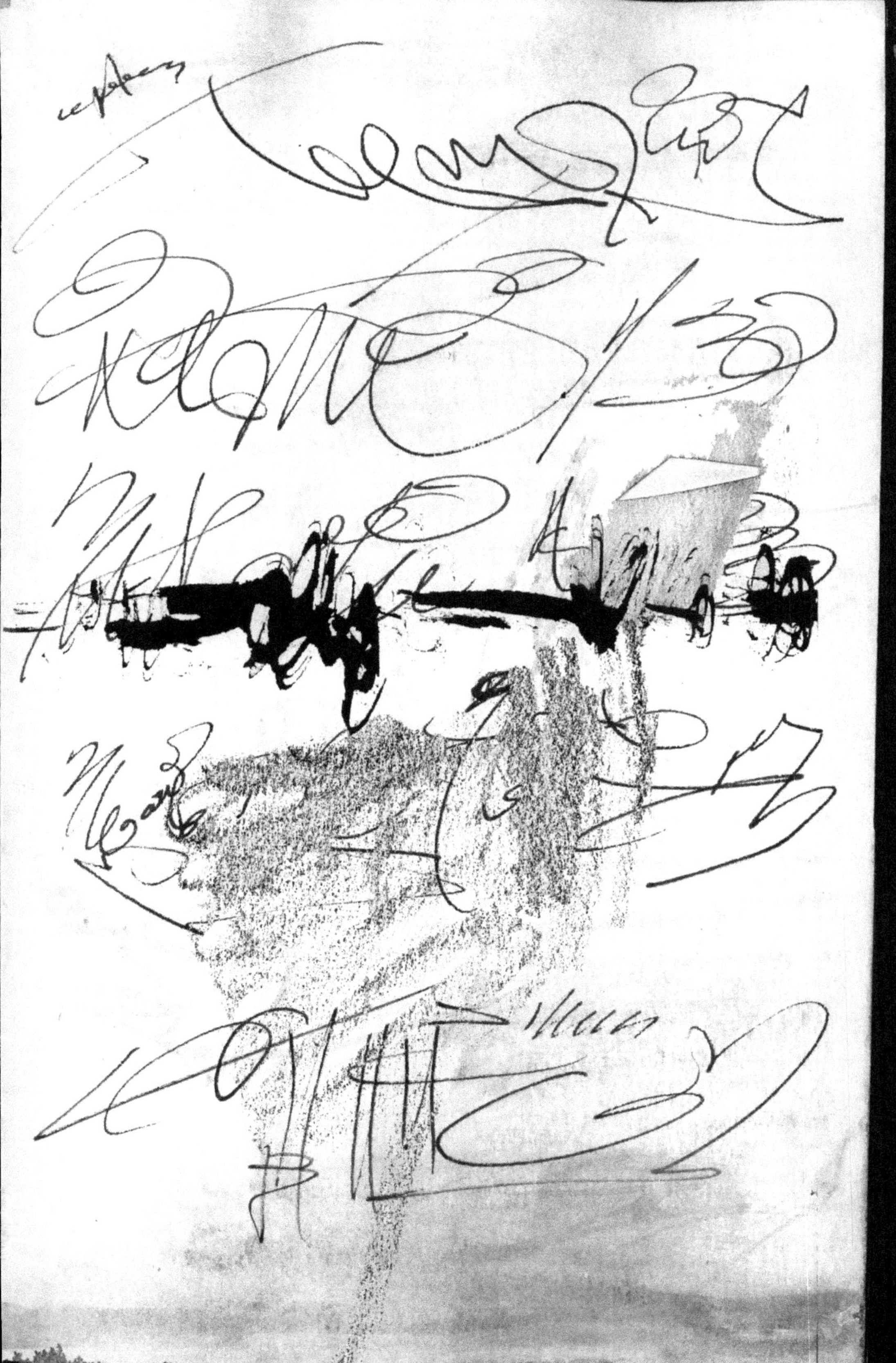

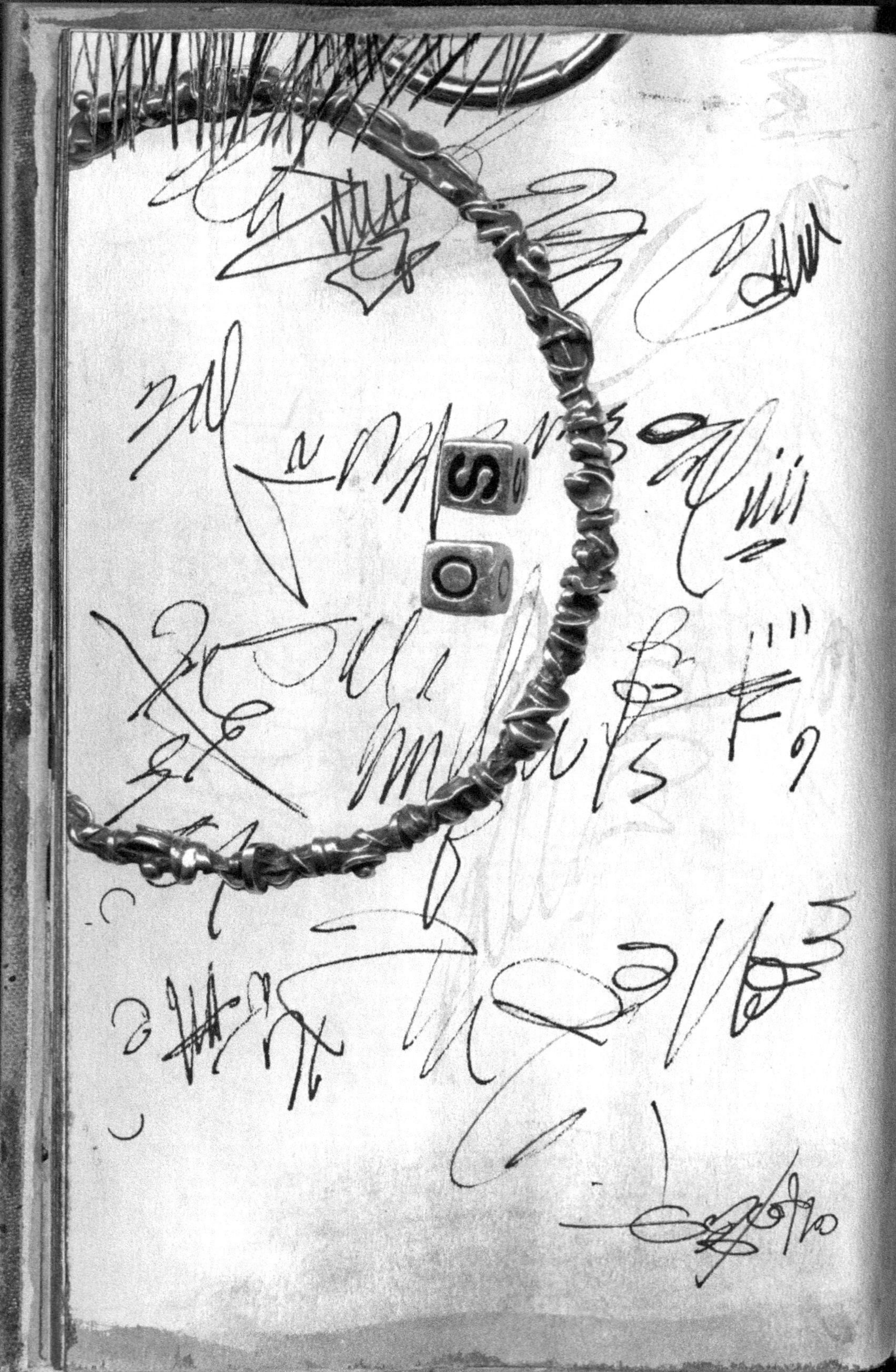
S
O

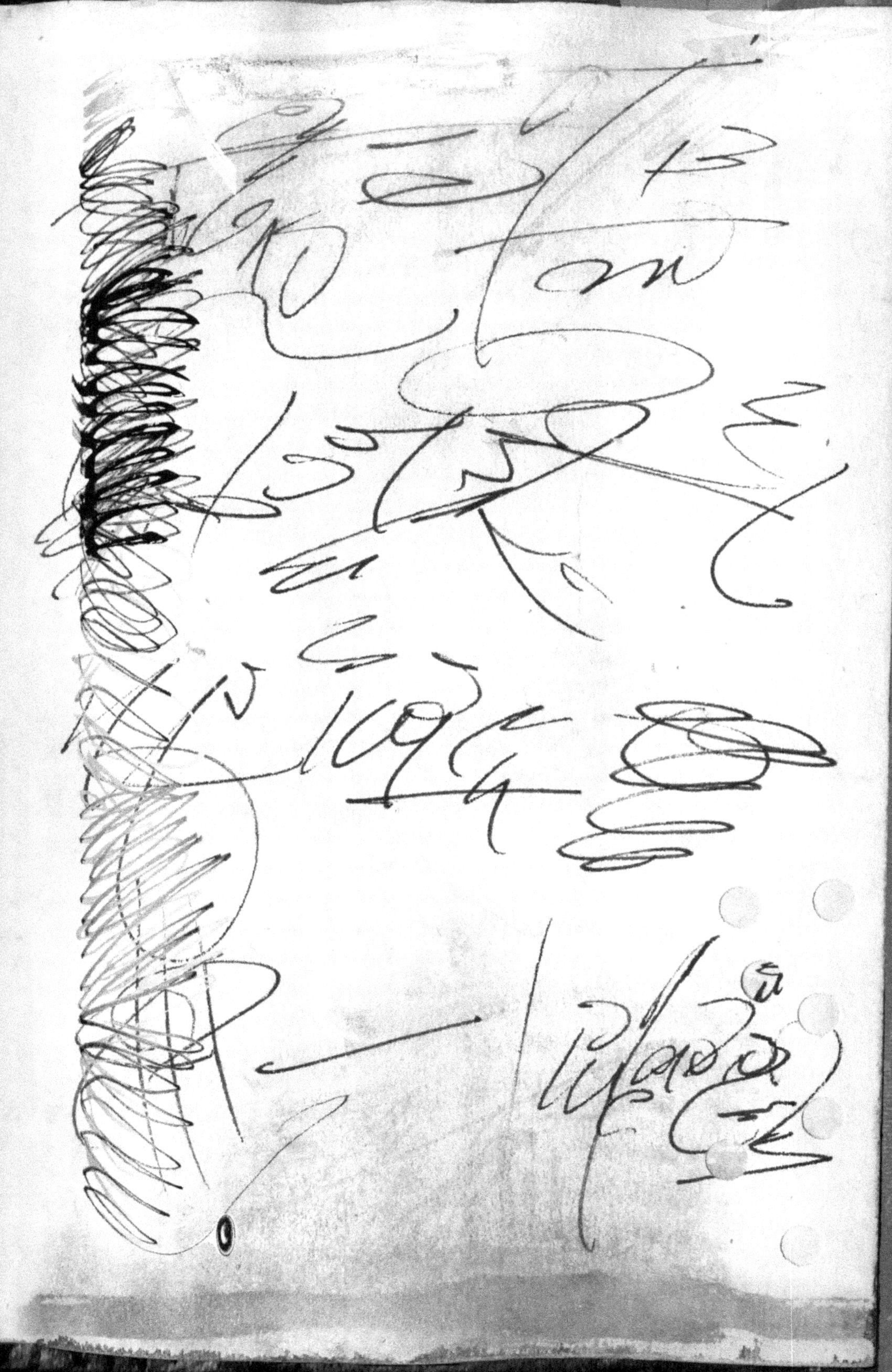

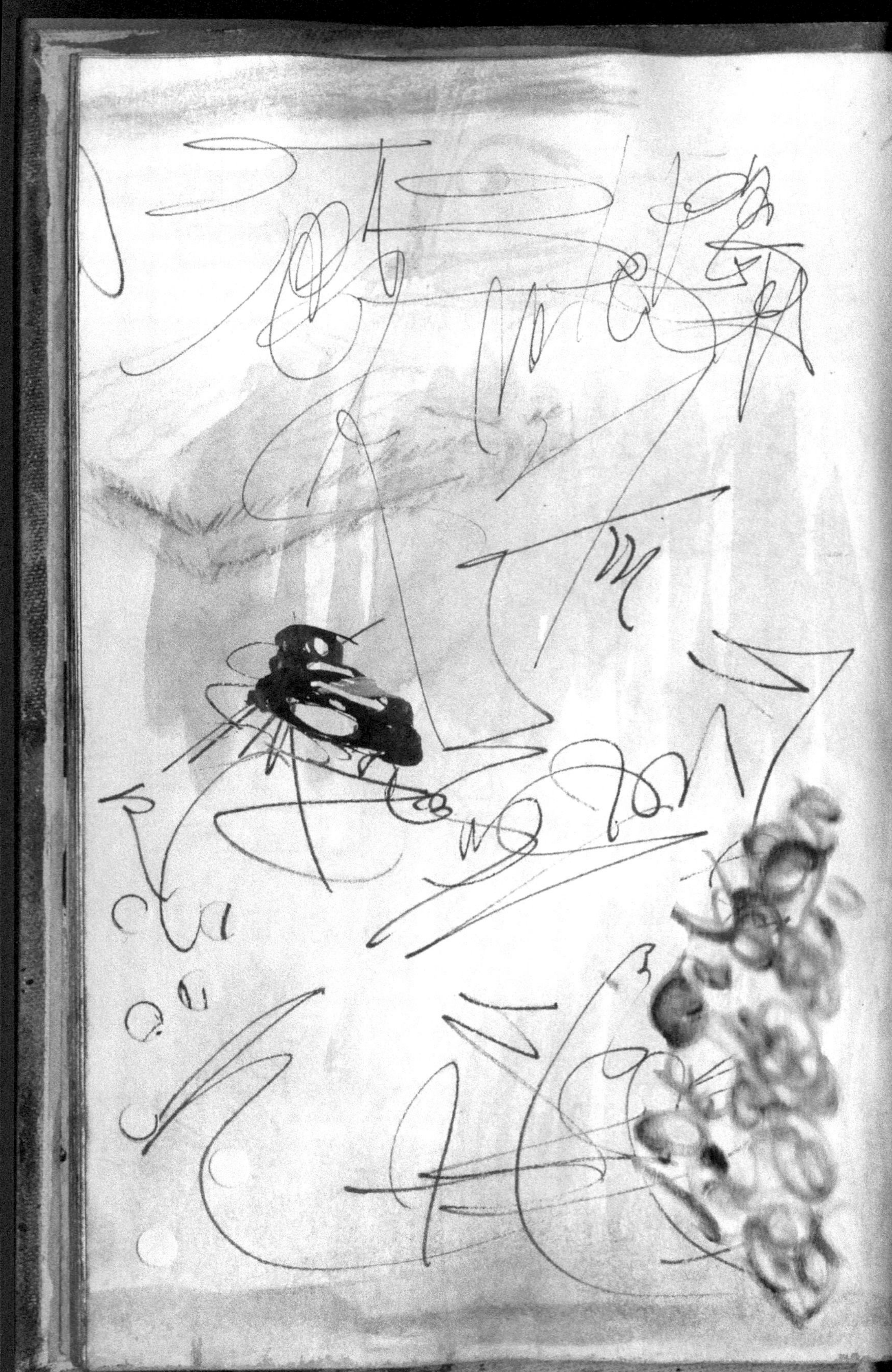

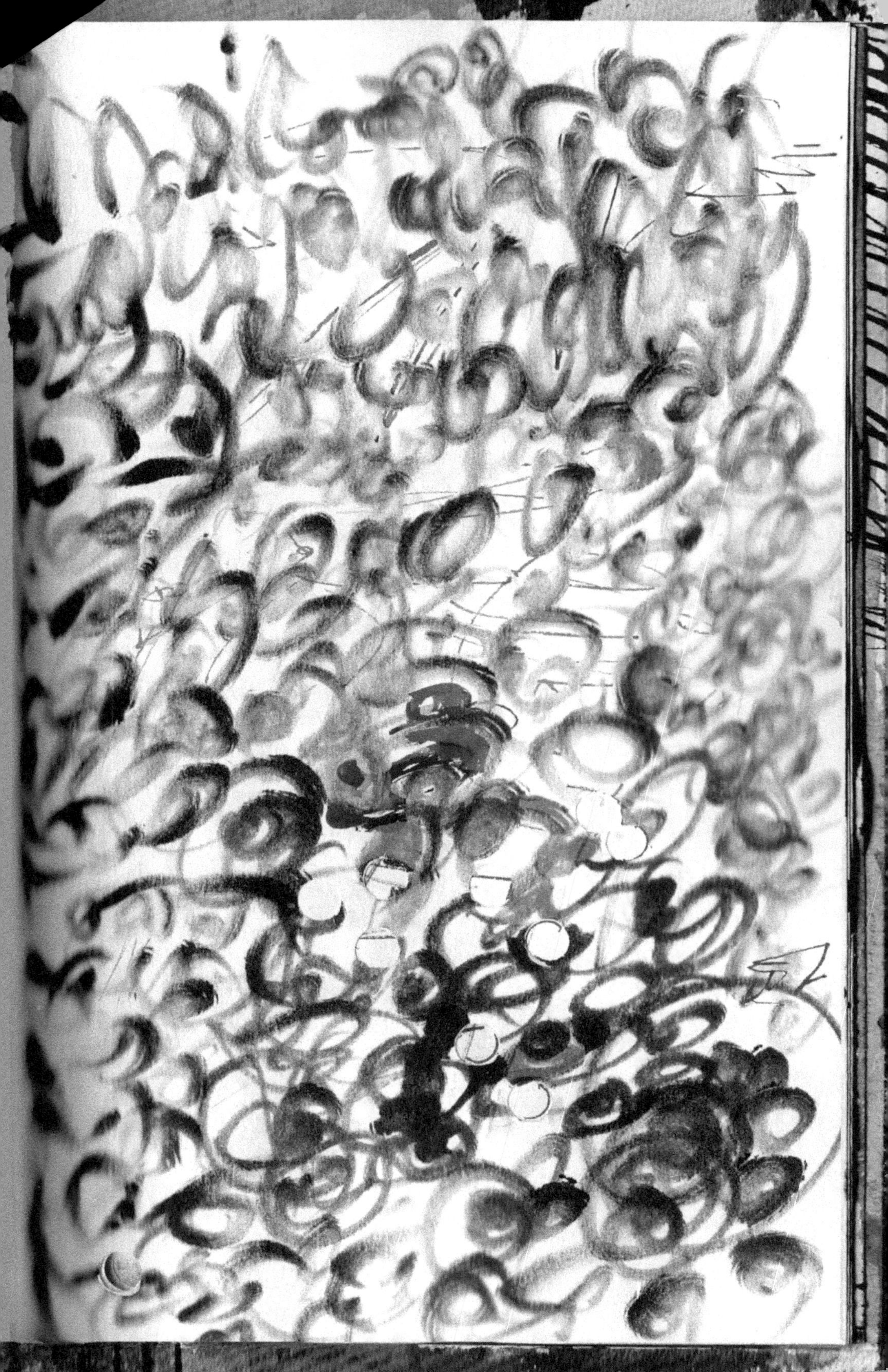

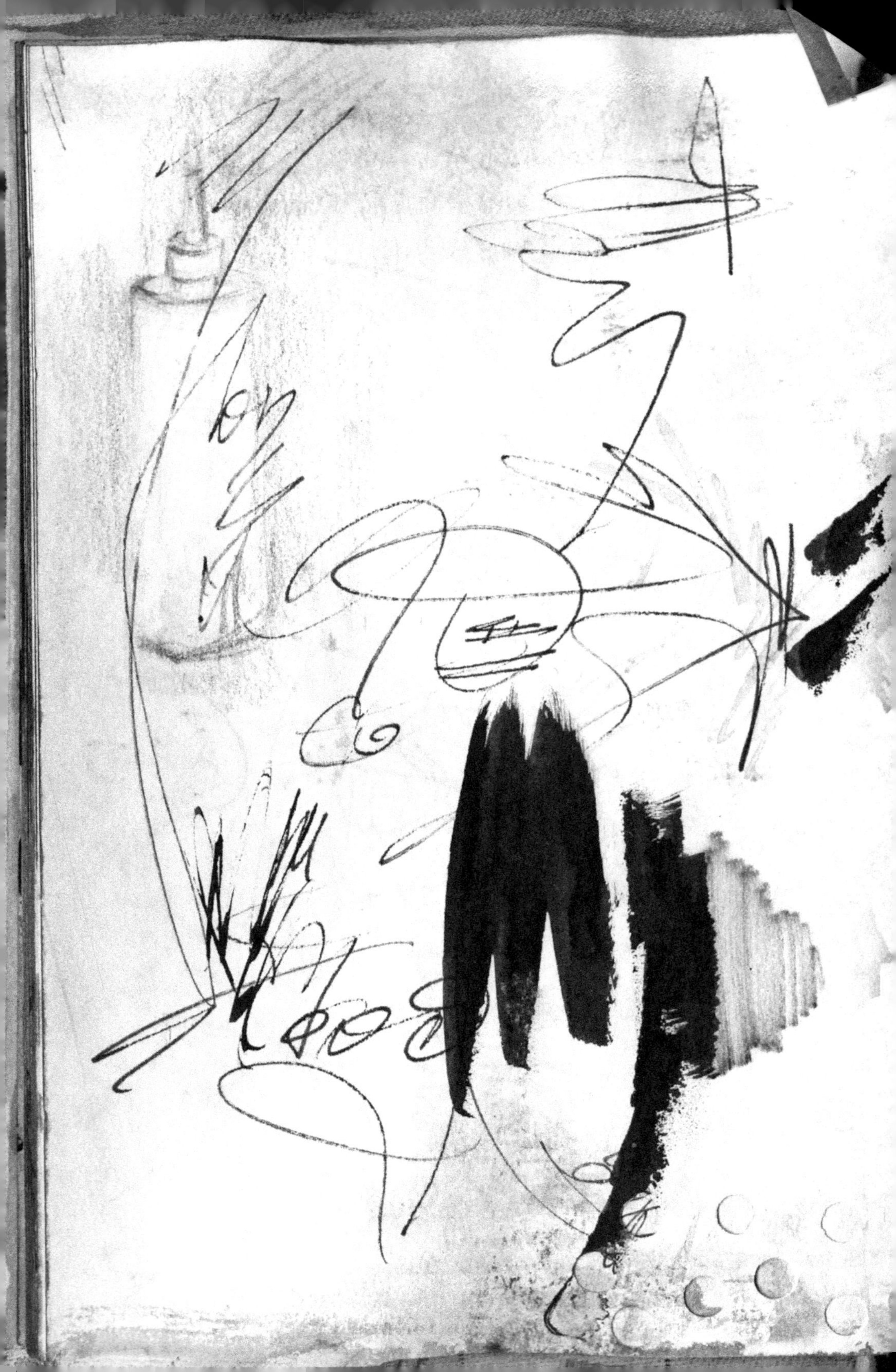

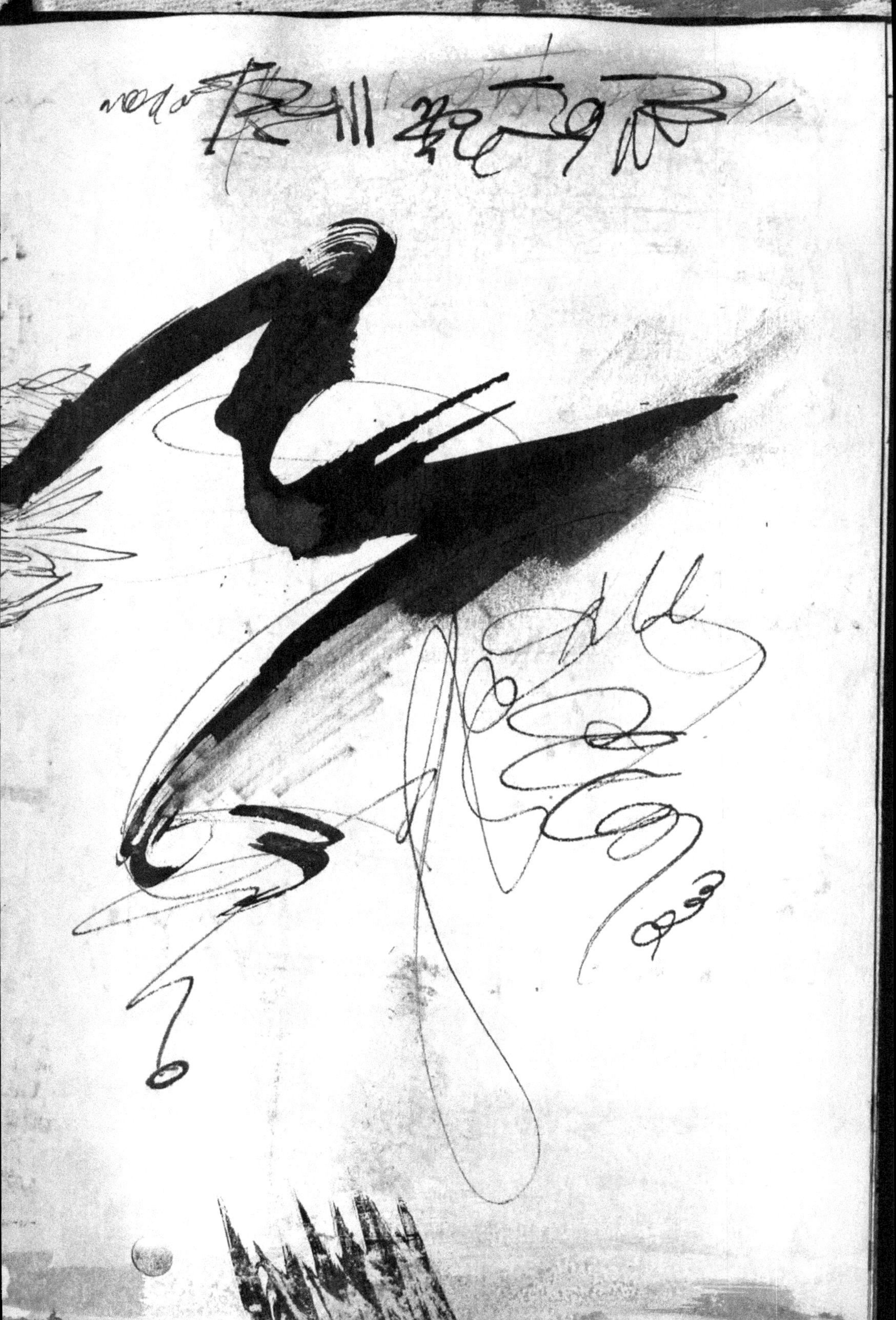

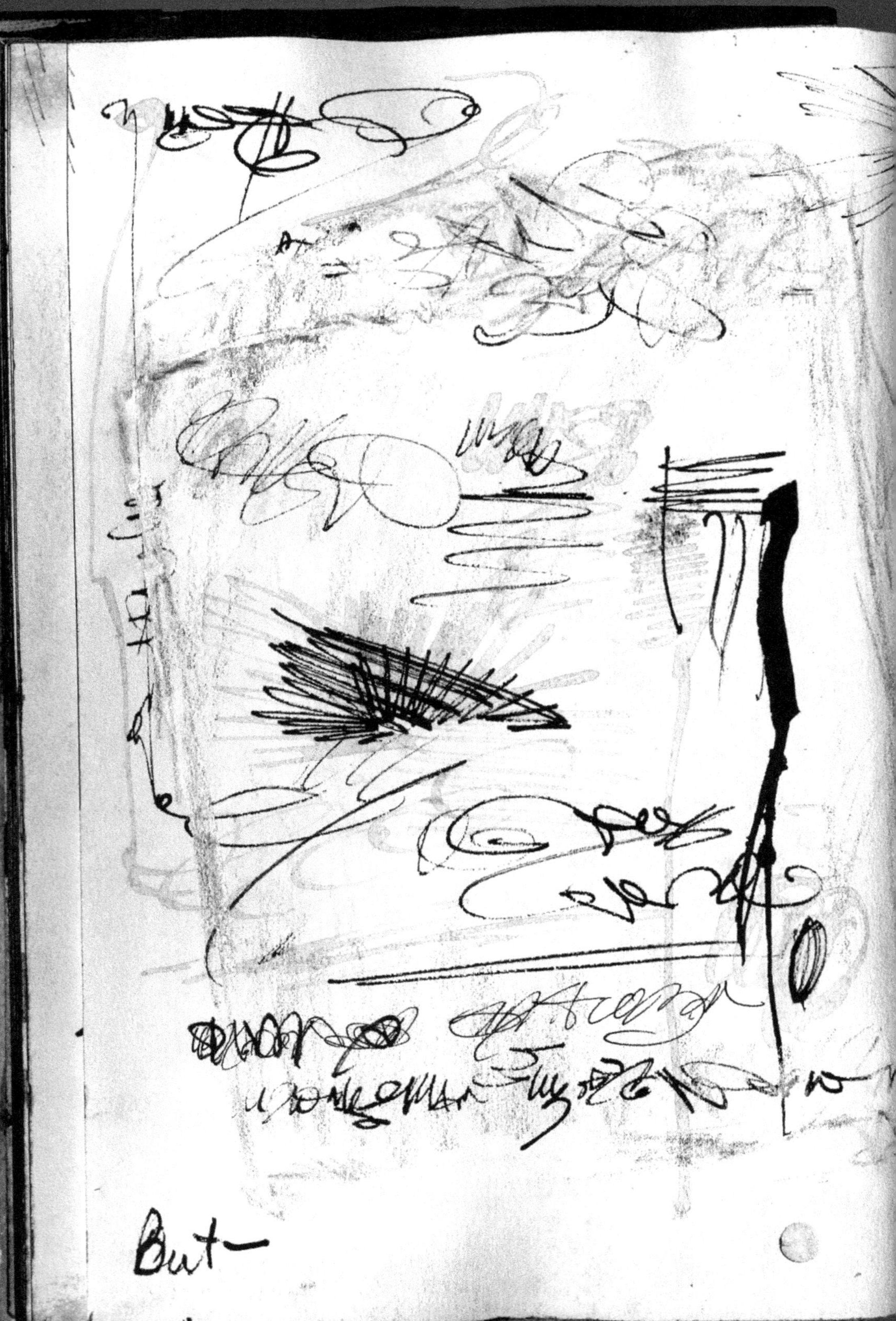
But—

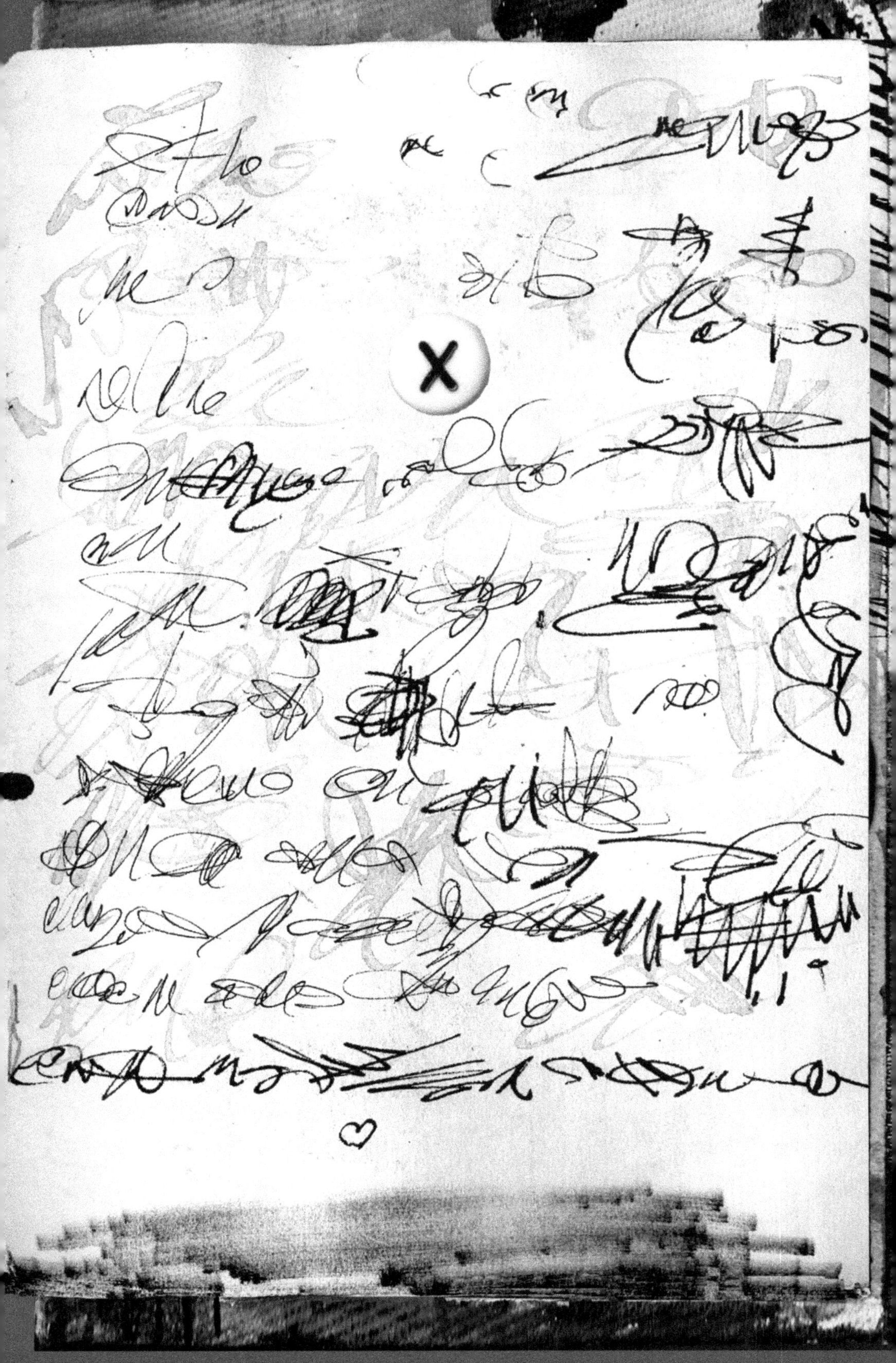

and-

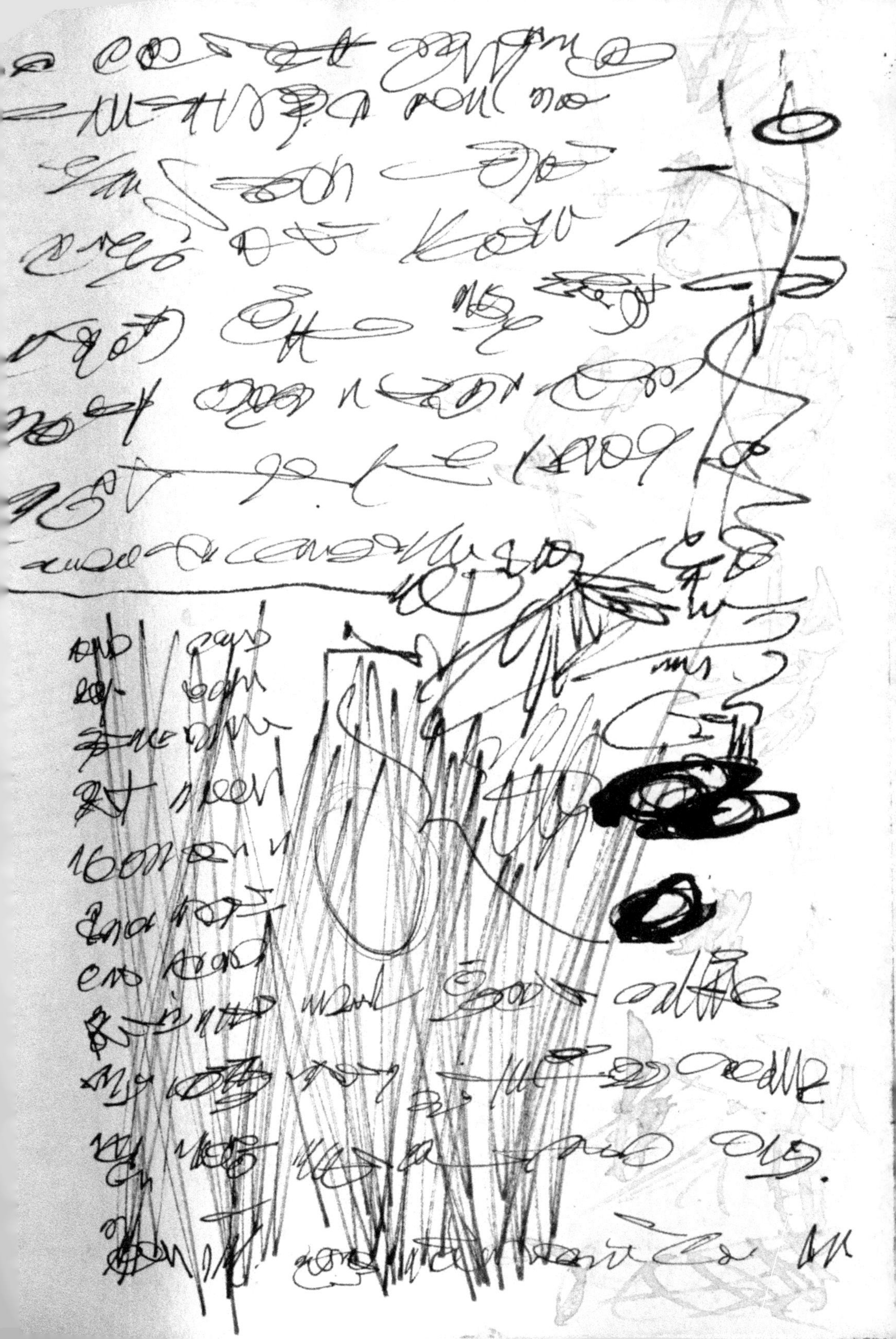

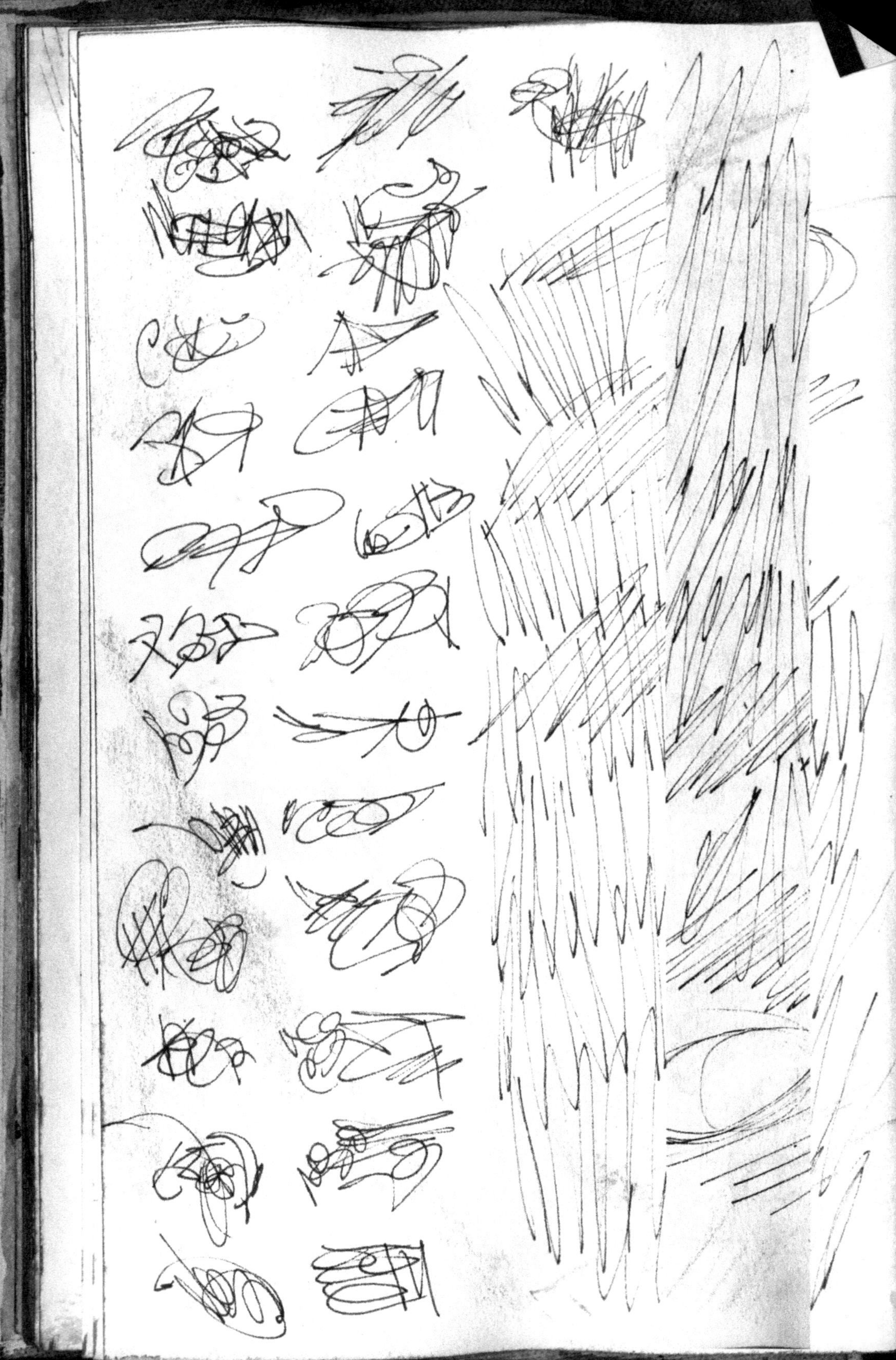

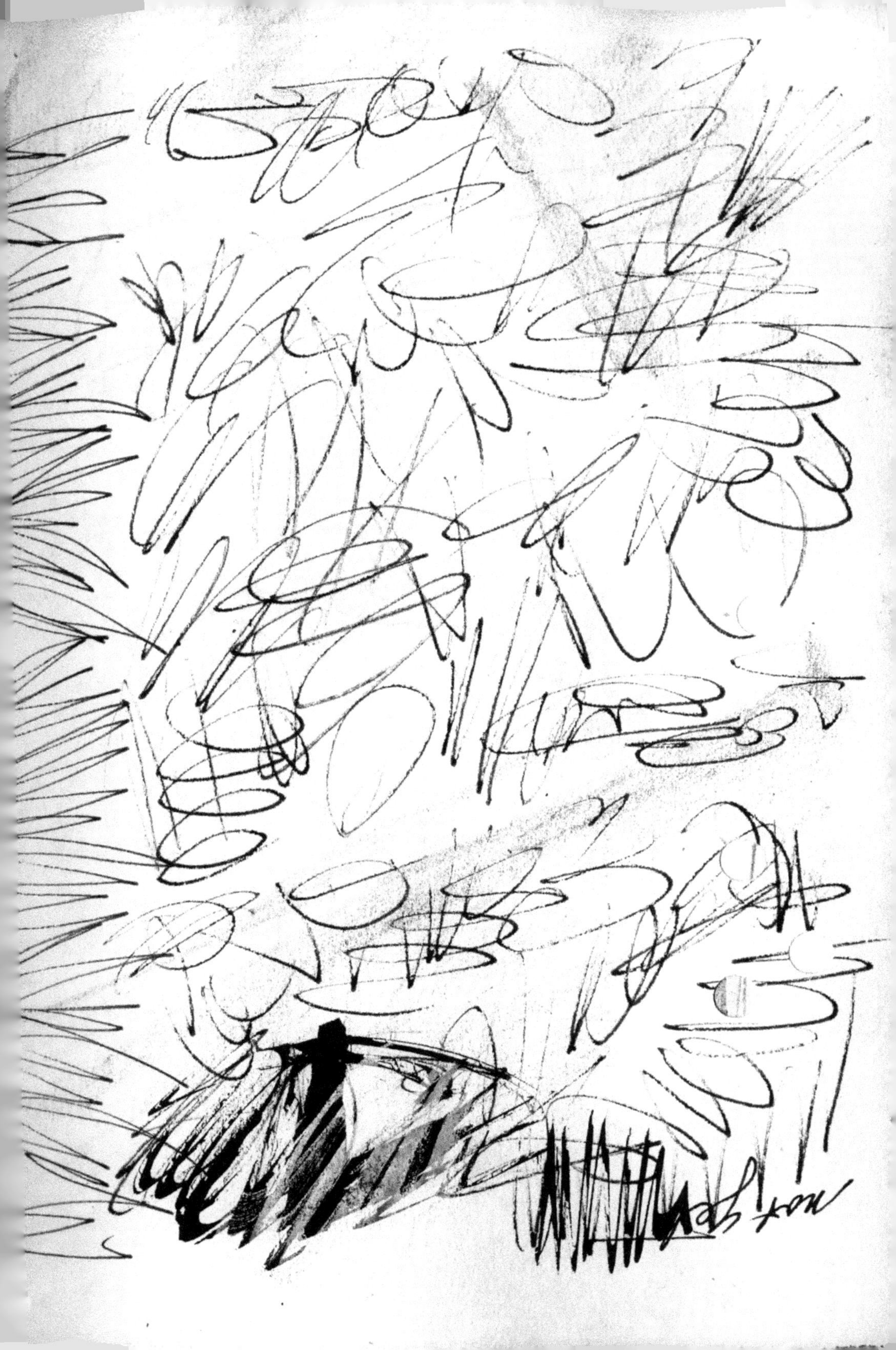

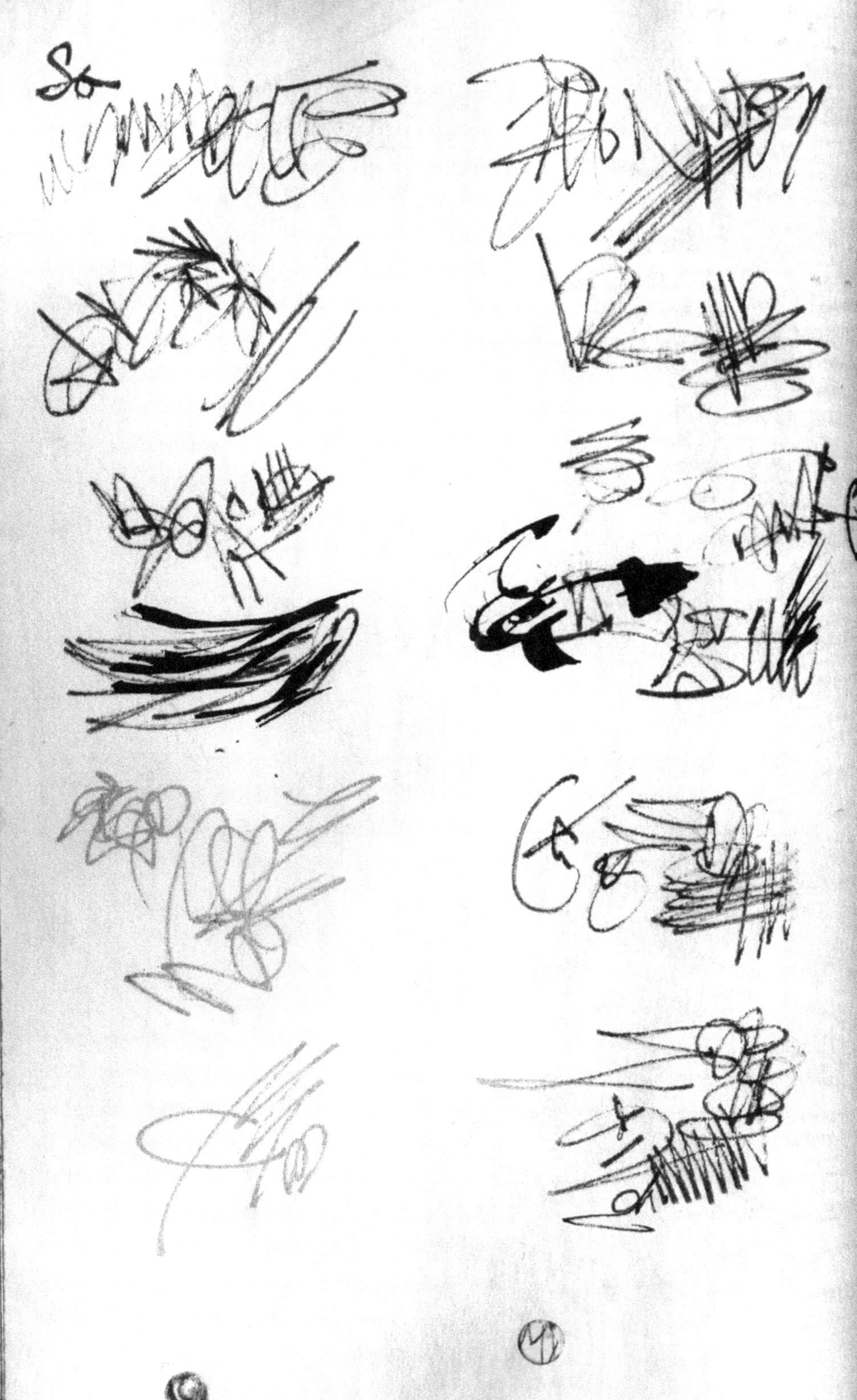

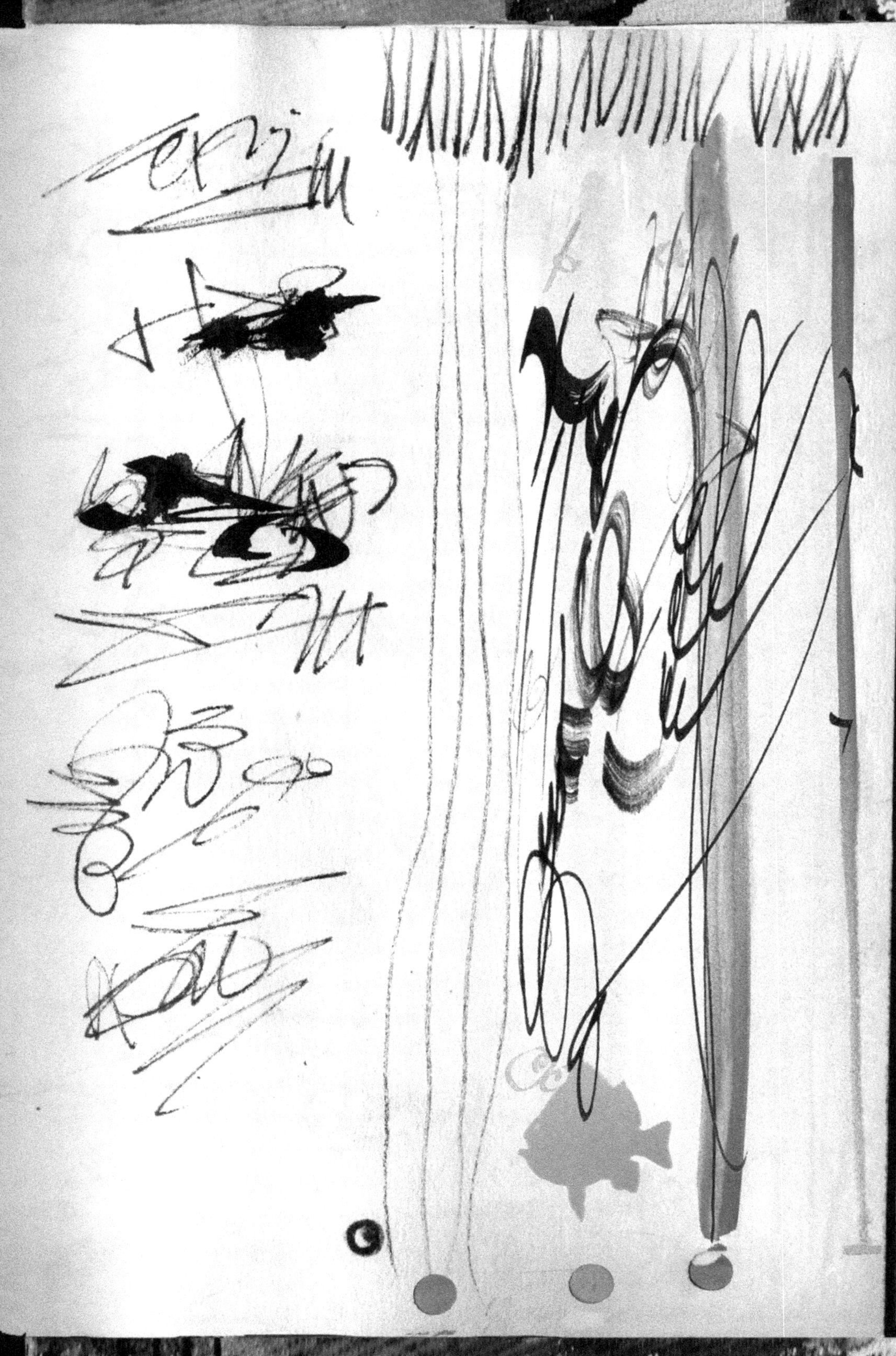

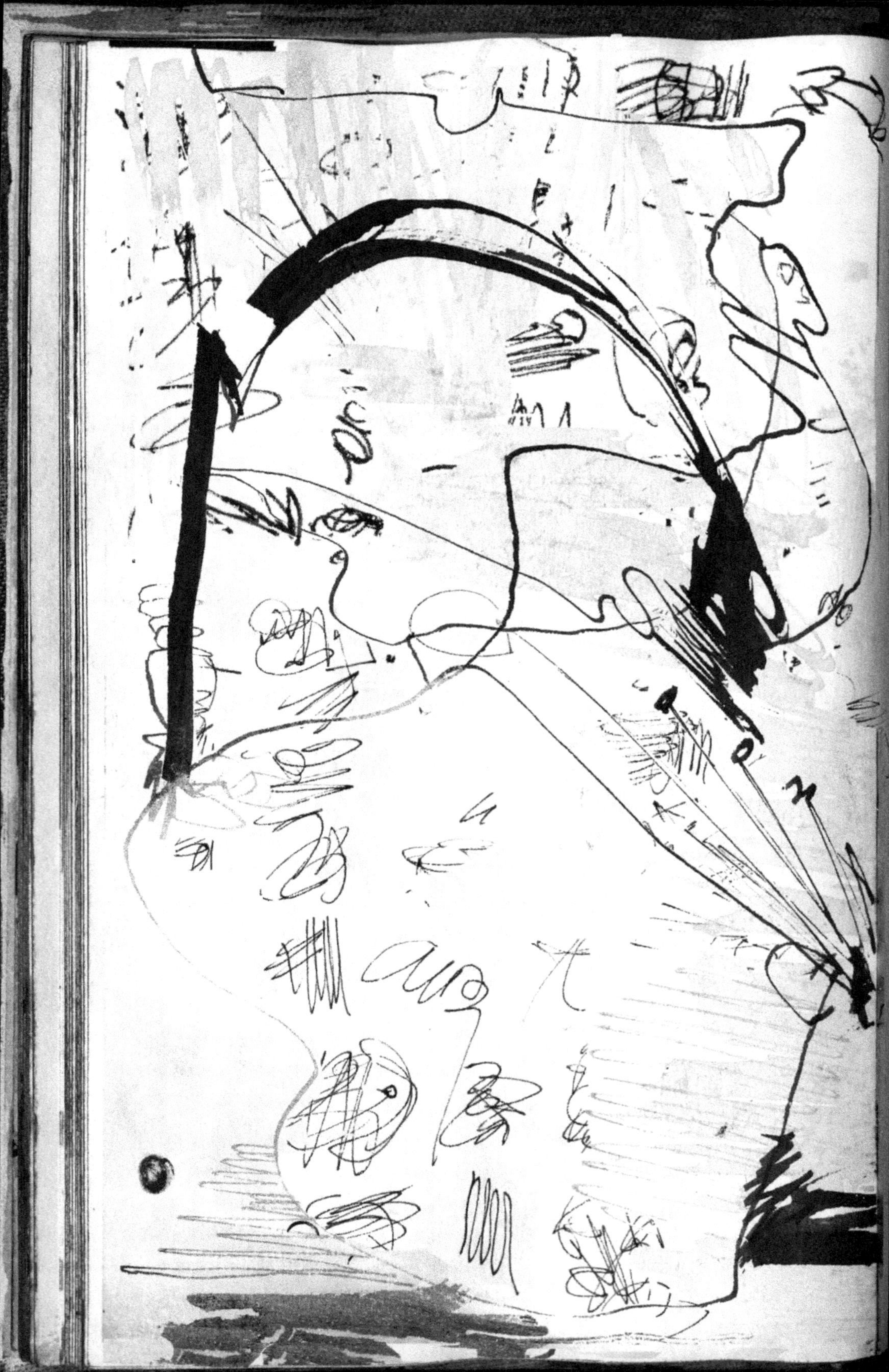

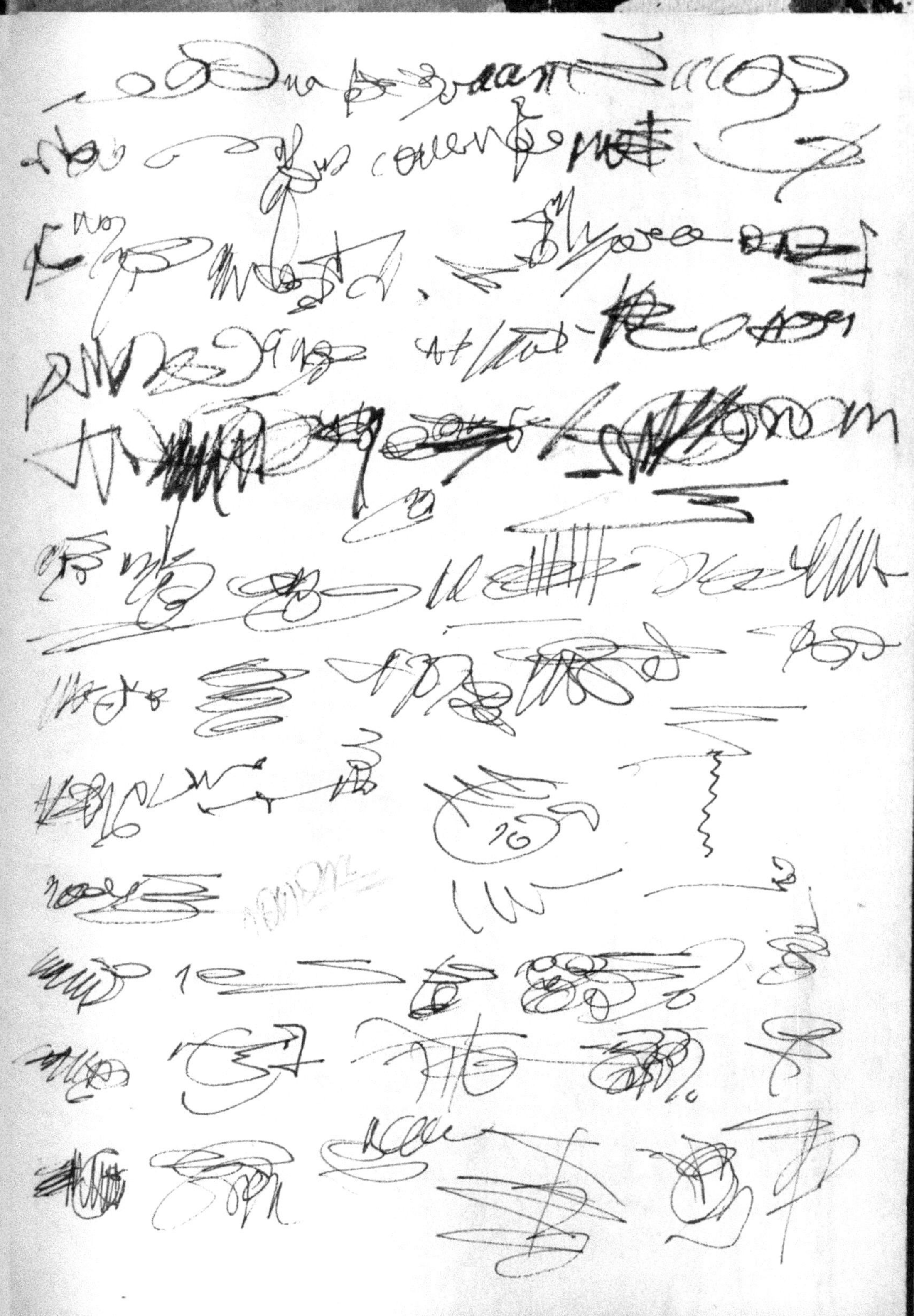

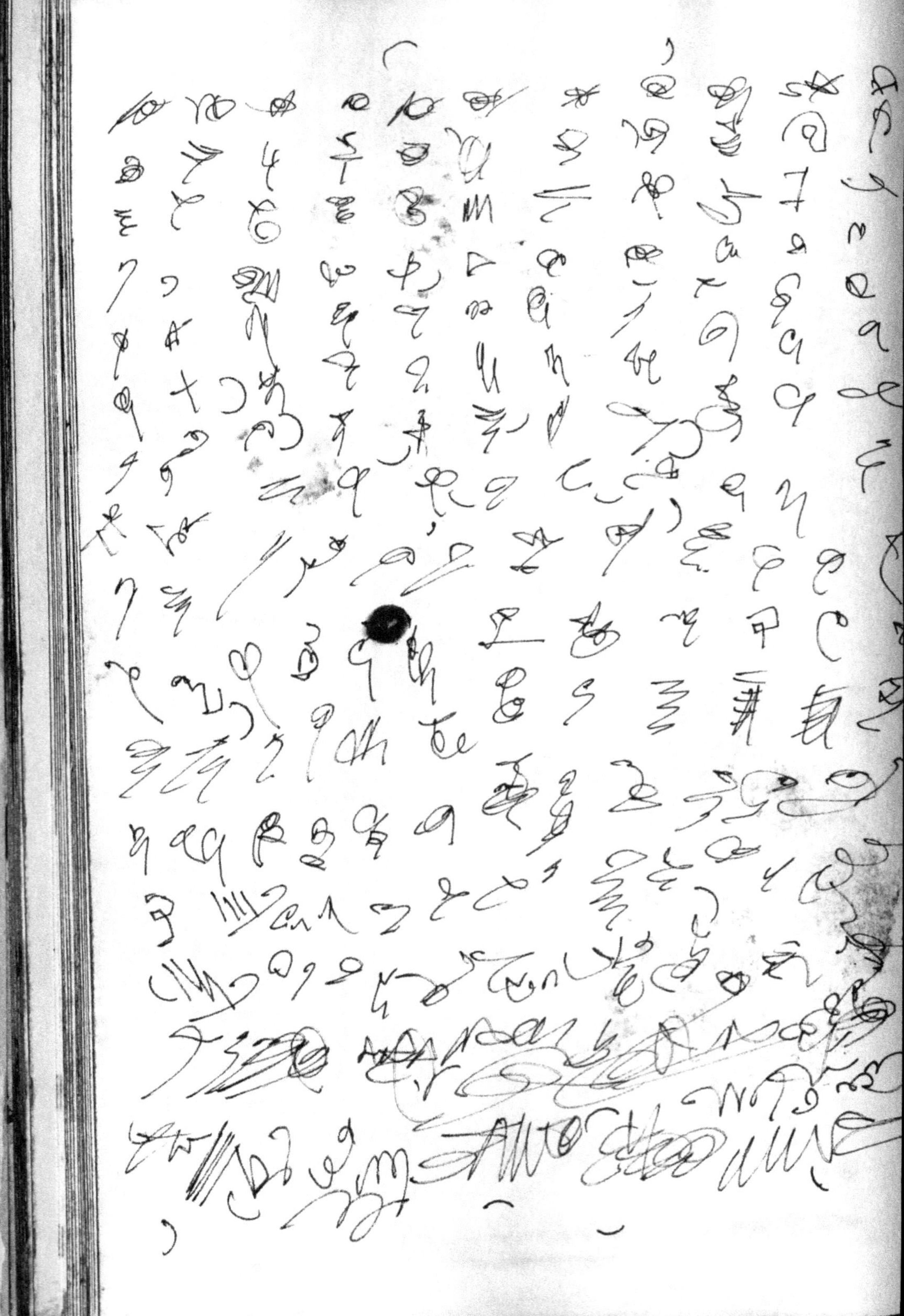

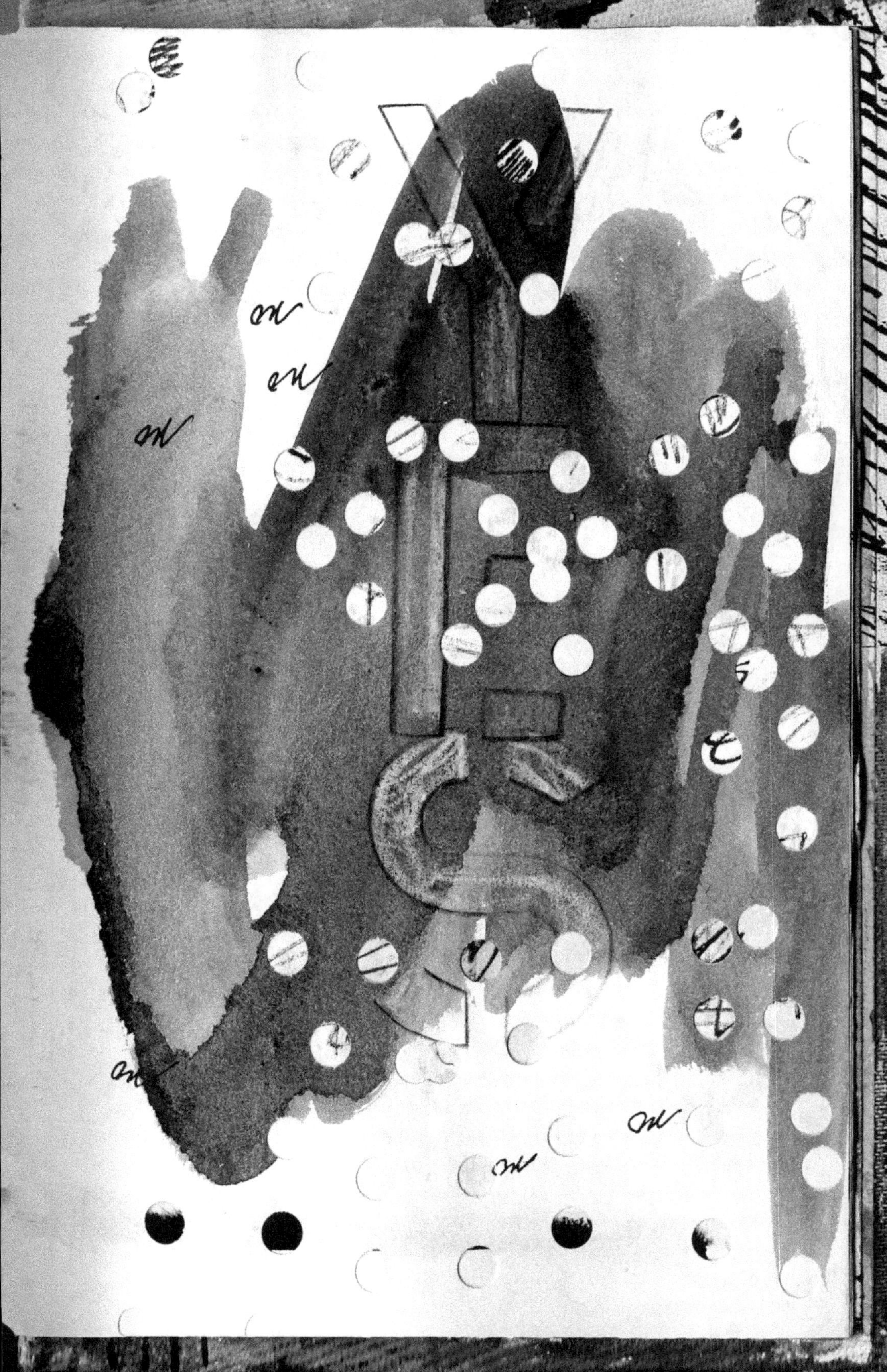

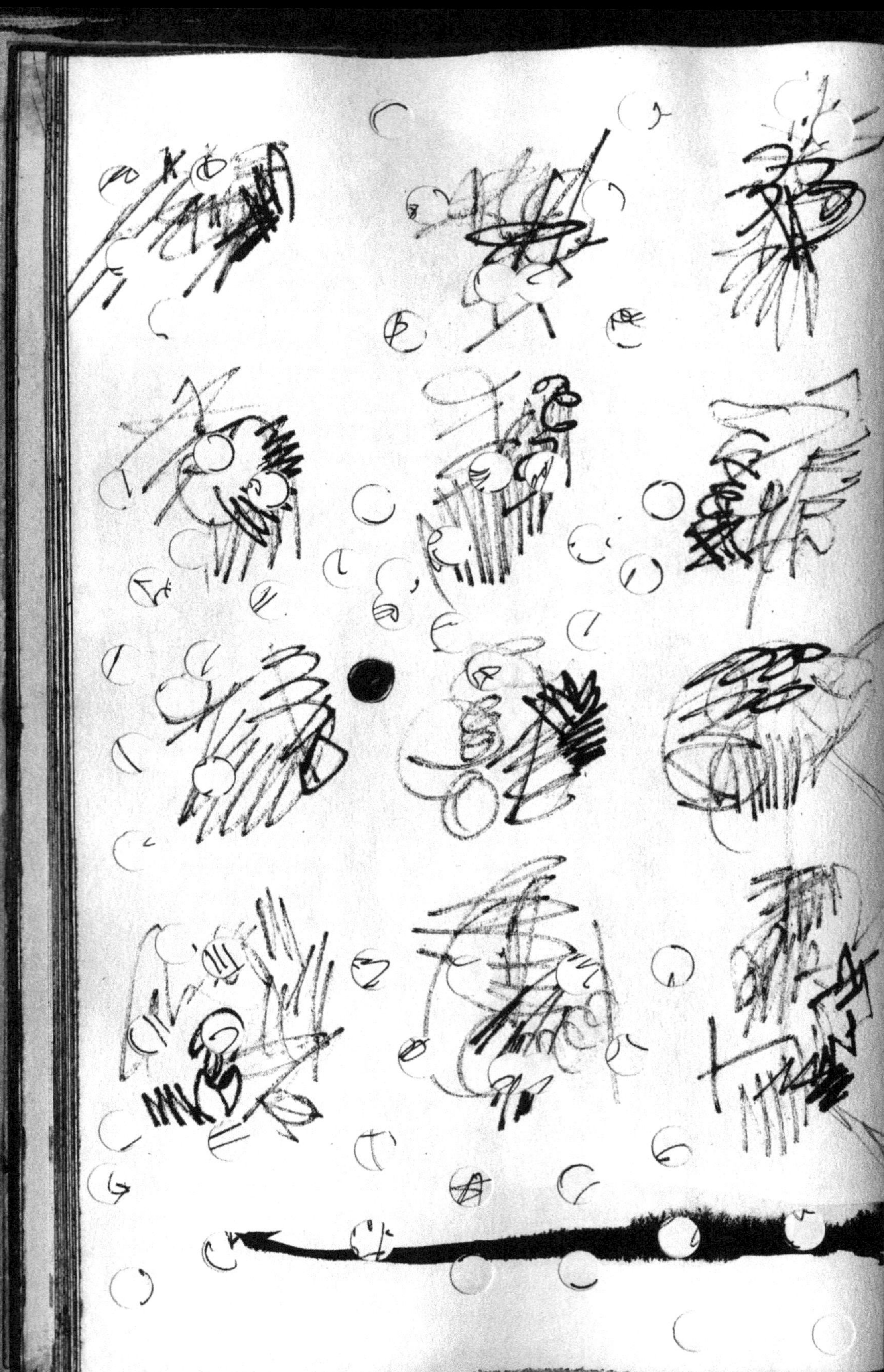

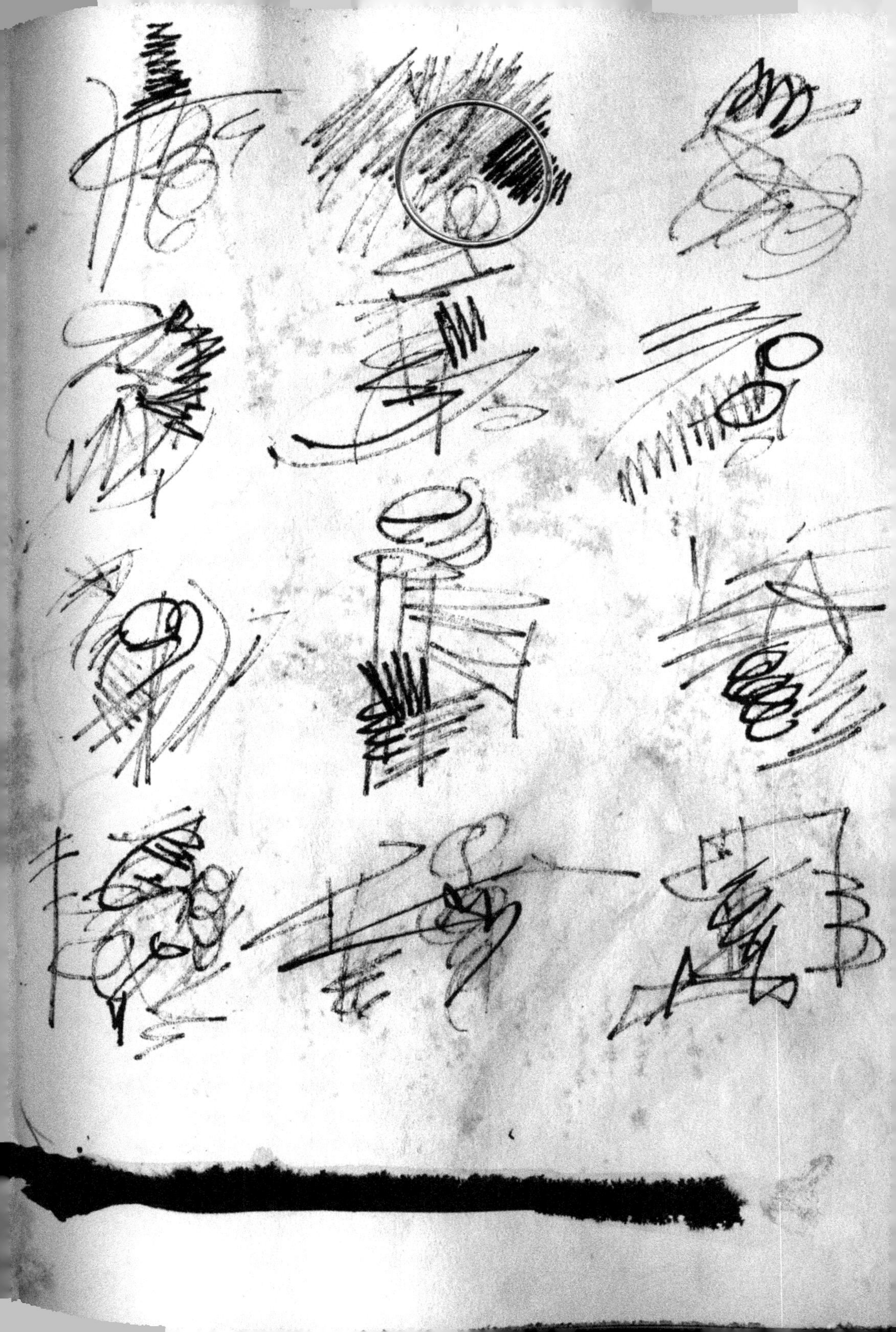

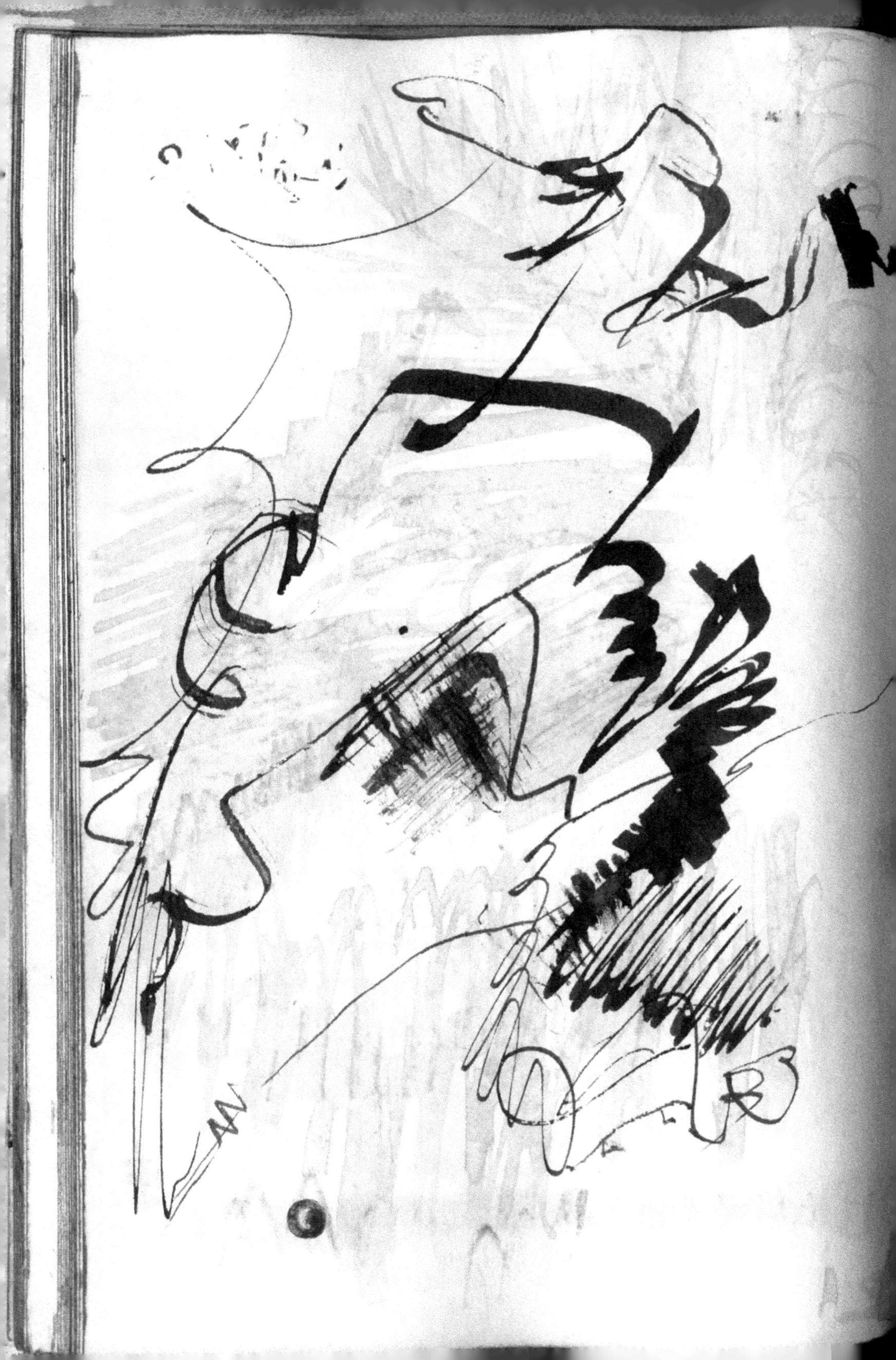

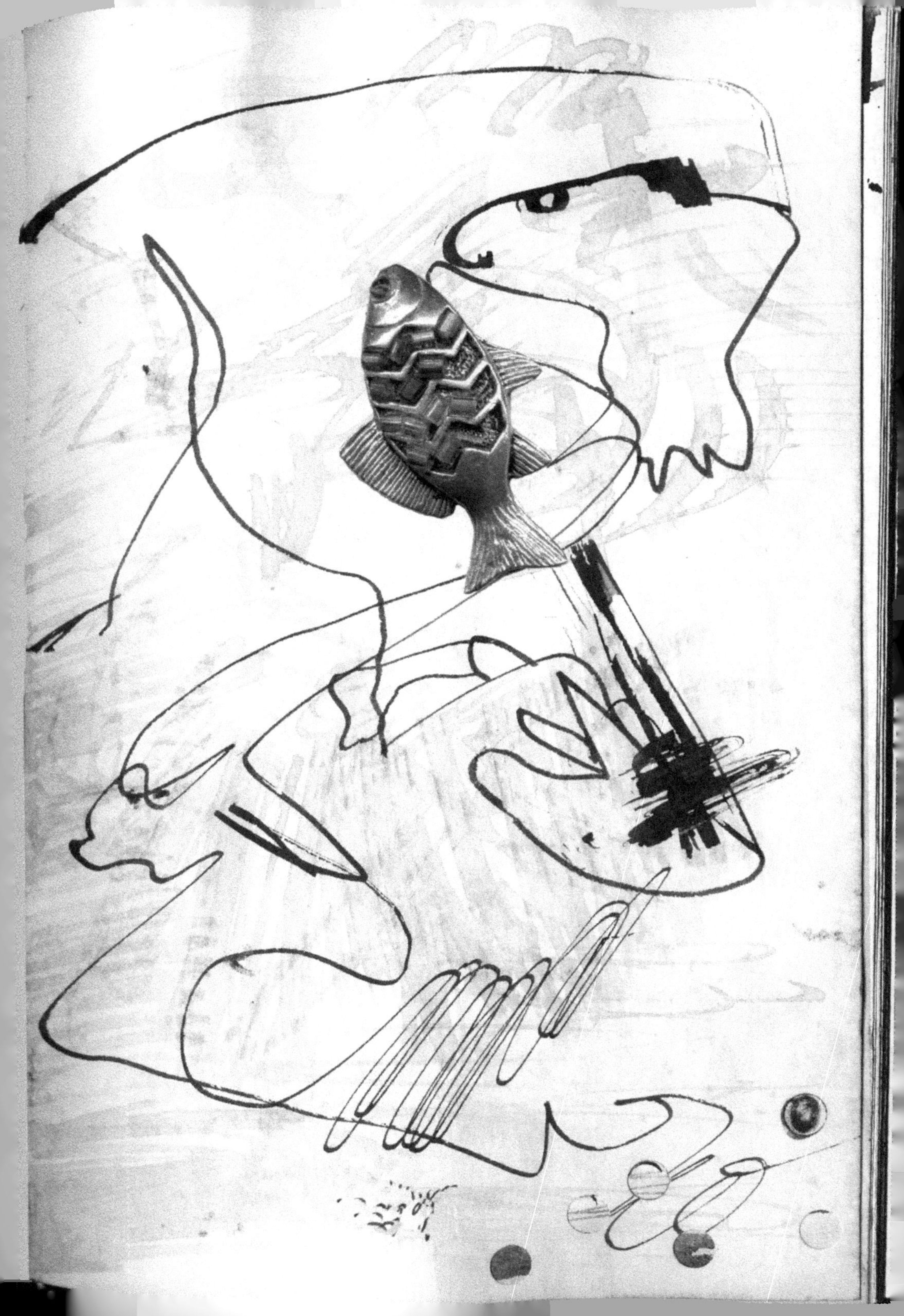

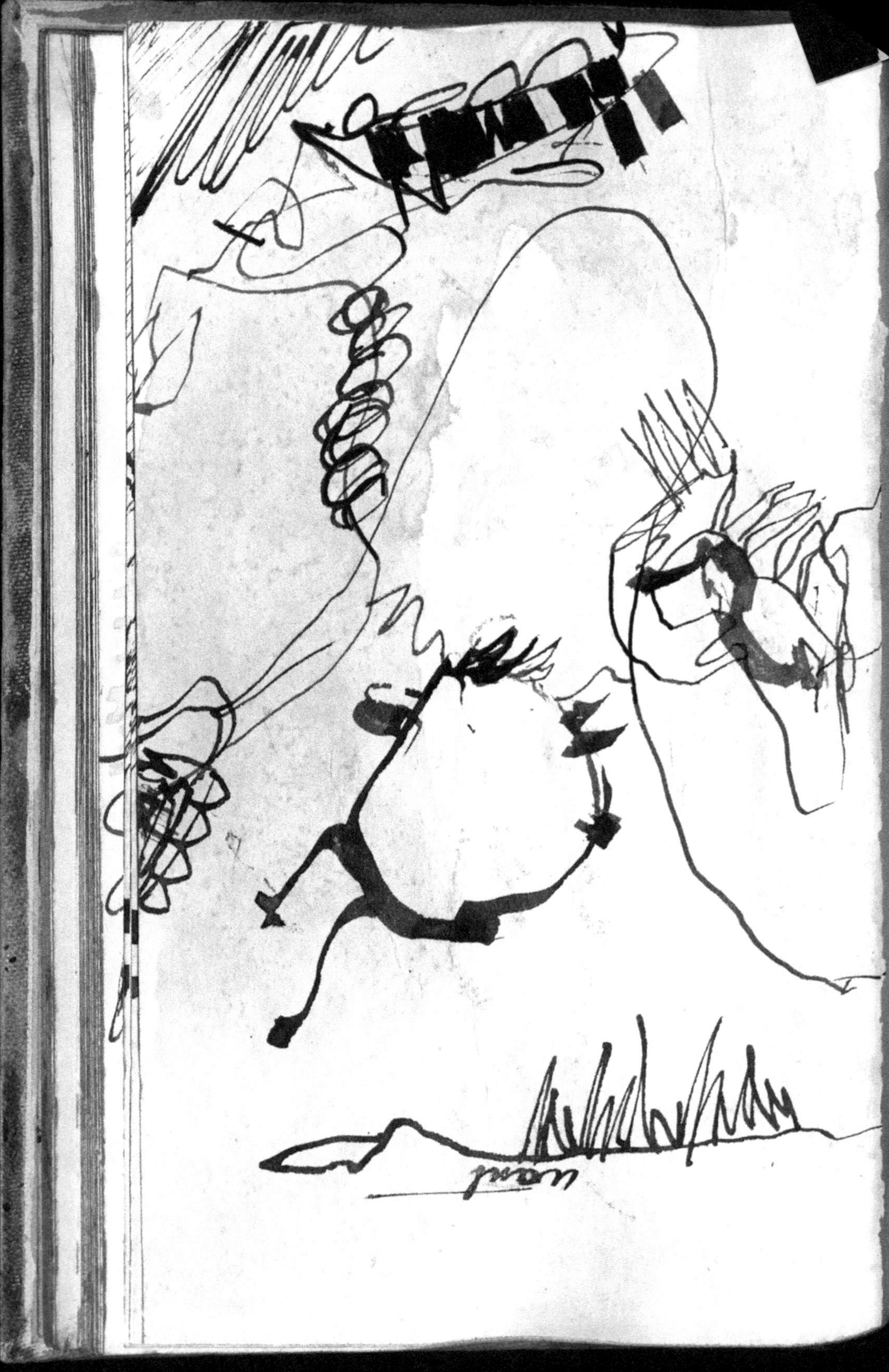

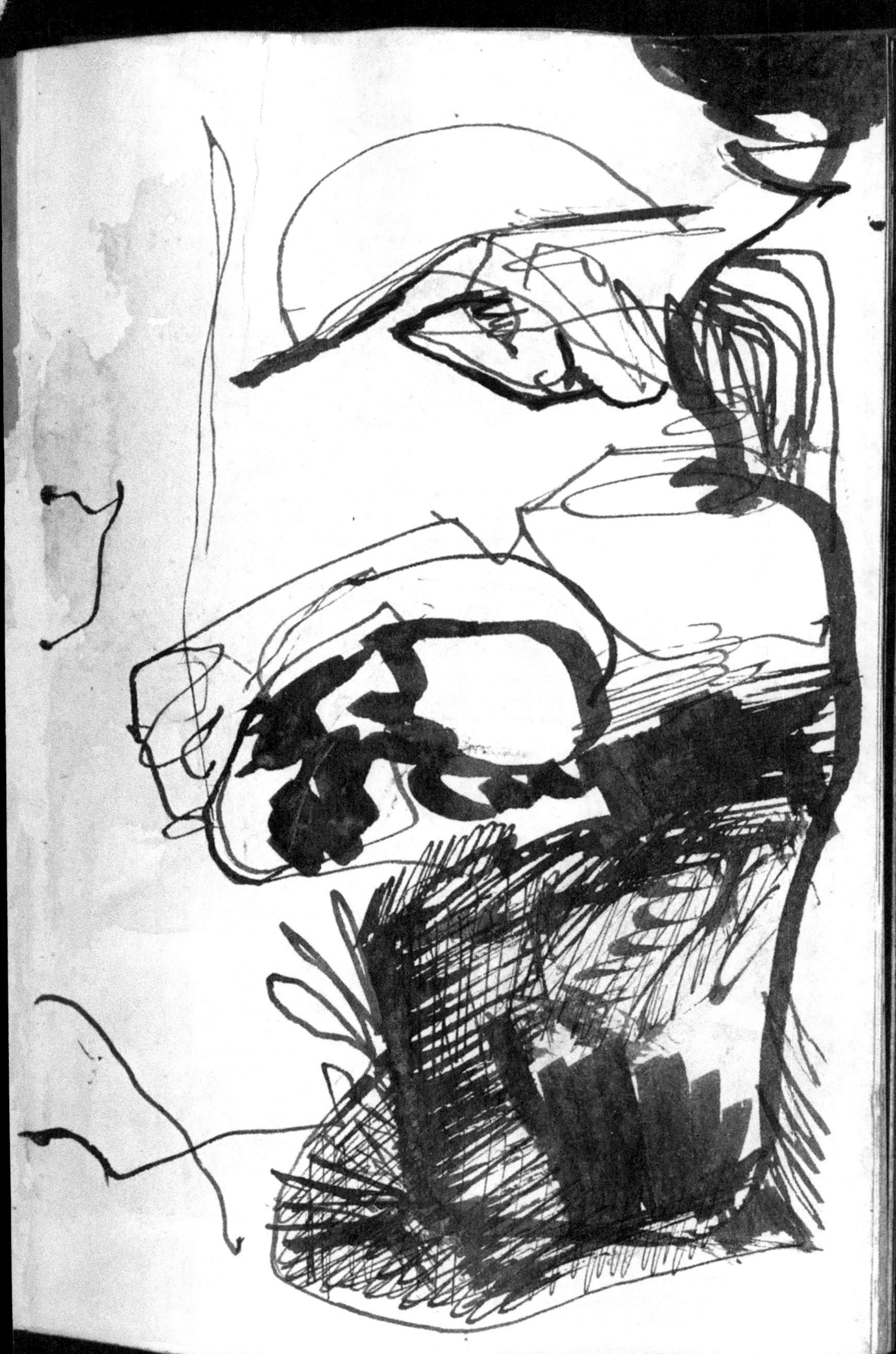

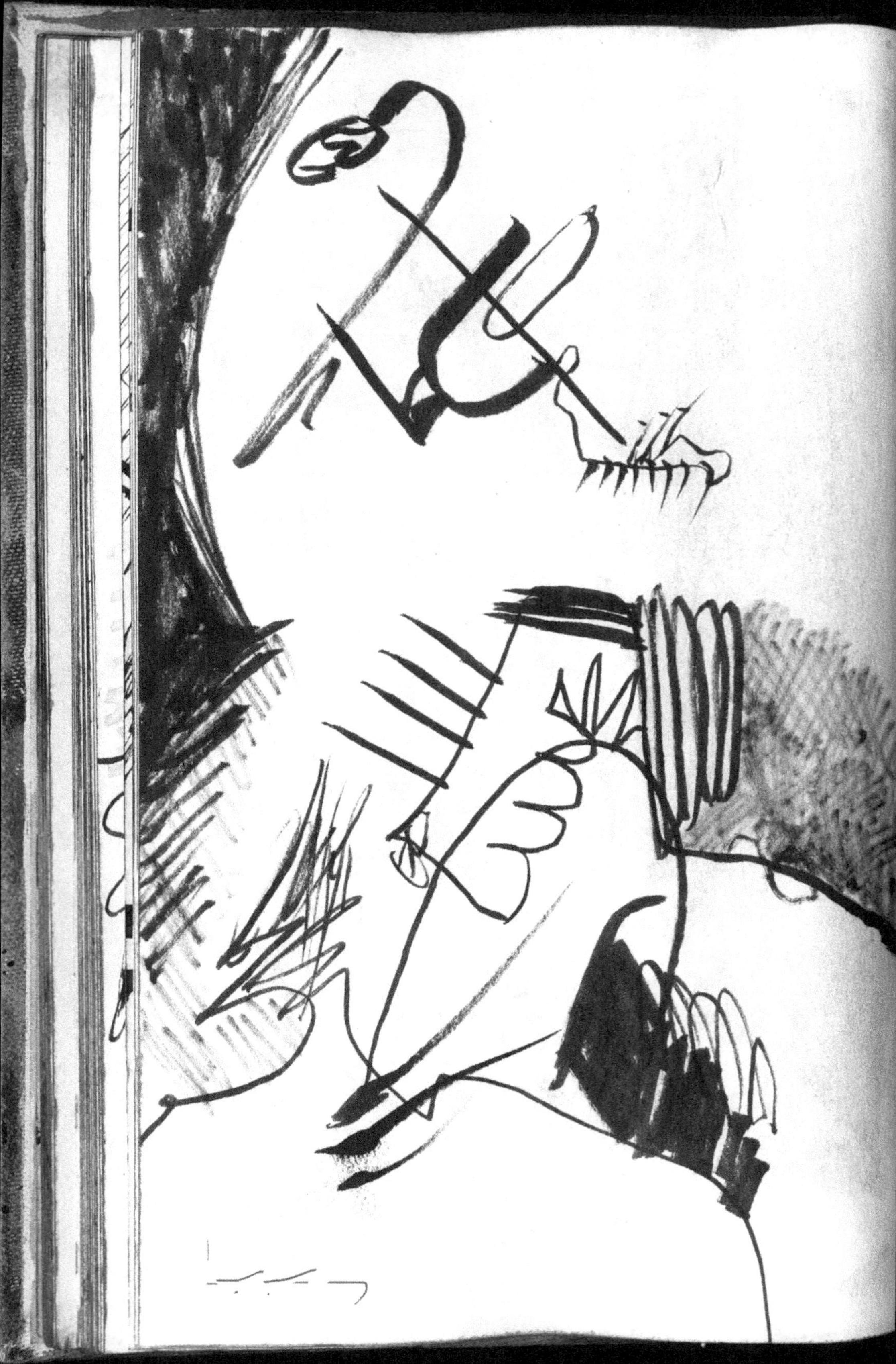

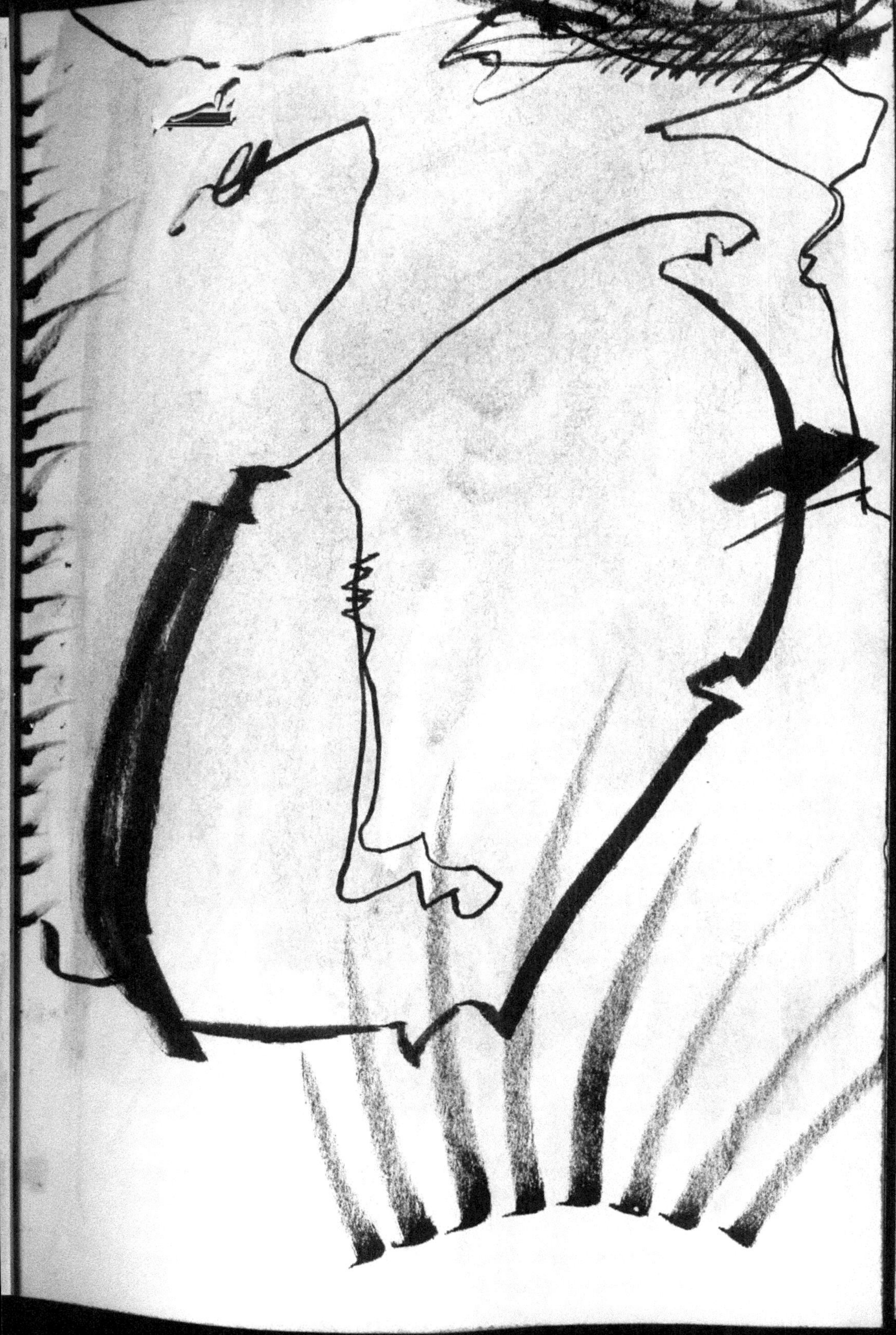

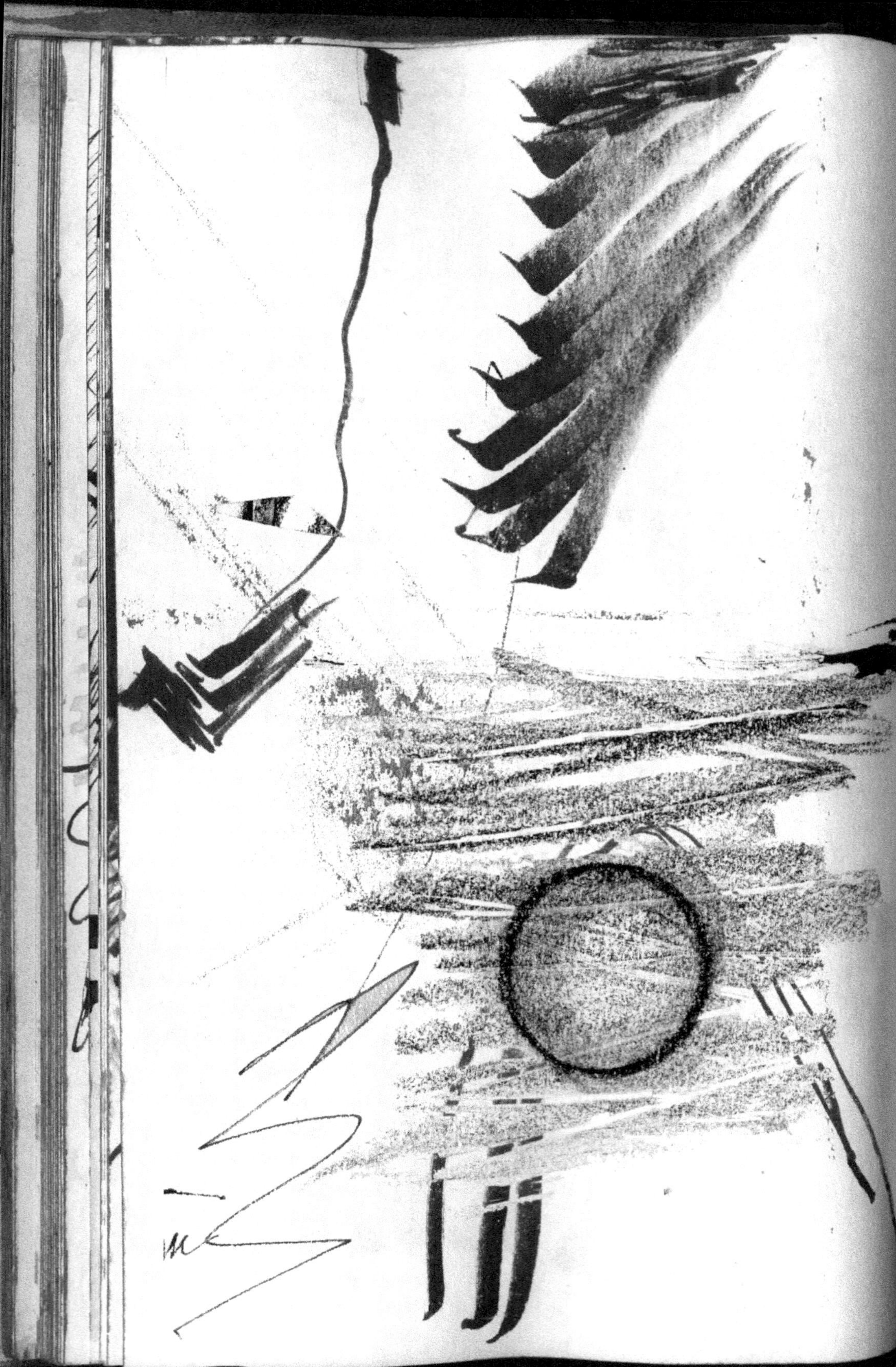

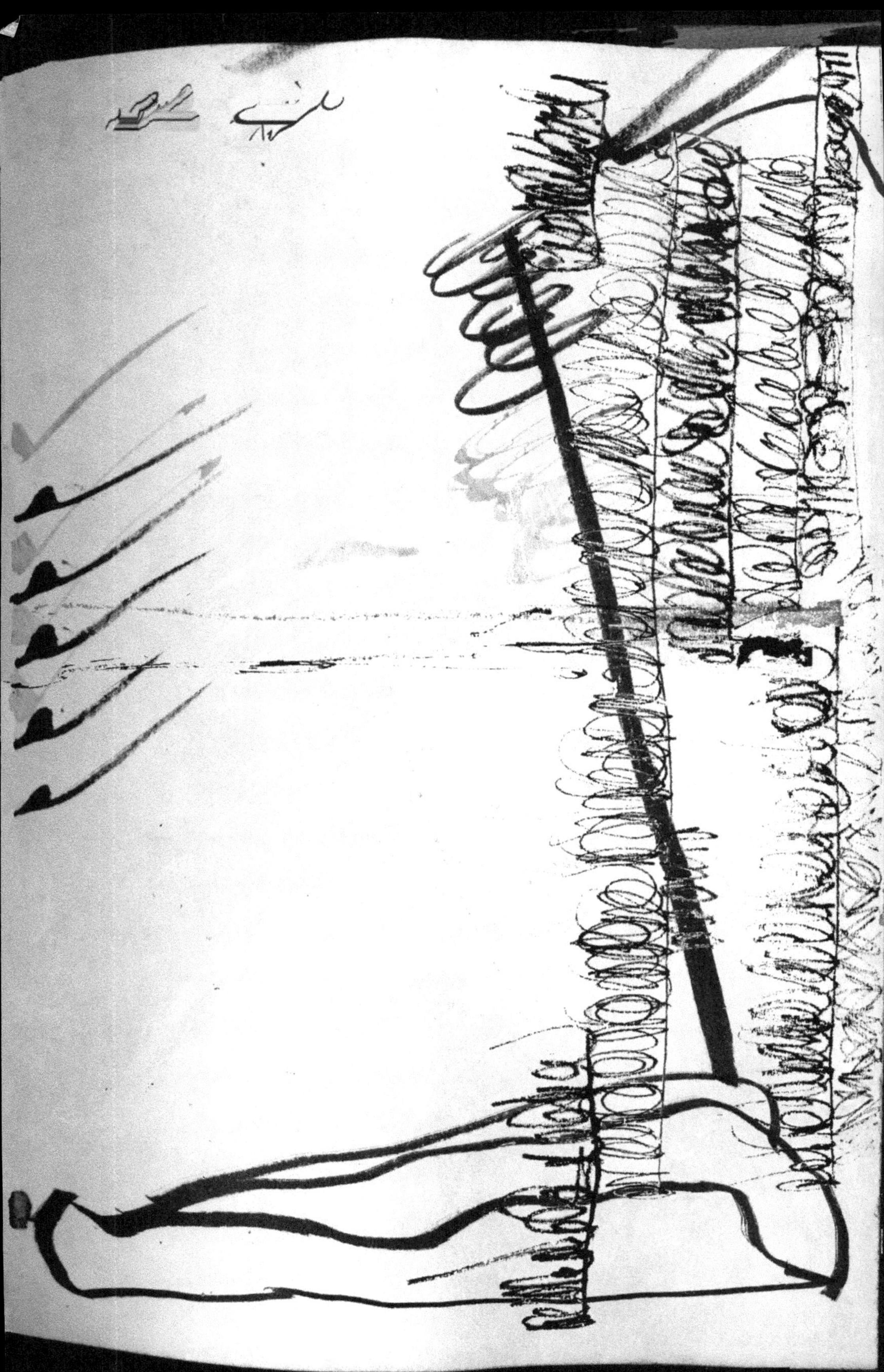

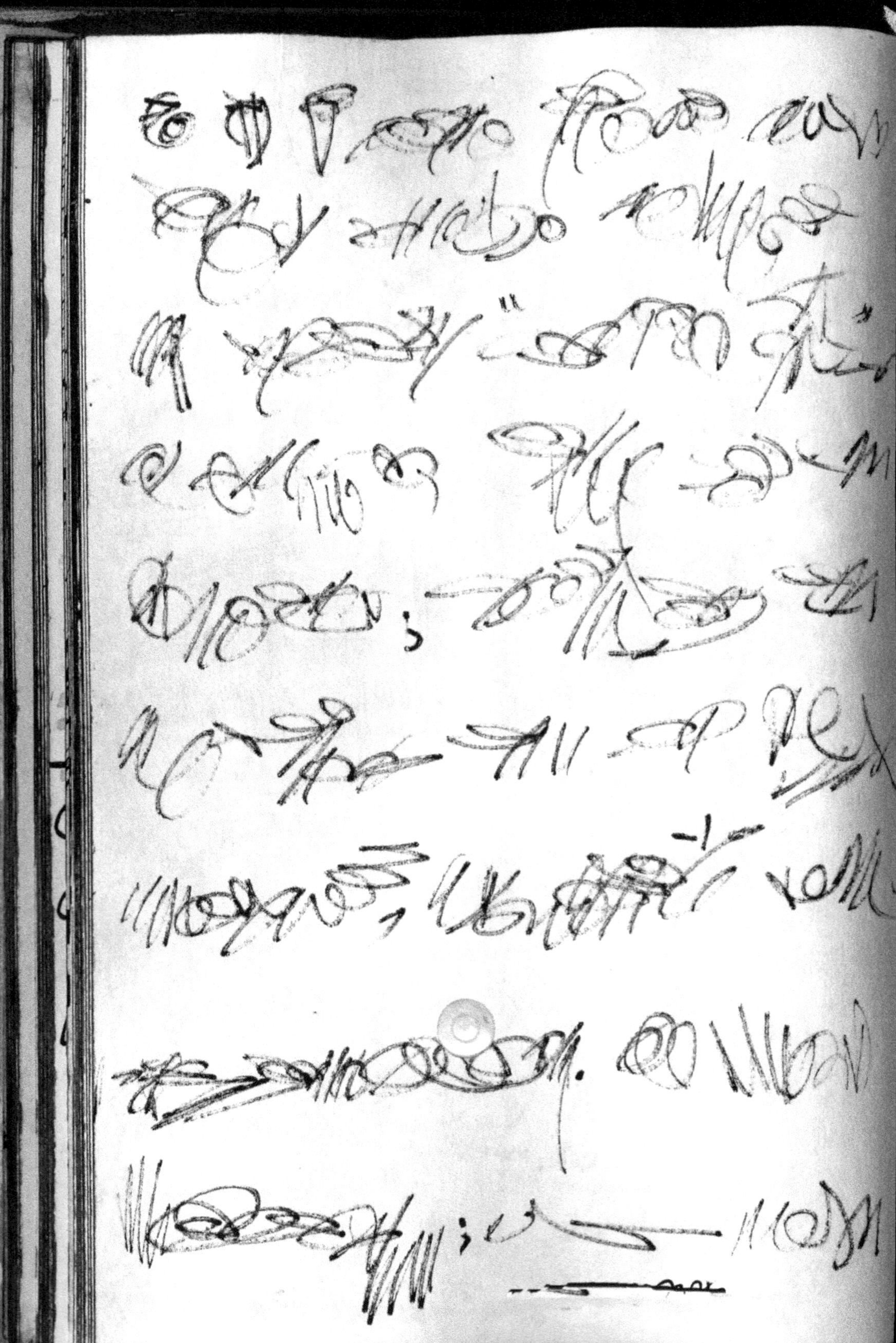

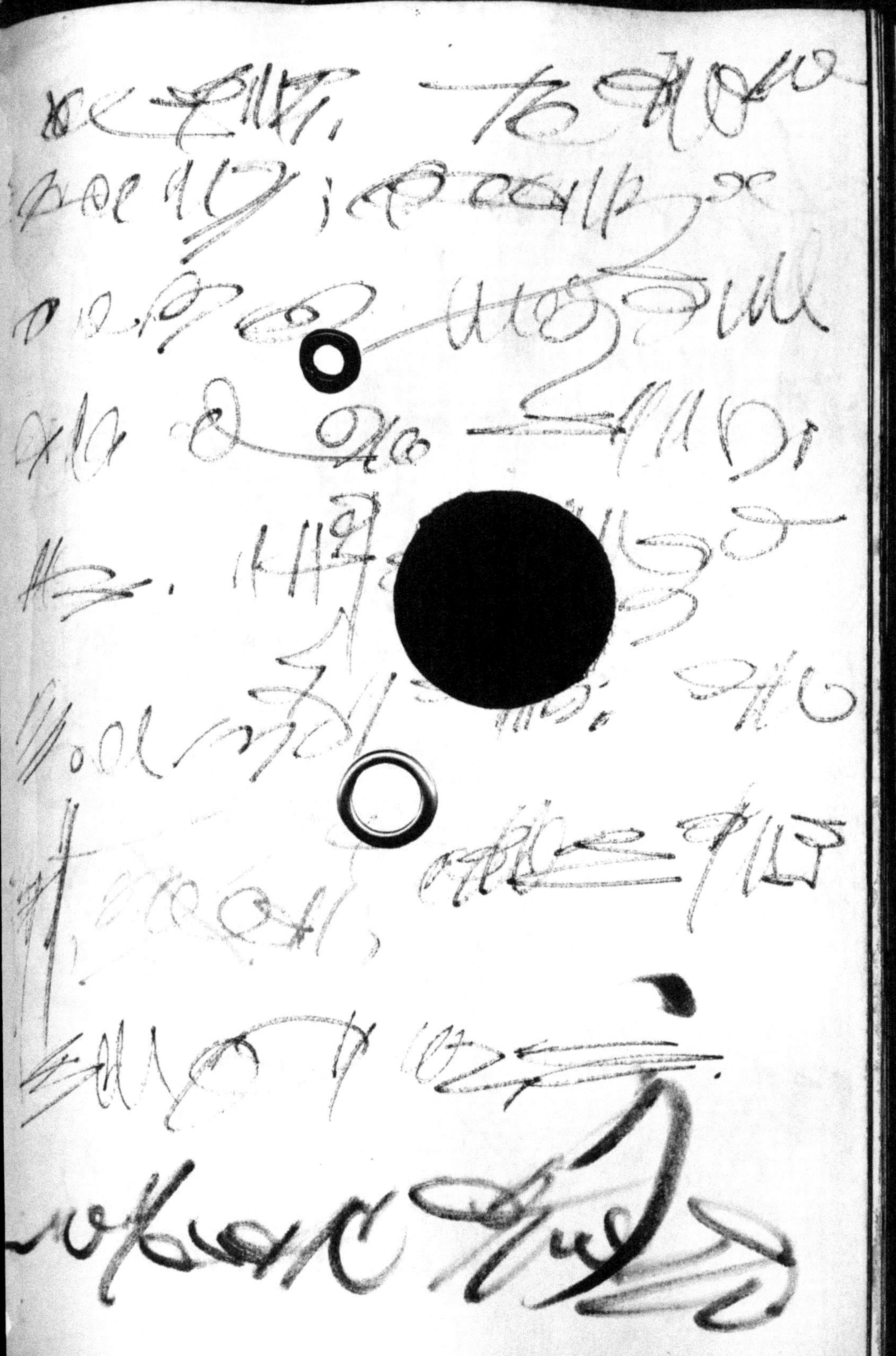

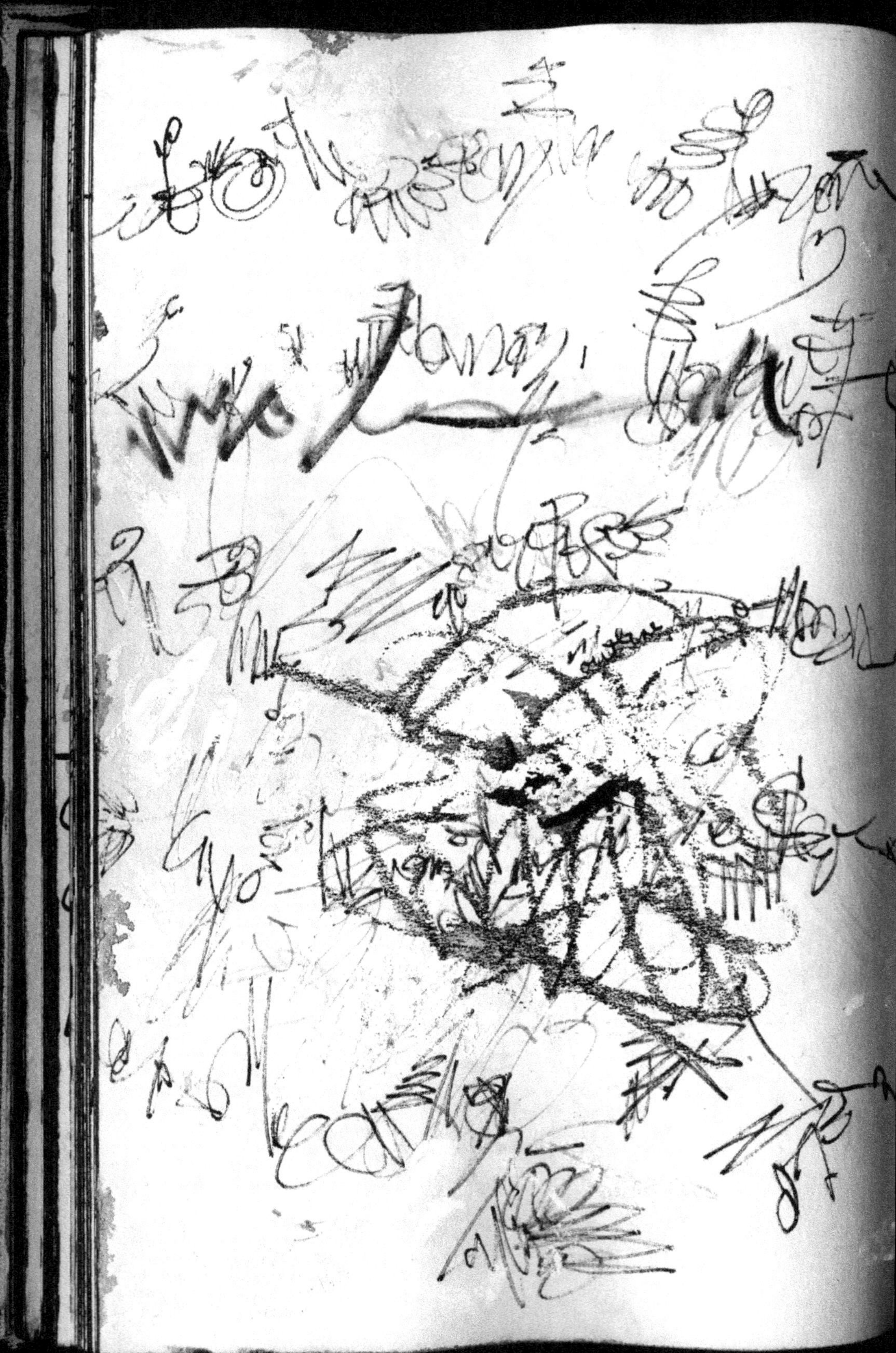

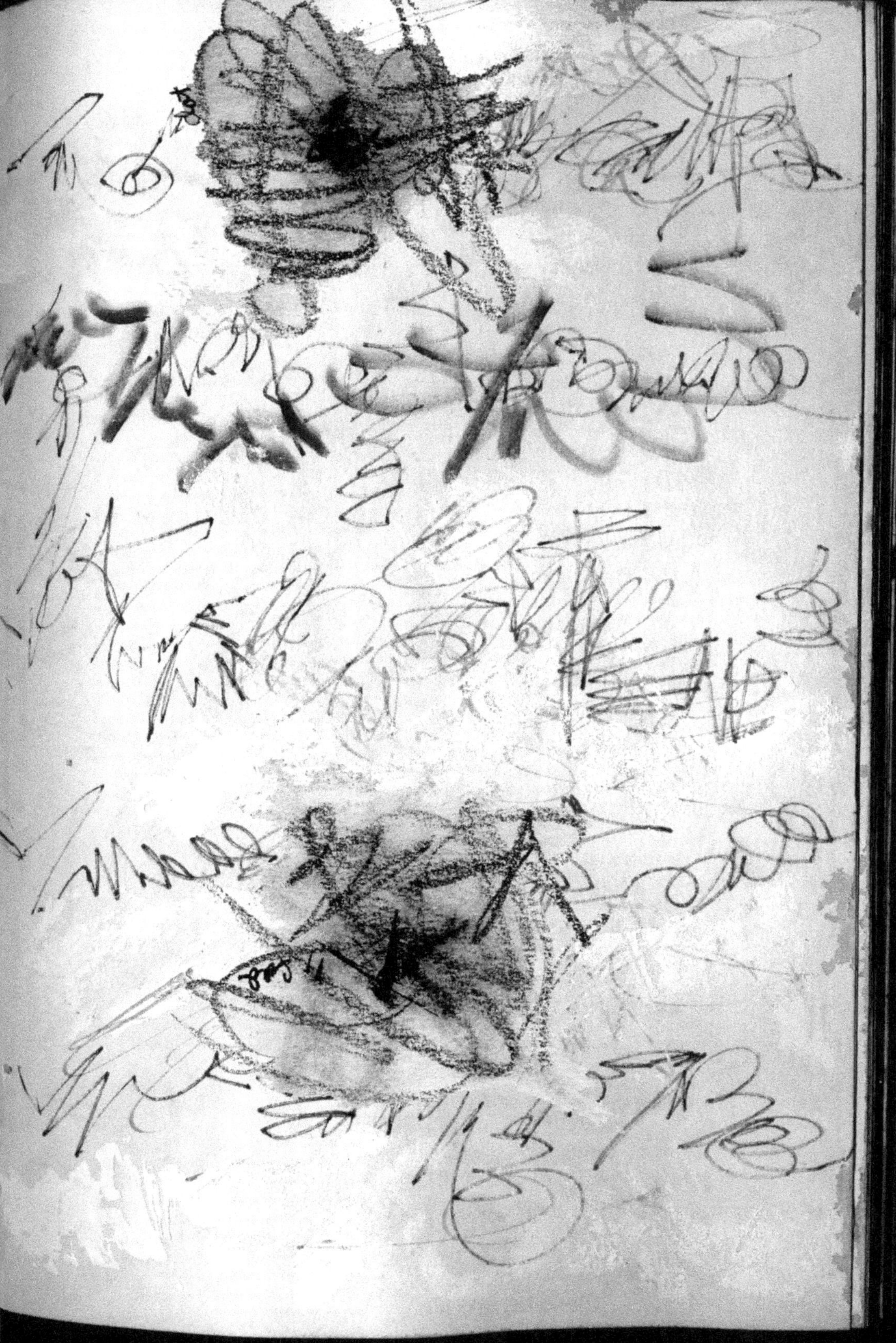

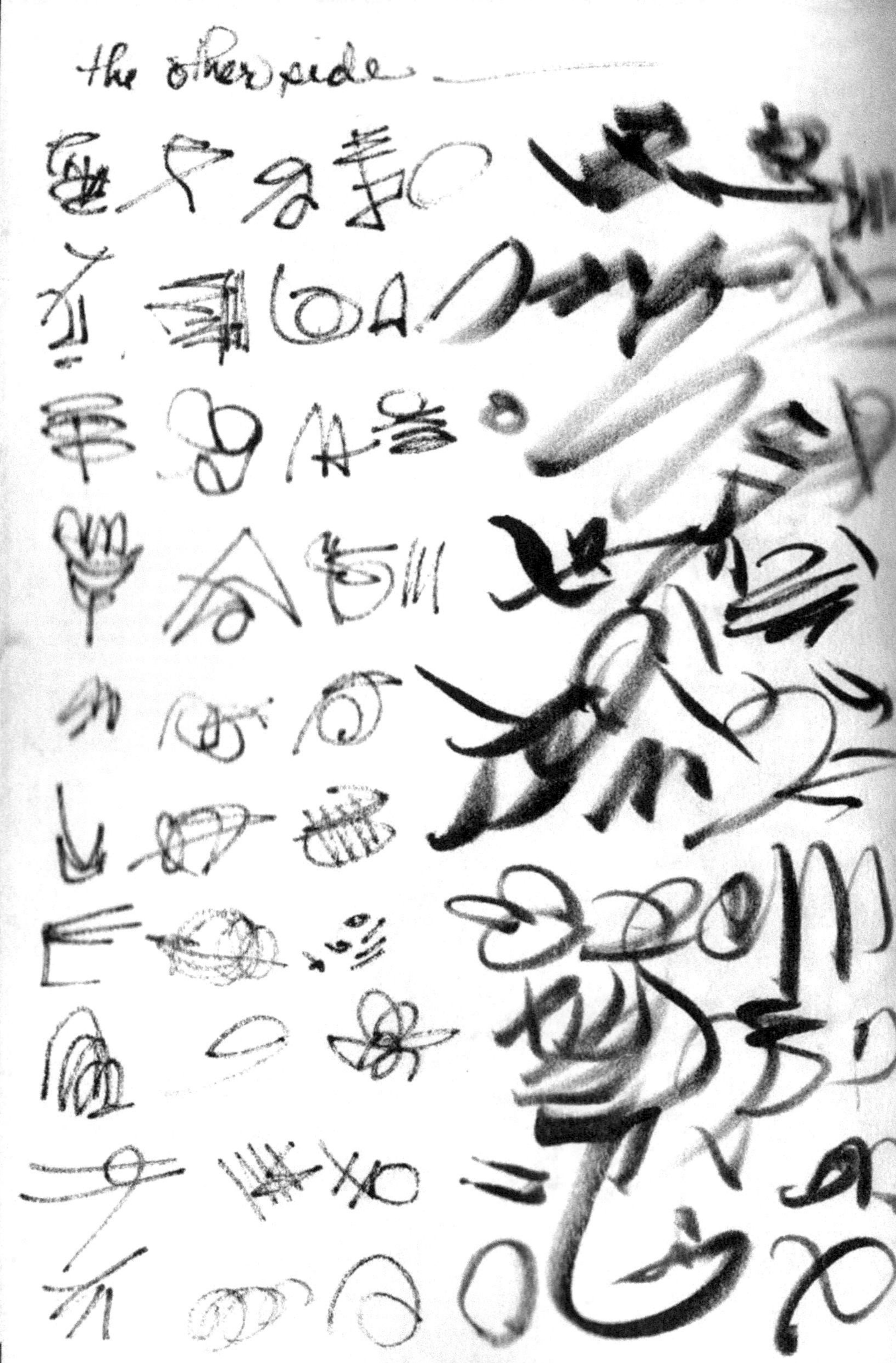
the other side

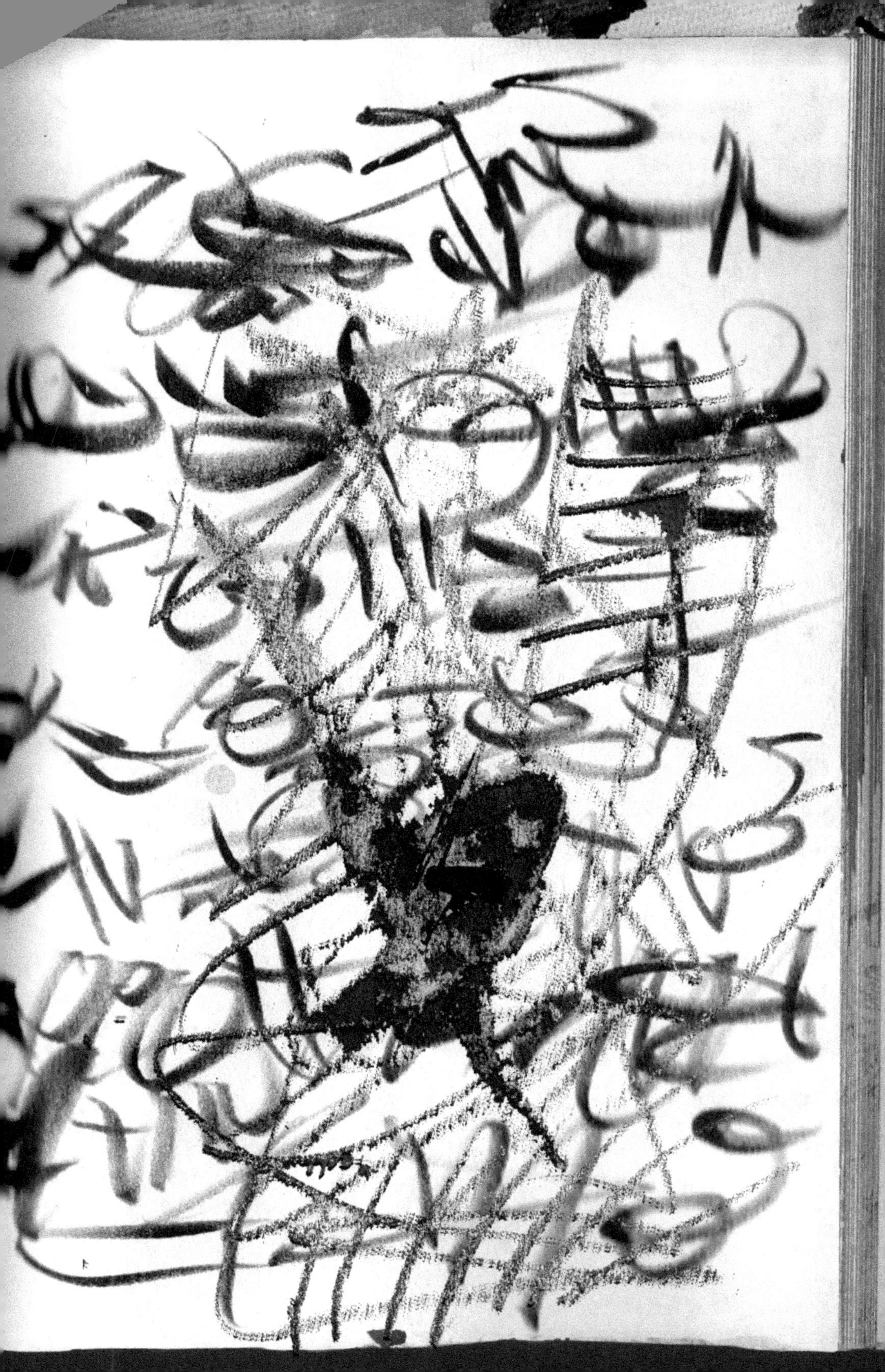

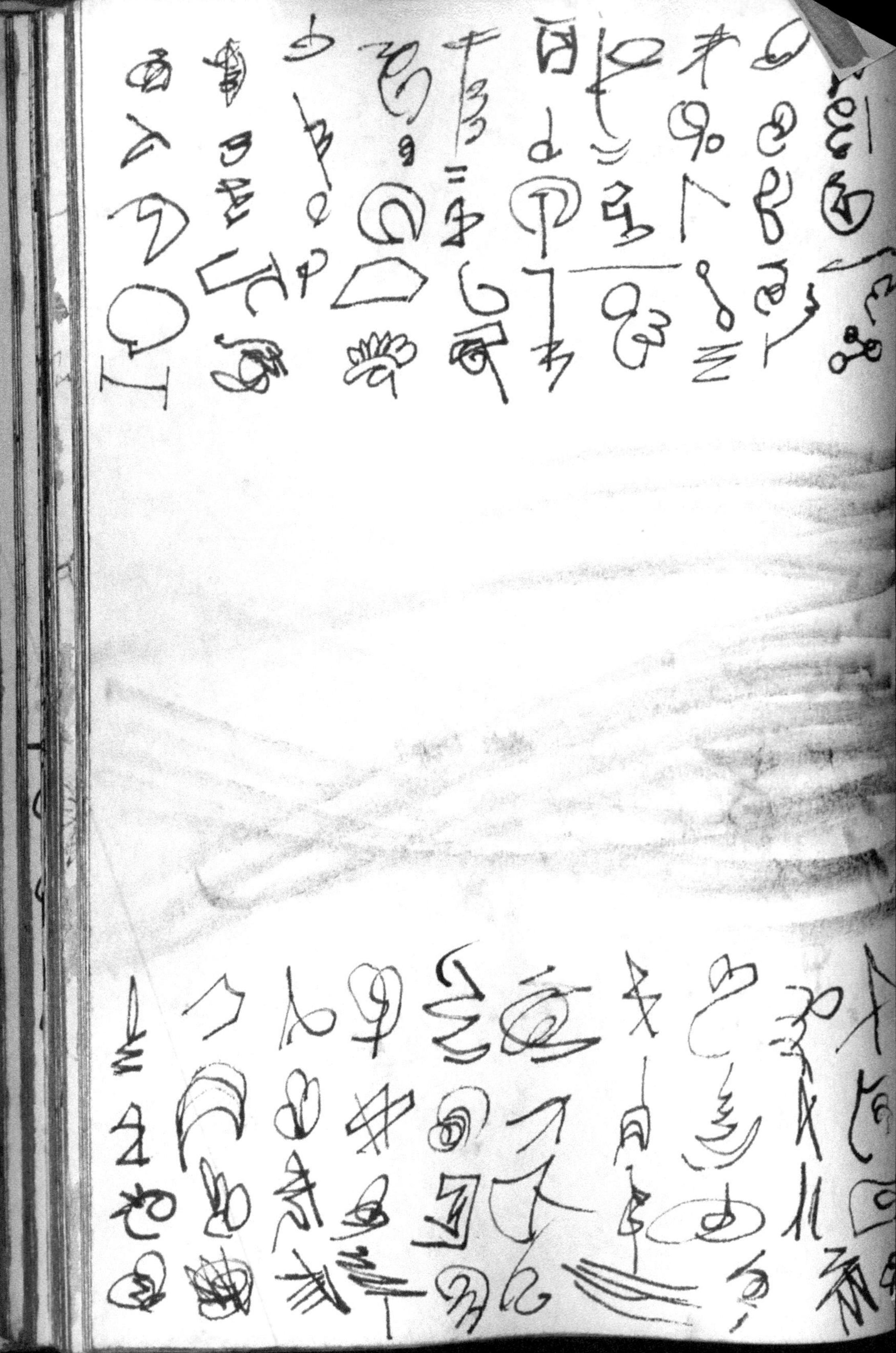

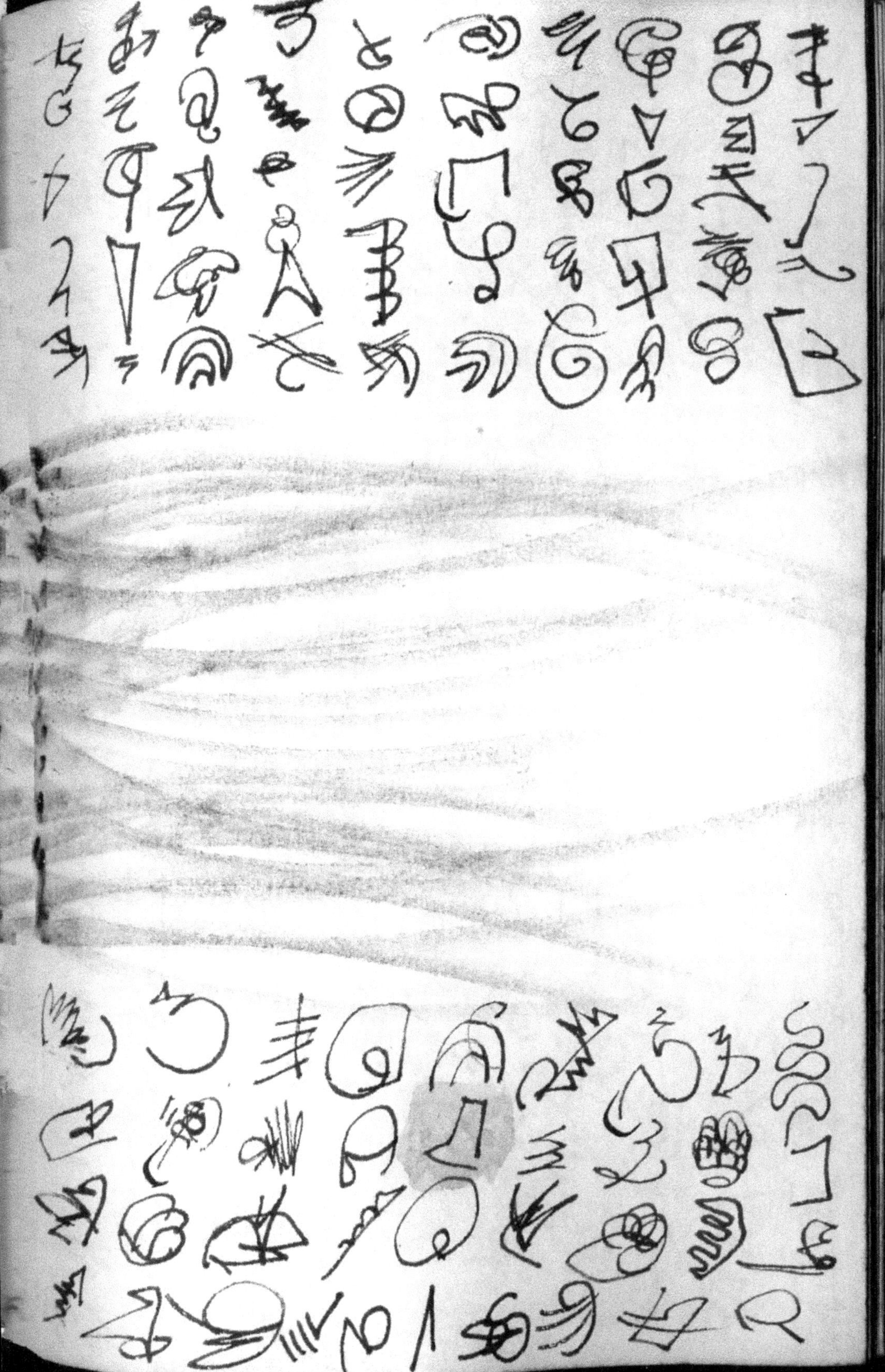

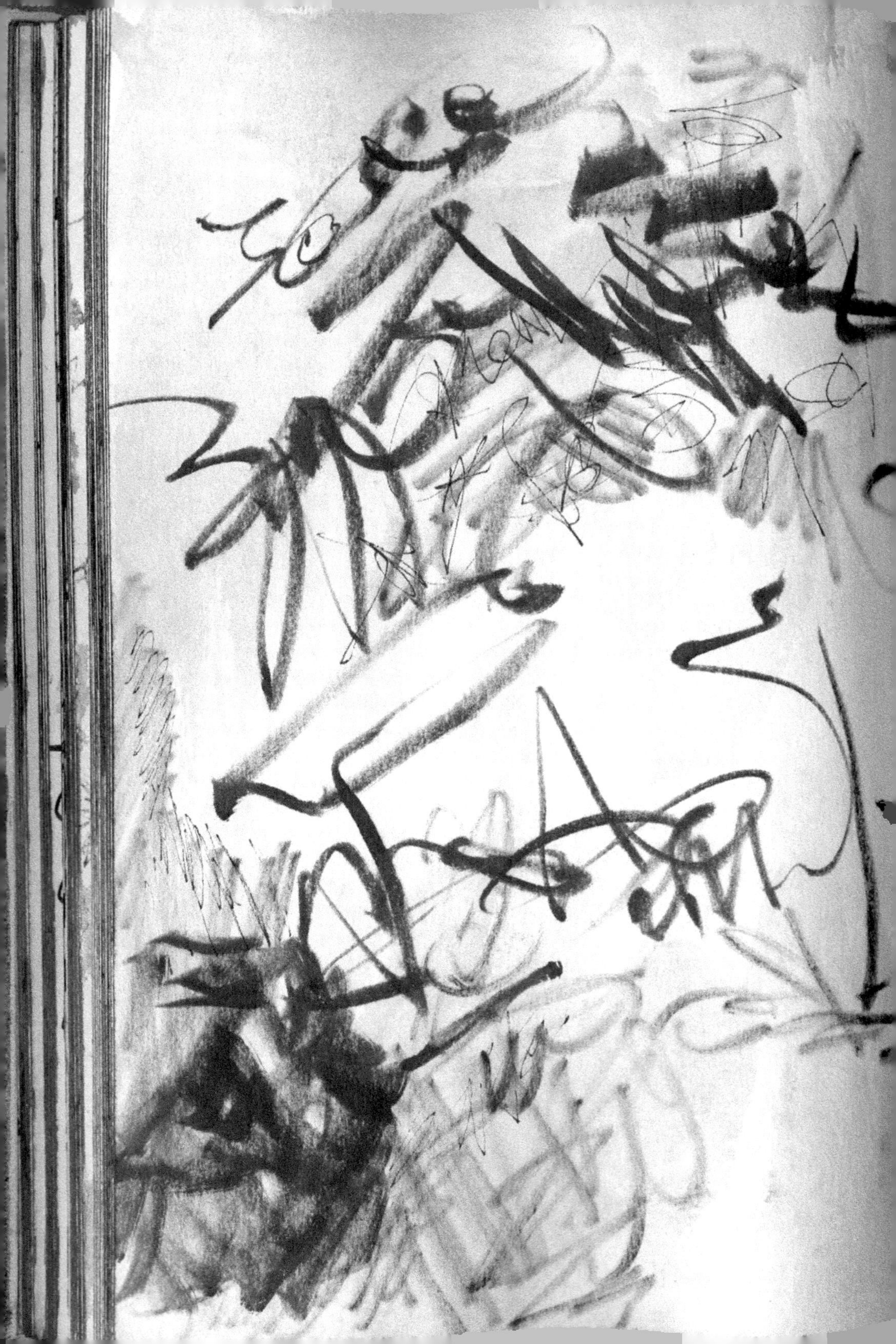

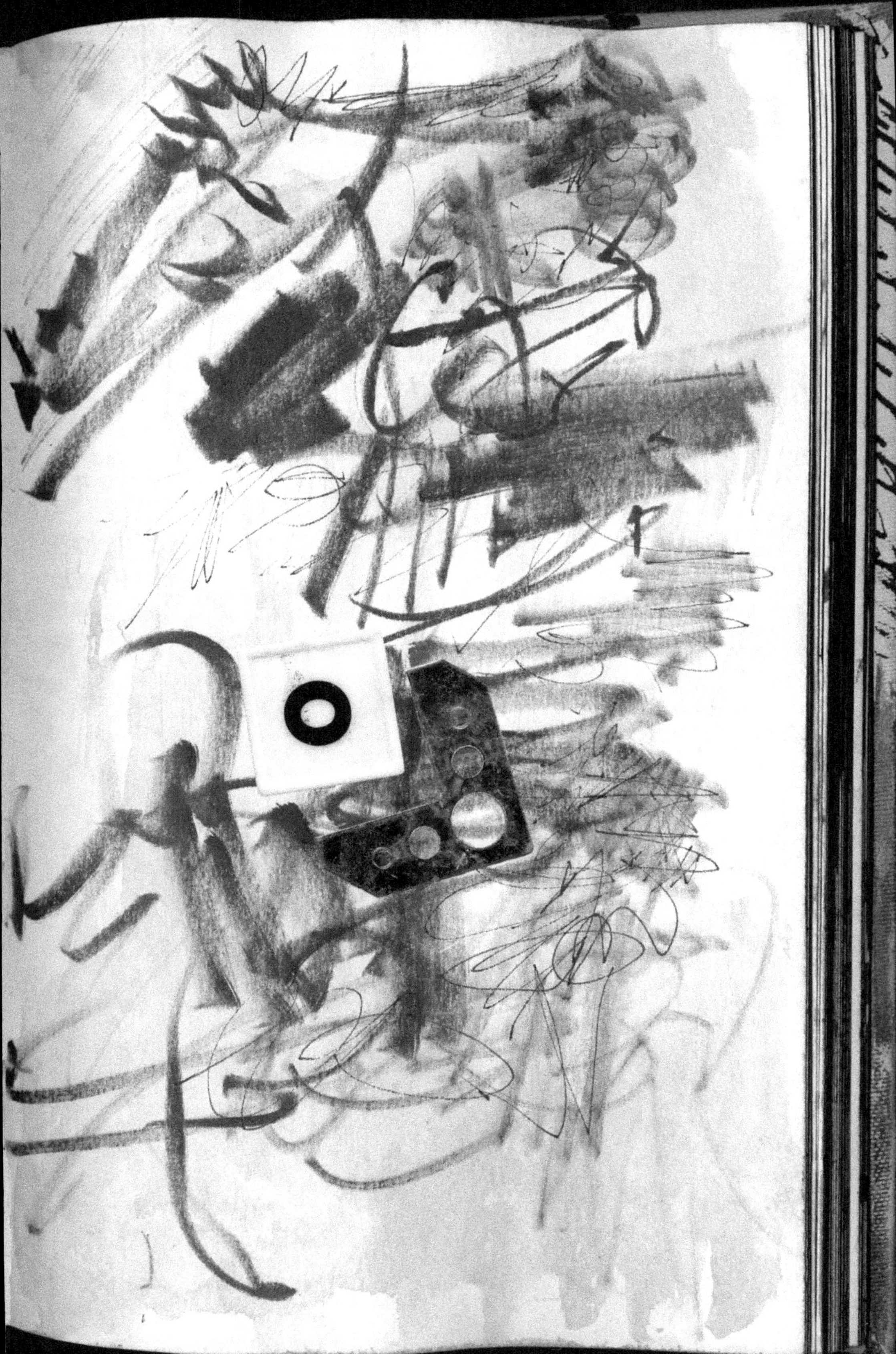

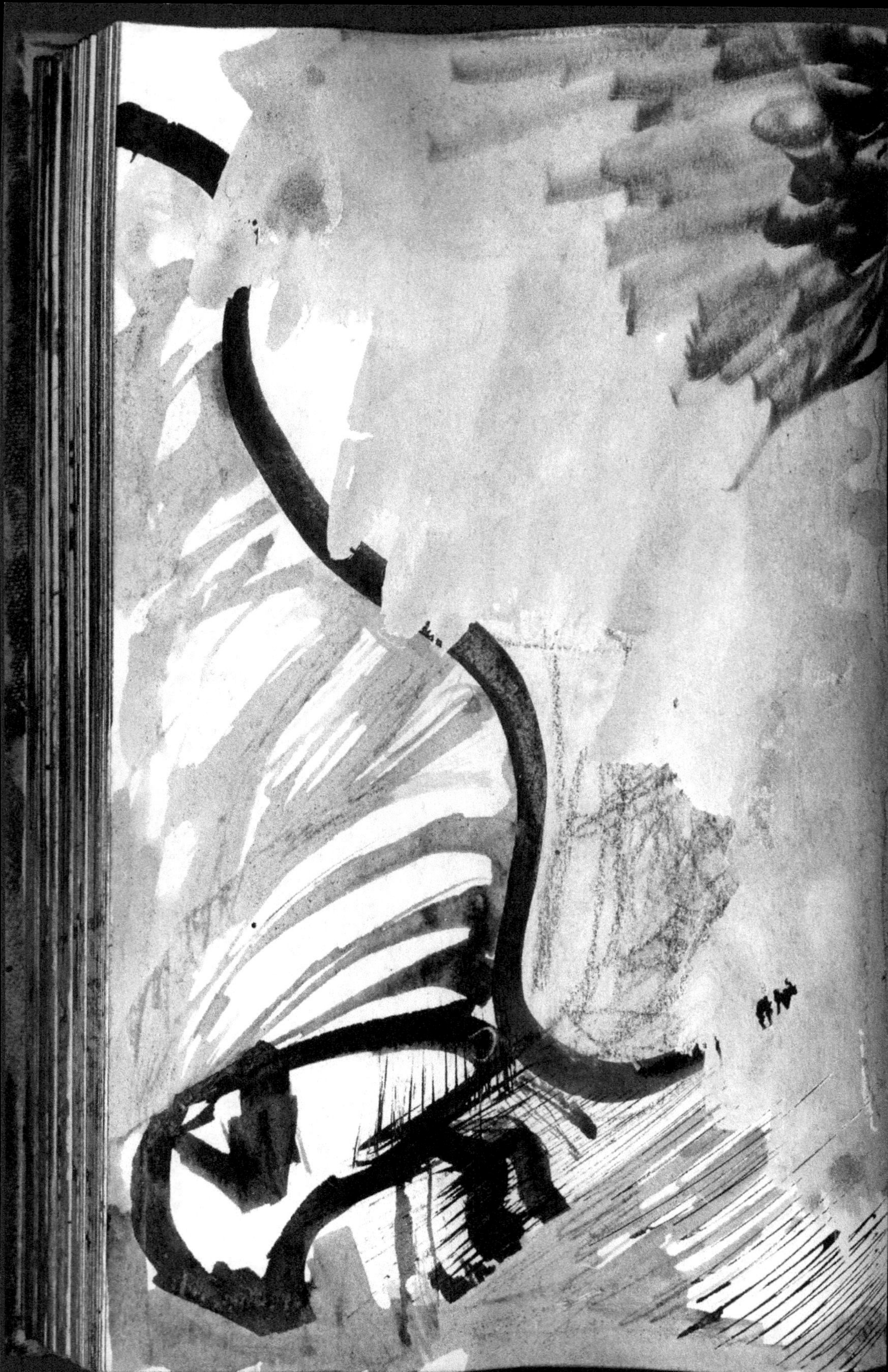

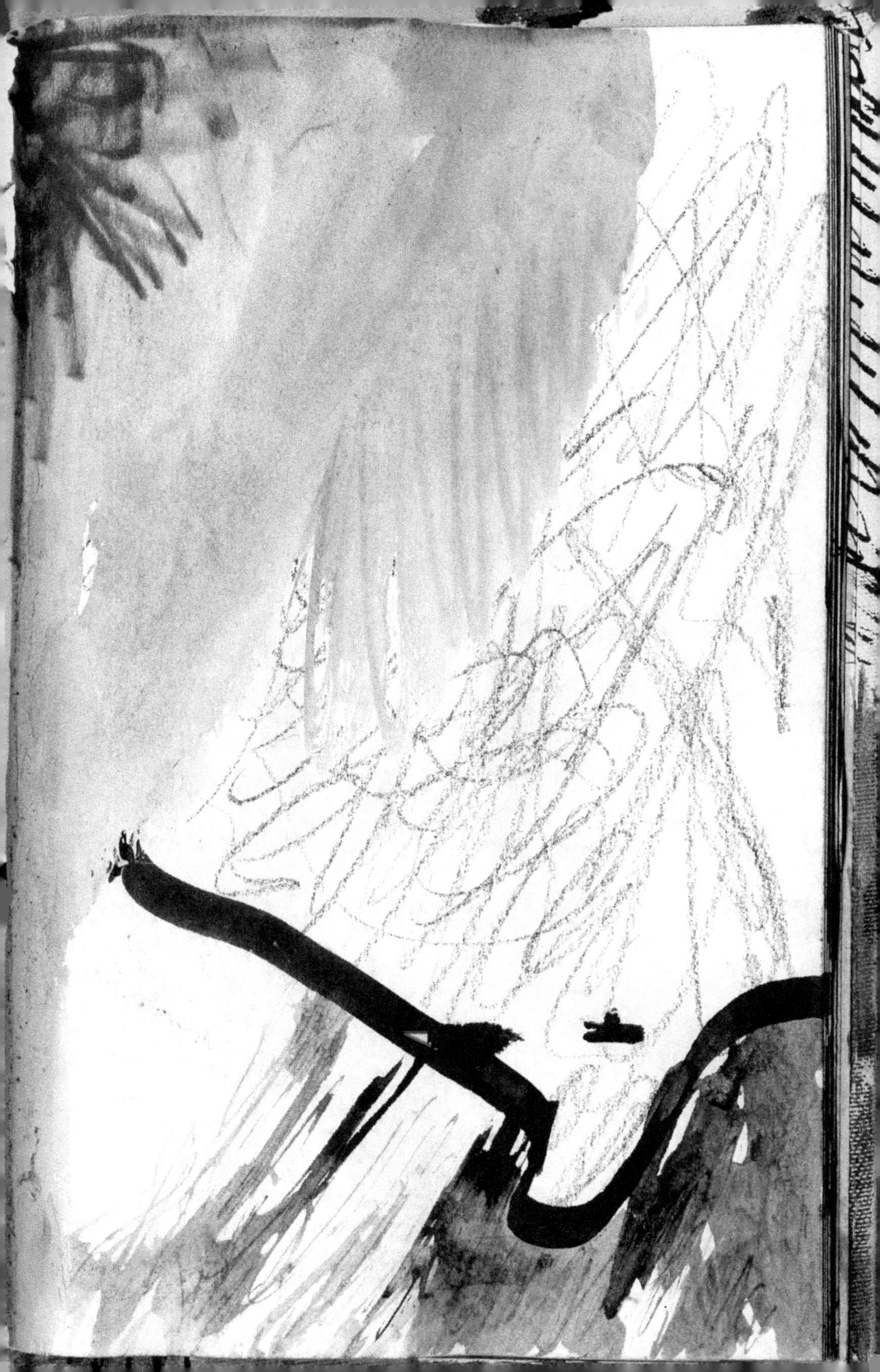

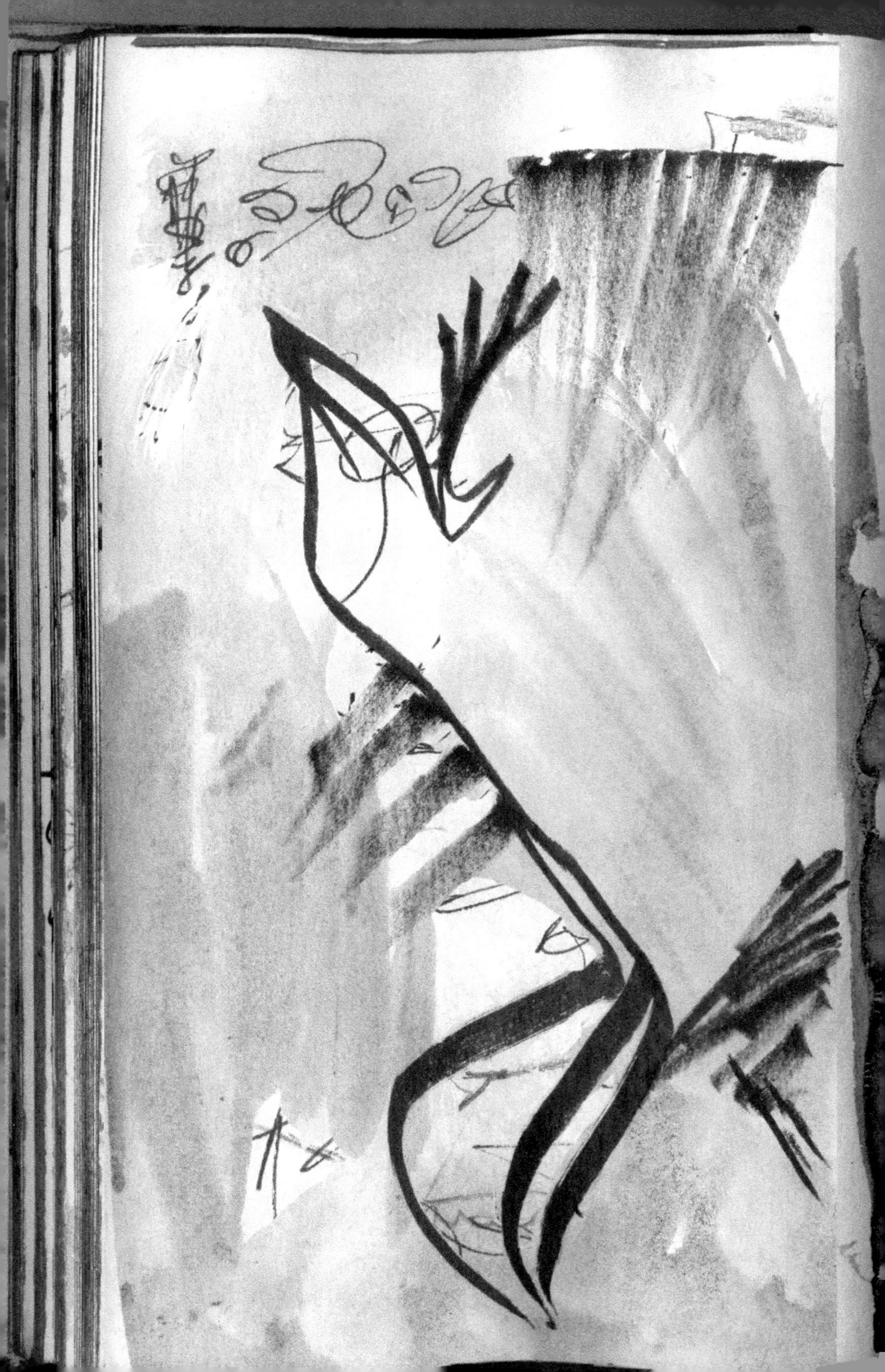

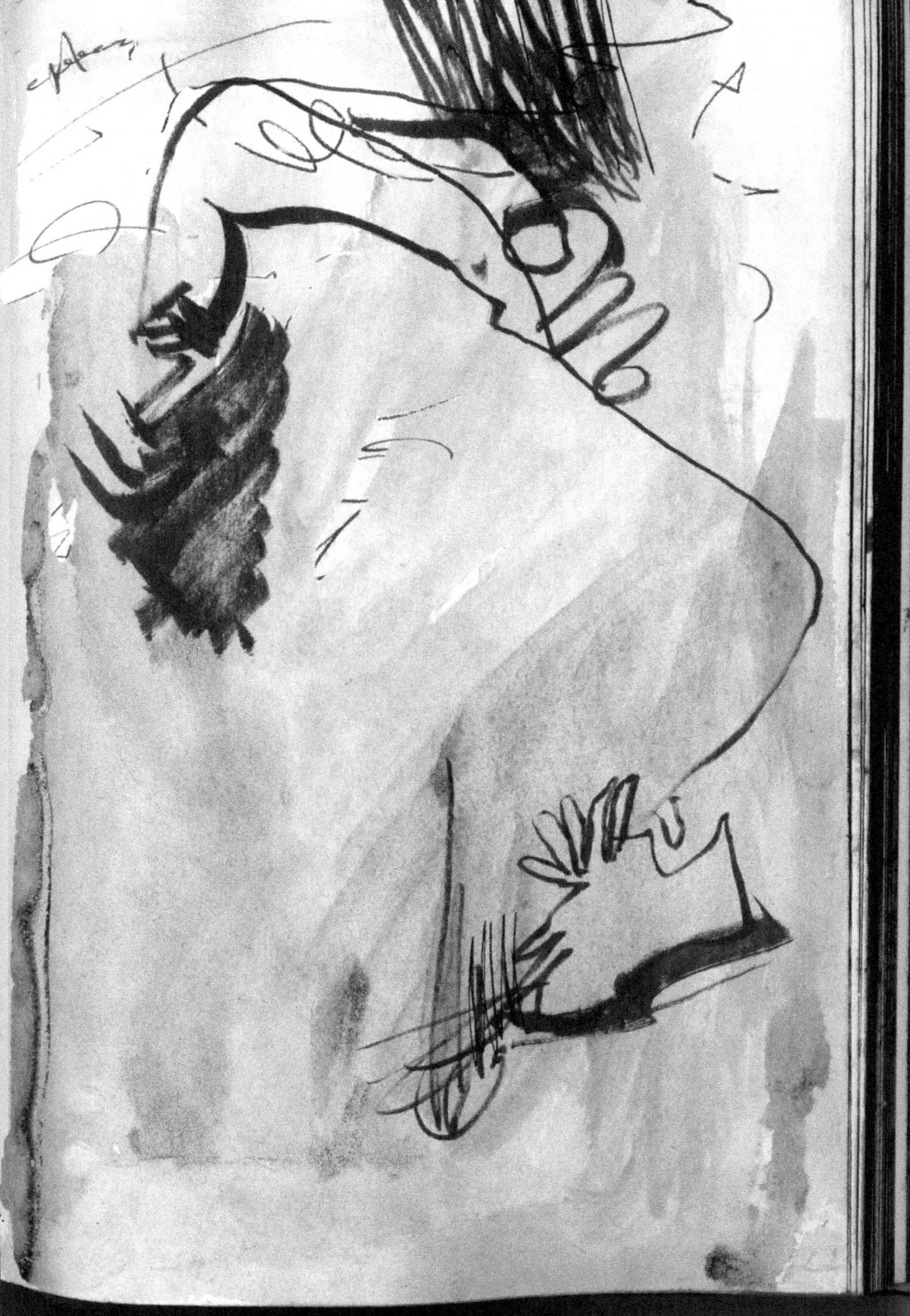

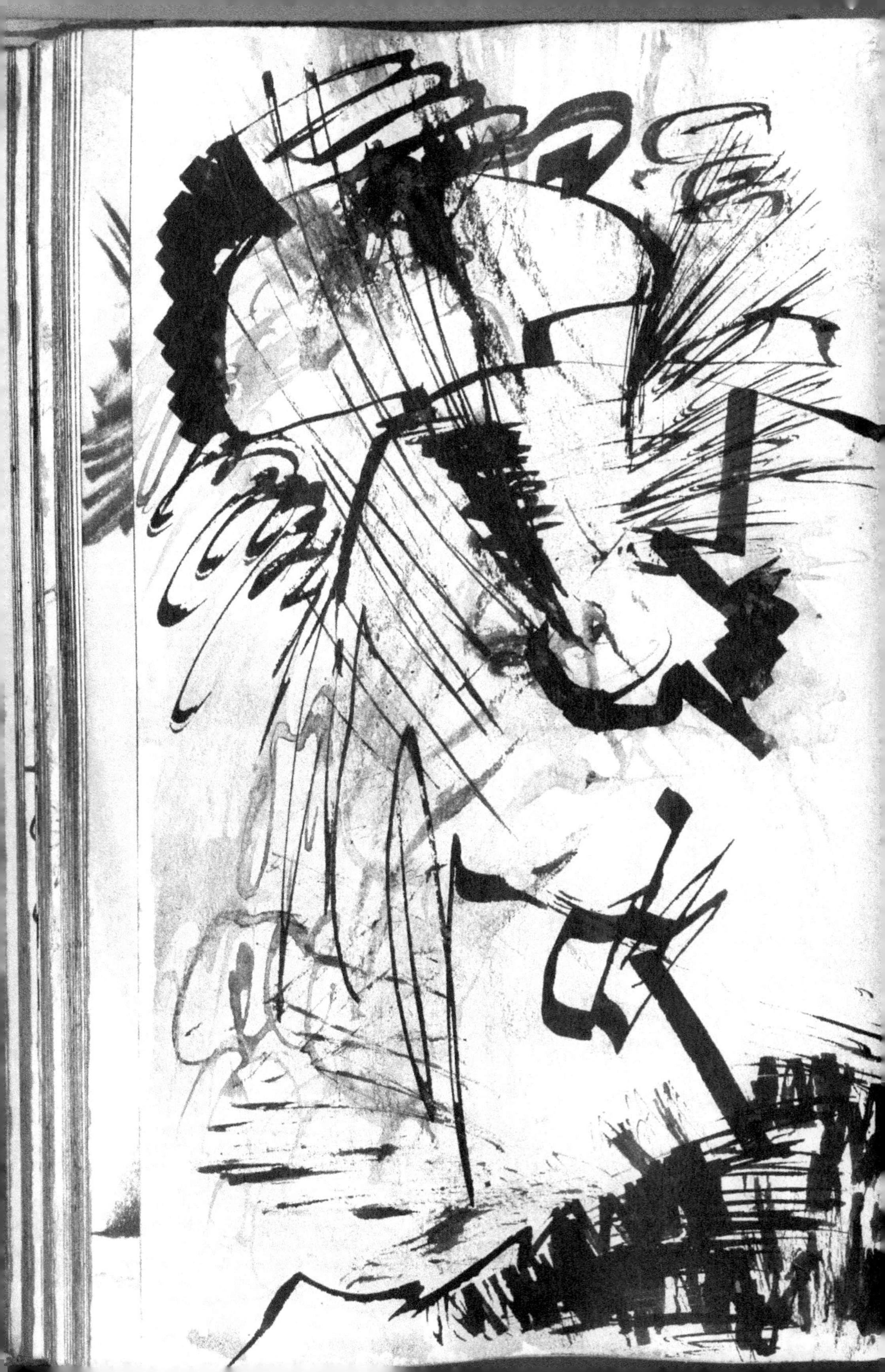

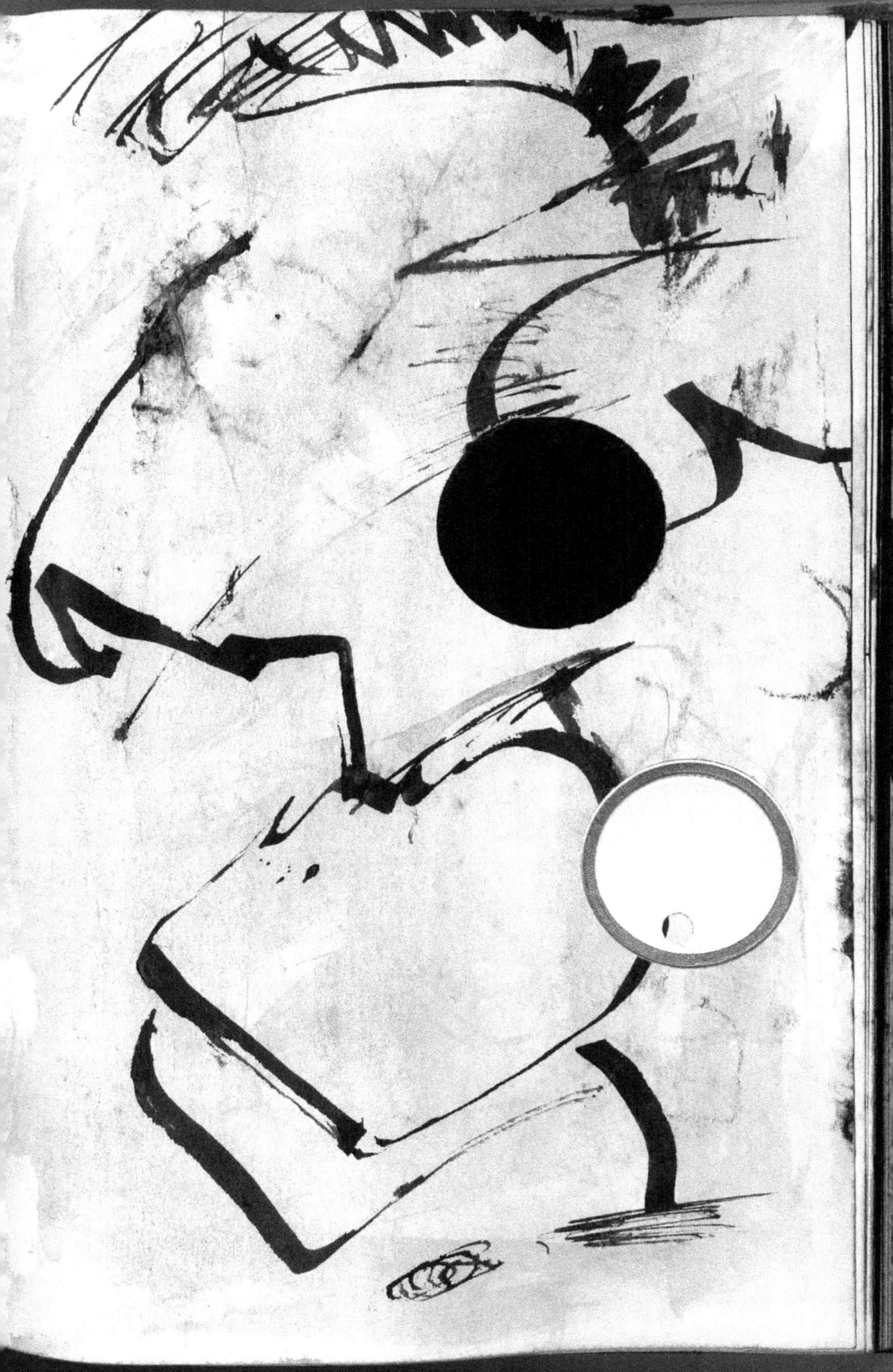

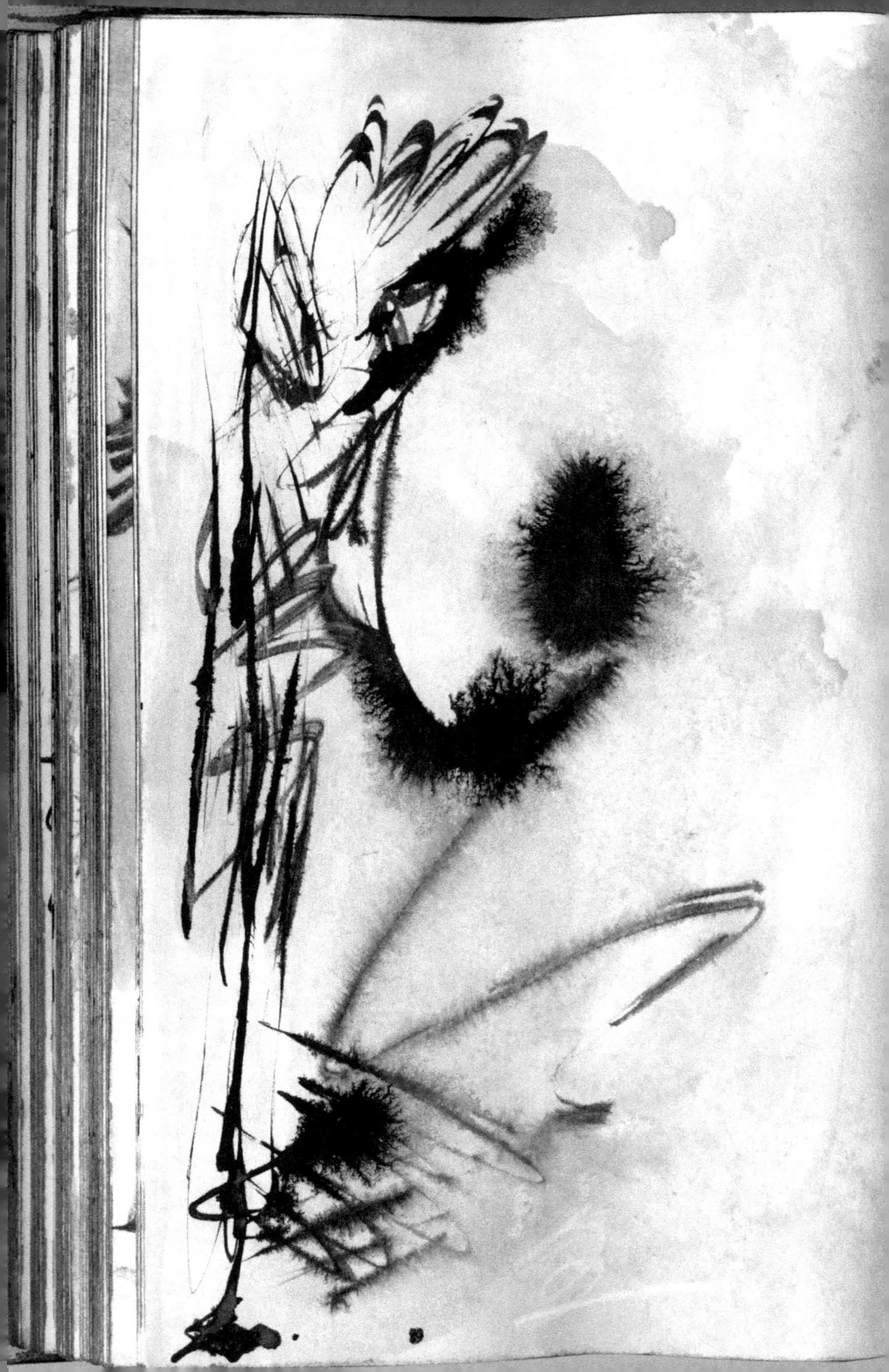

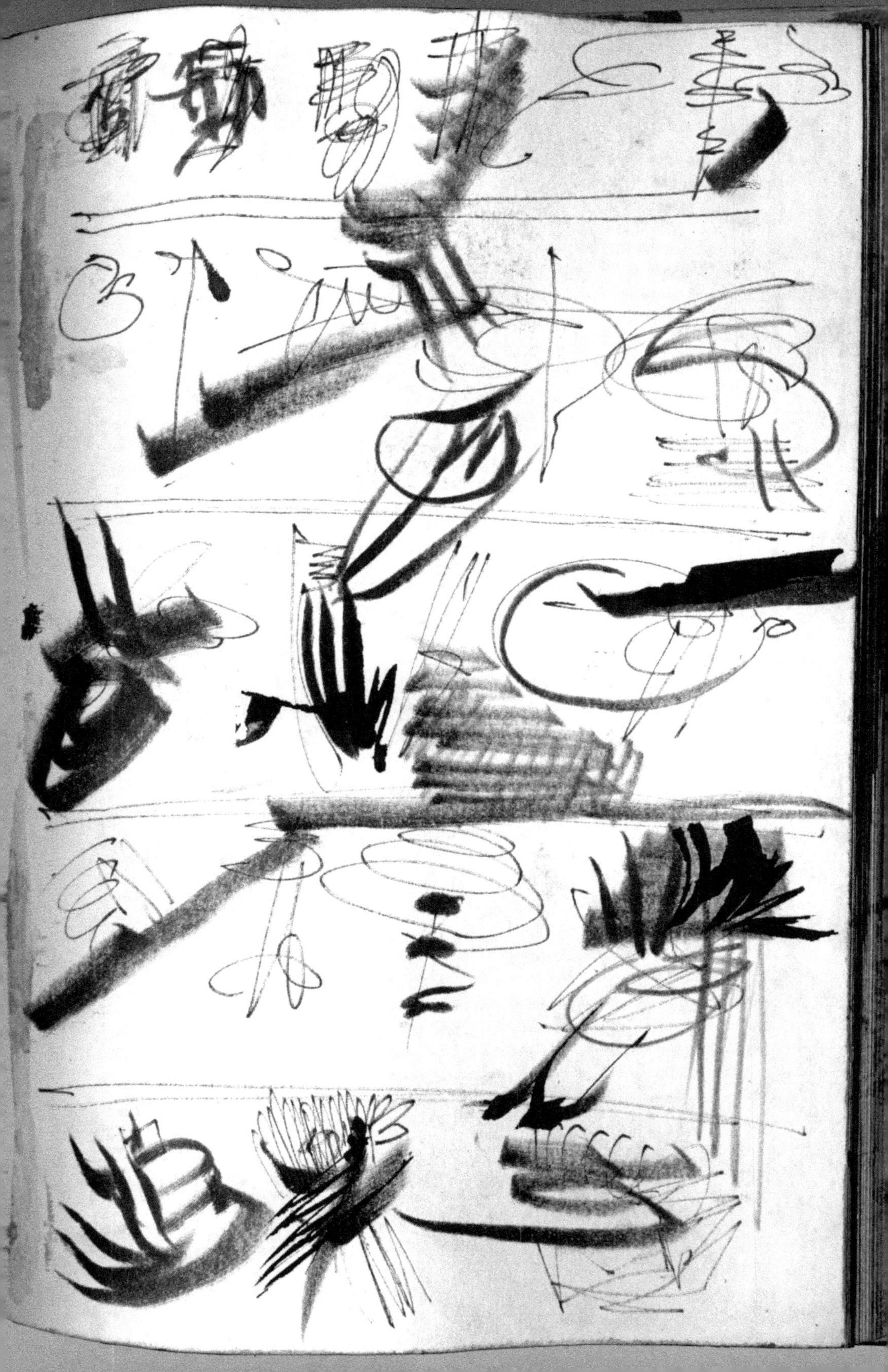

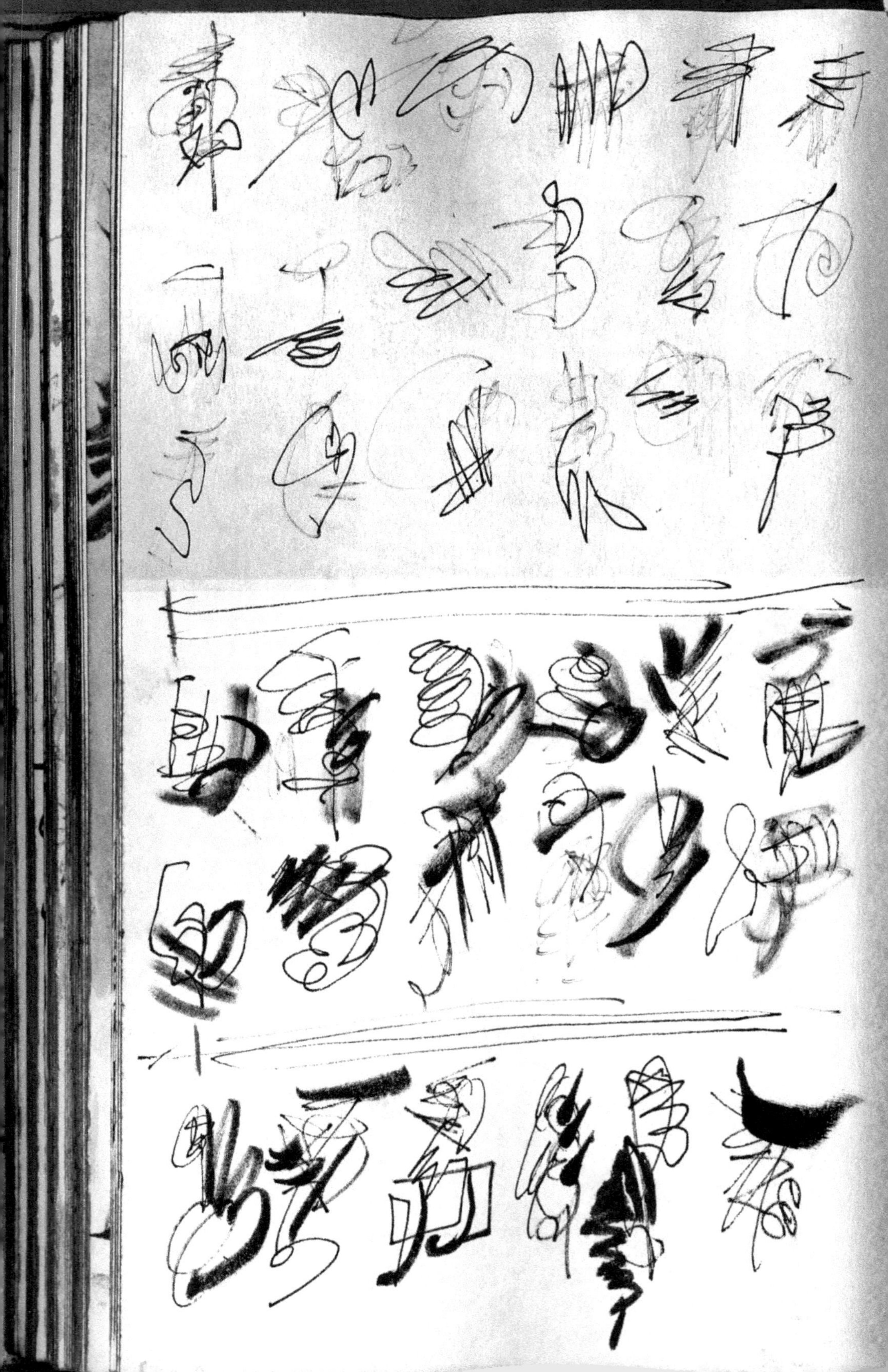

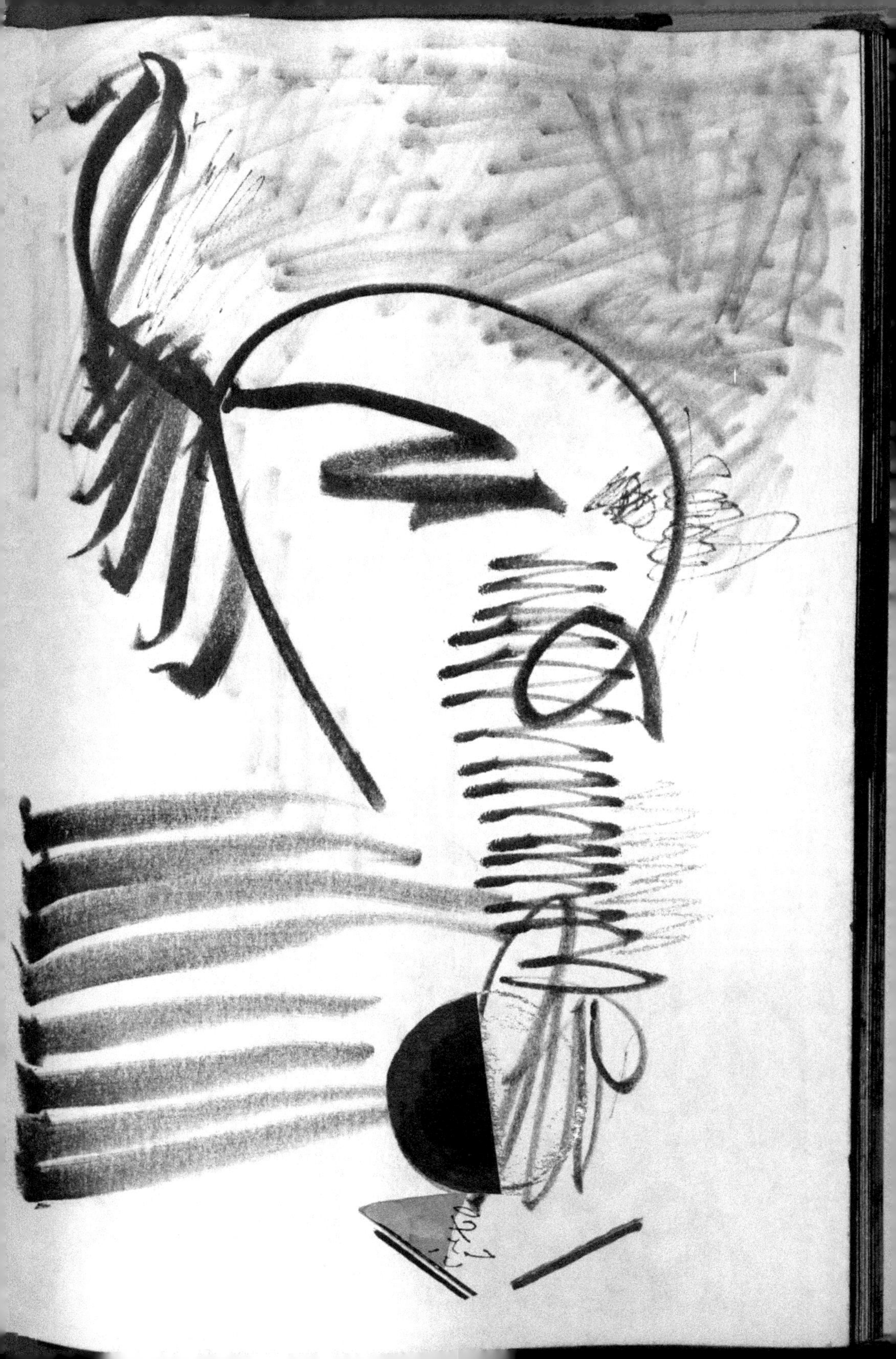

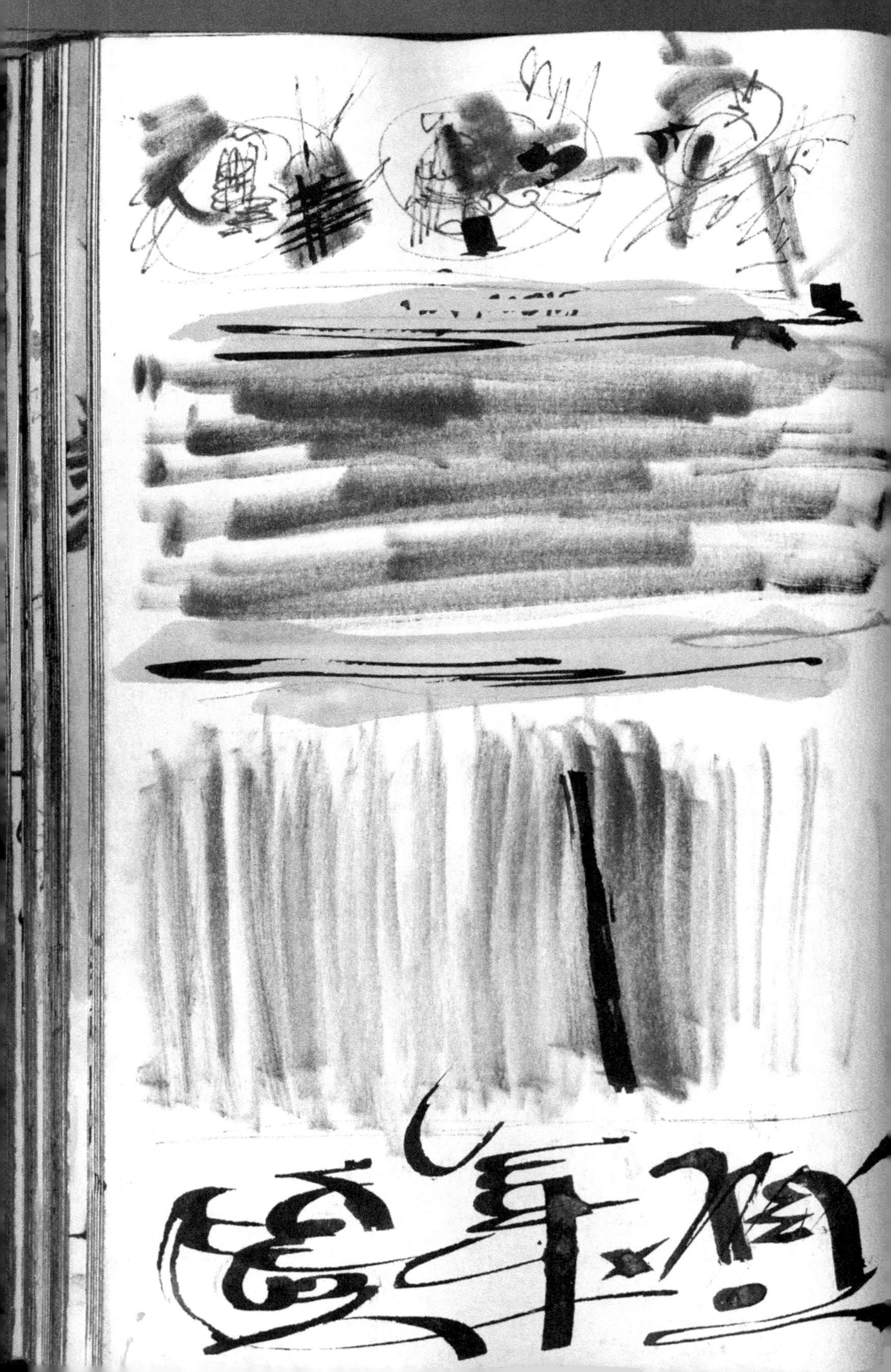

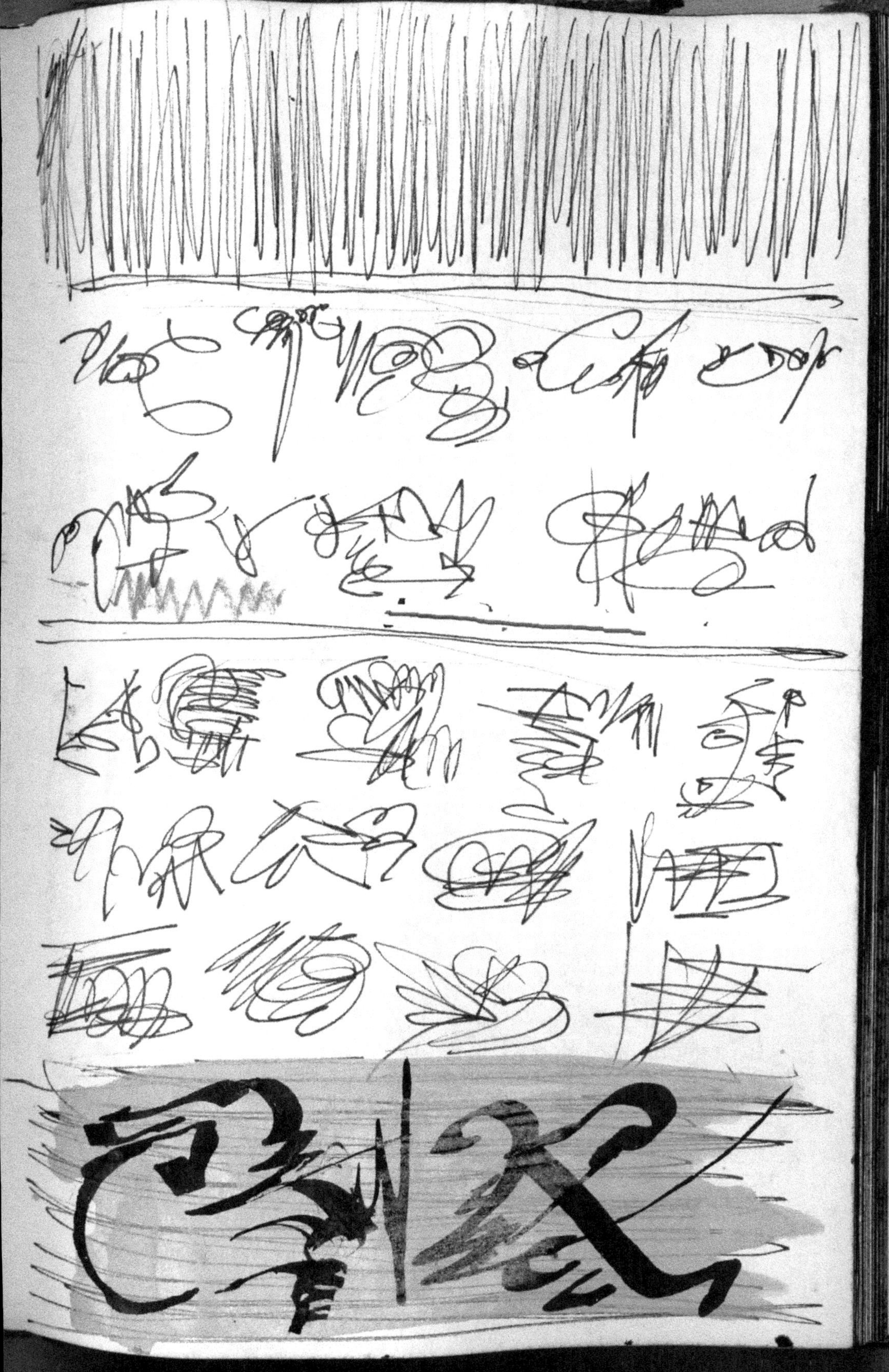

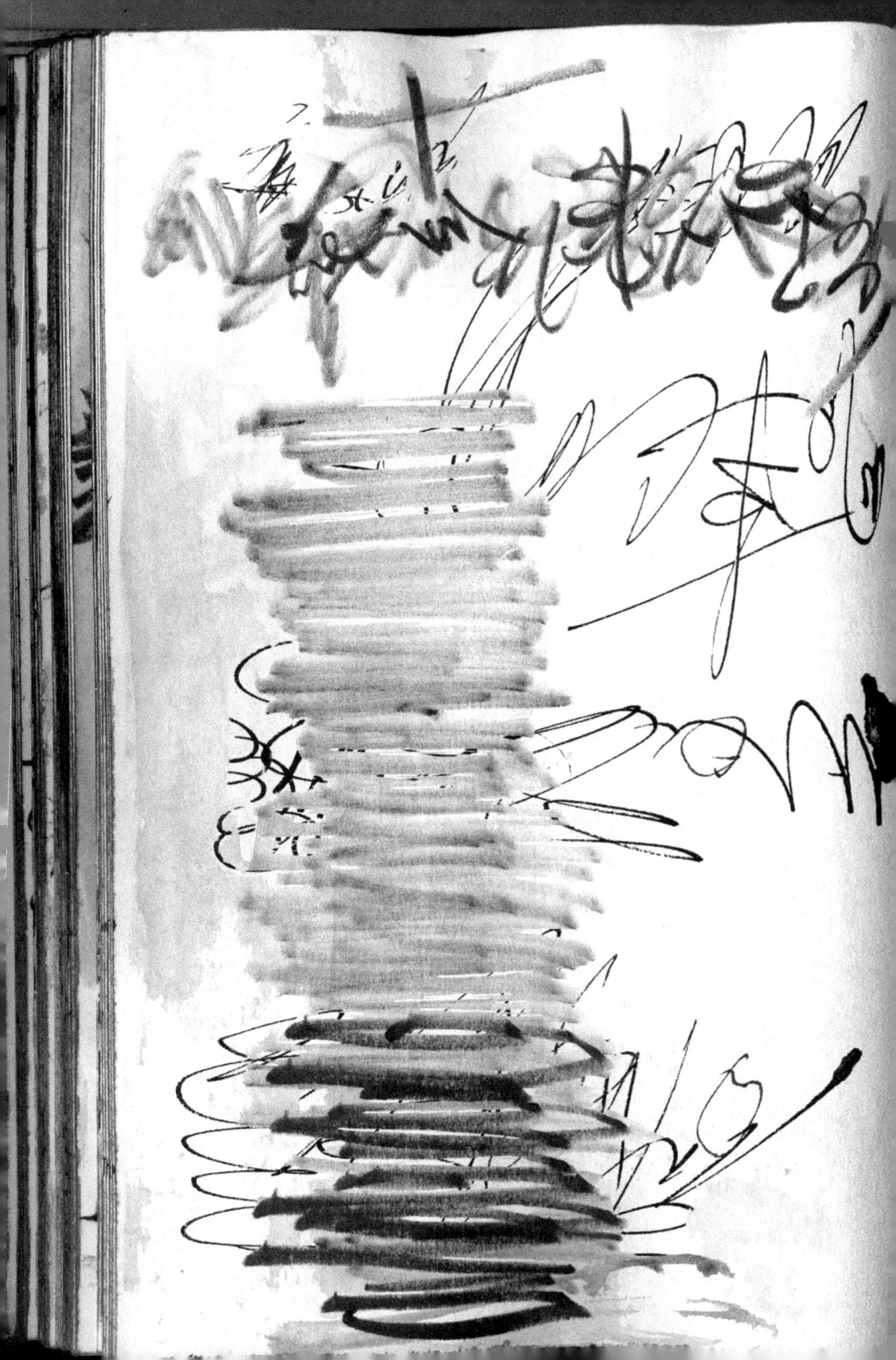

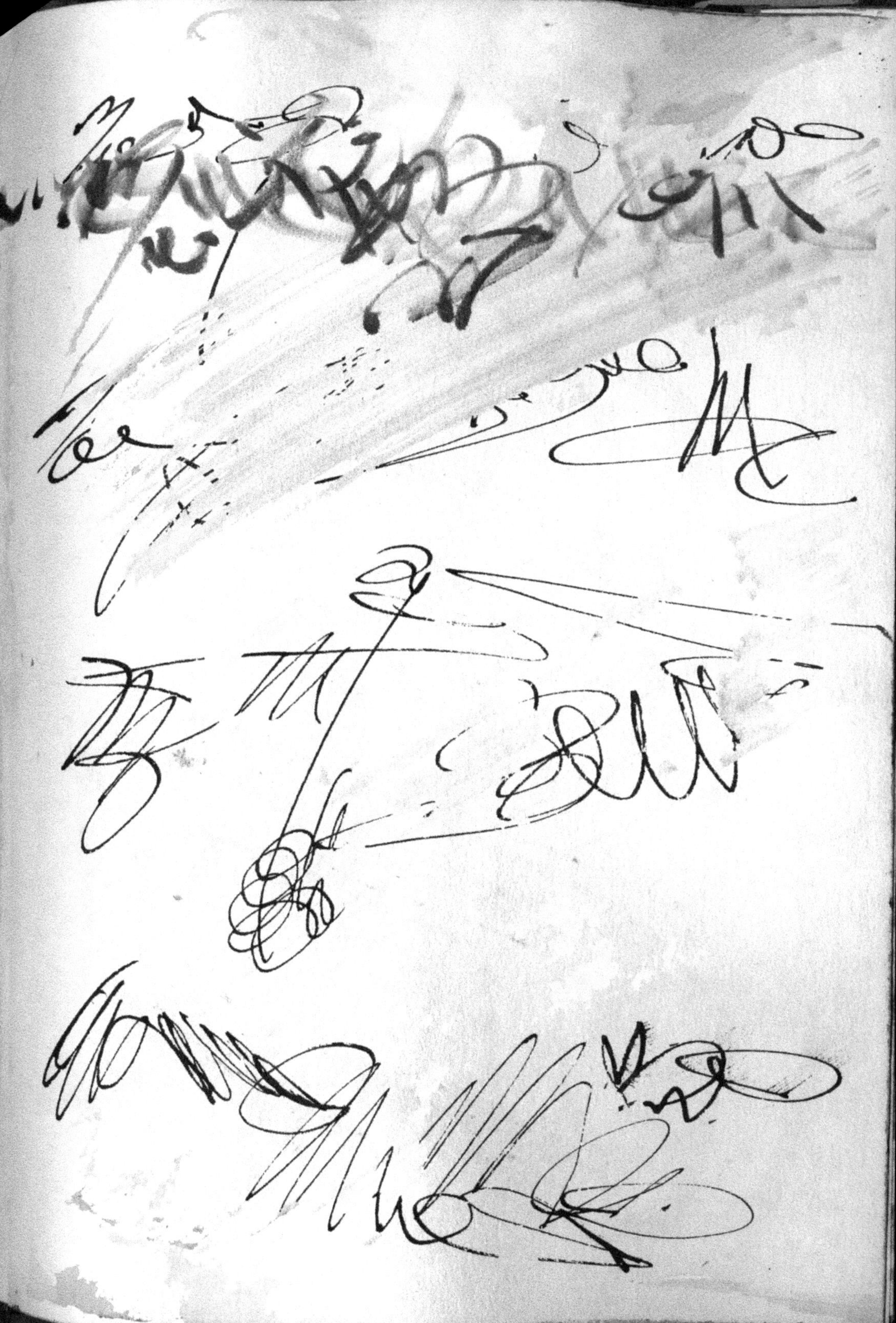

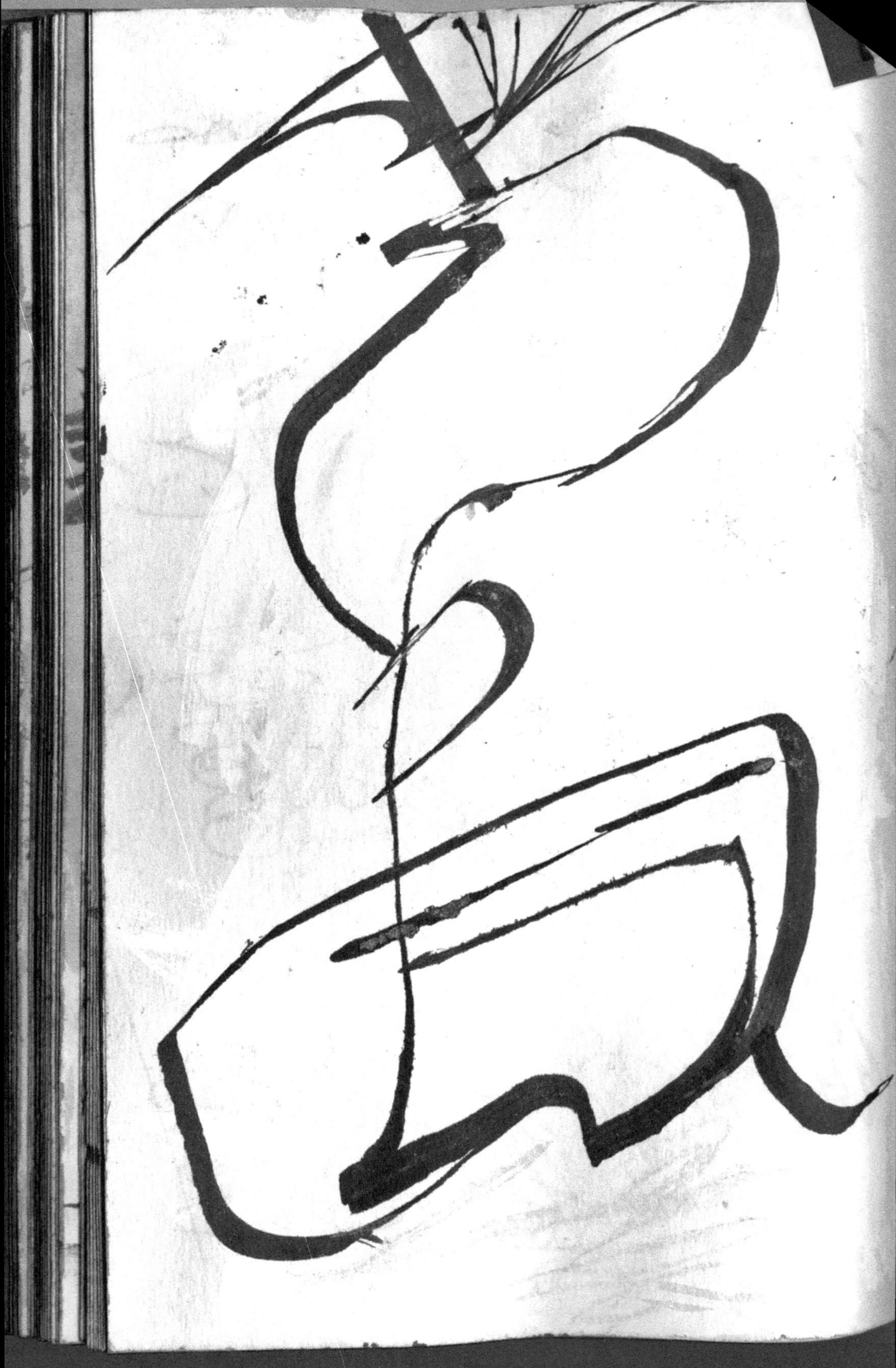

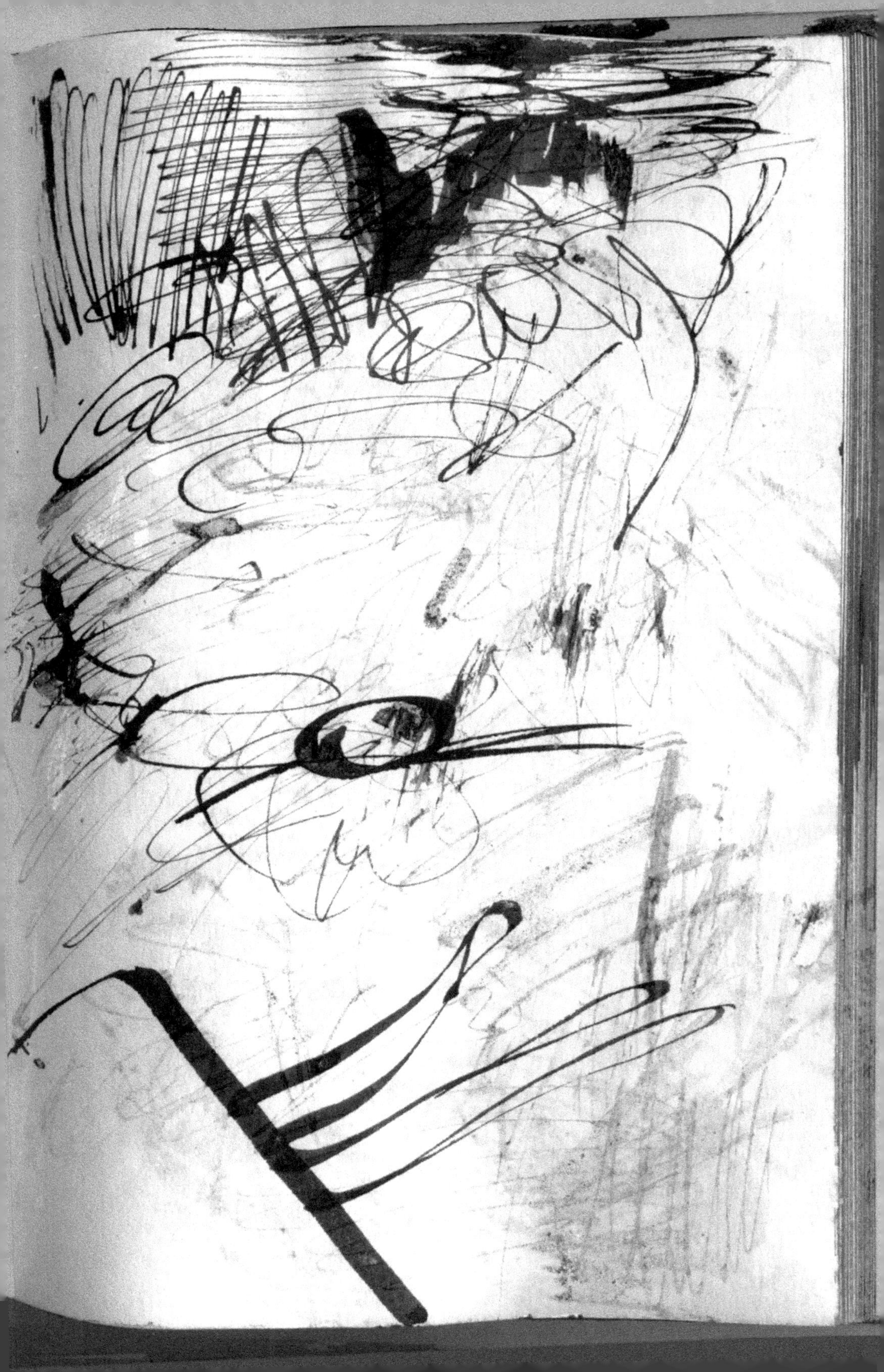

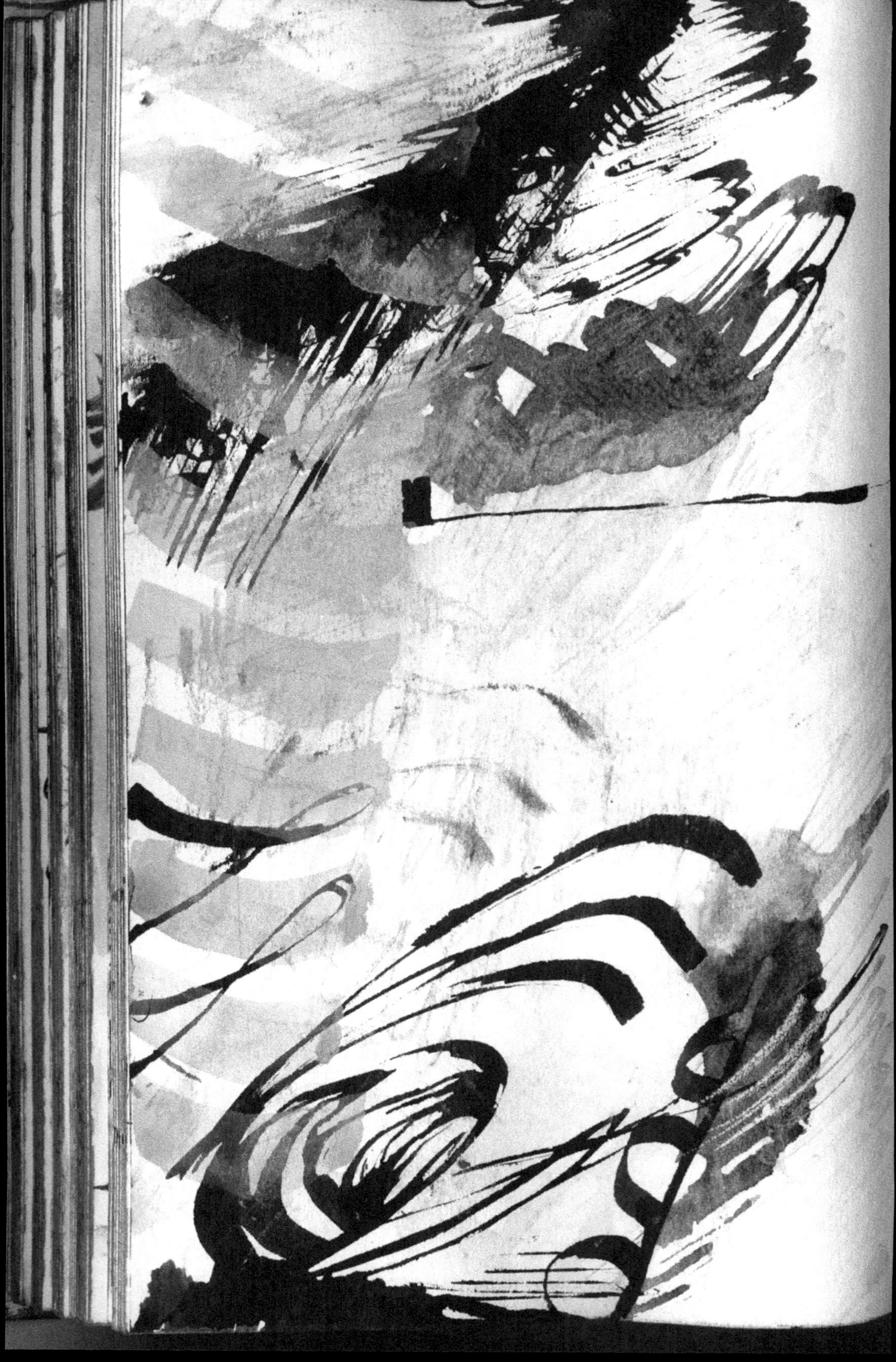

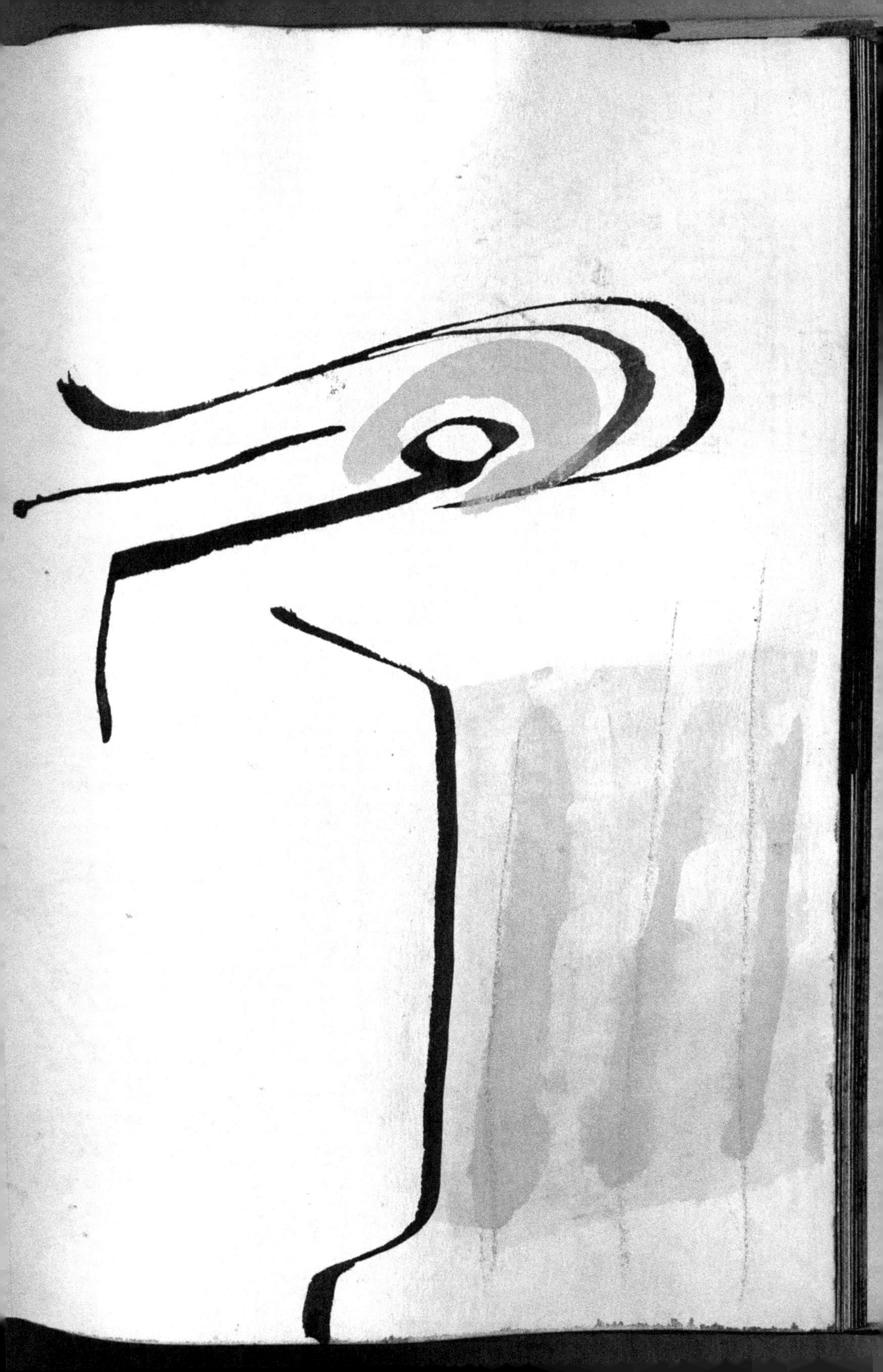

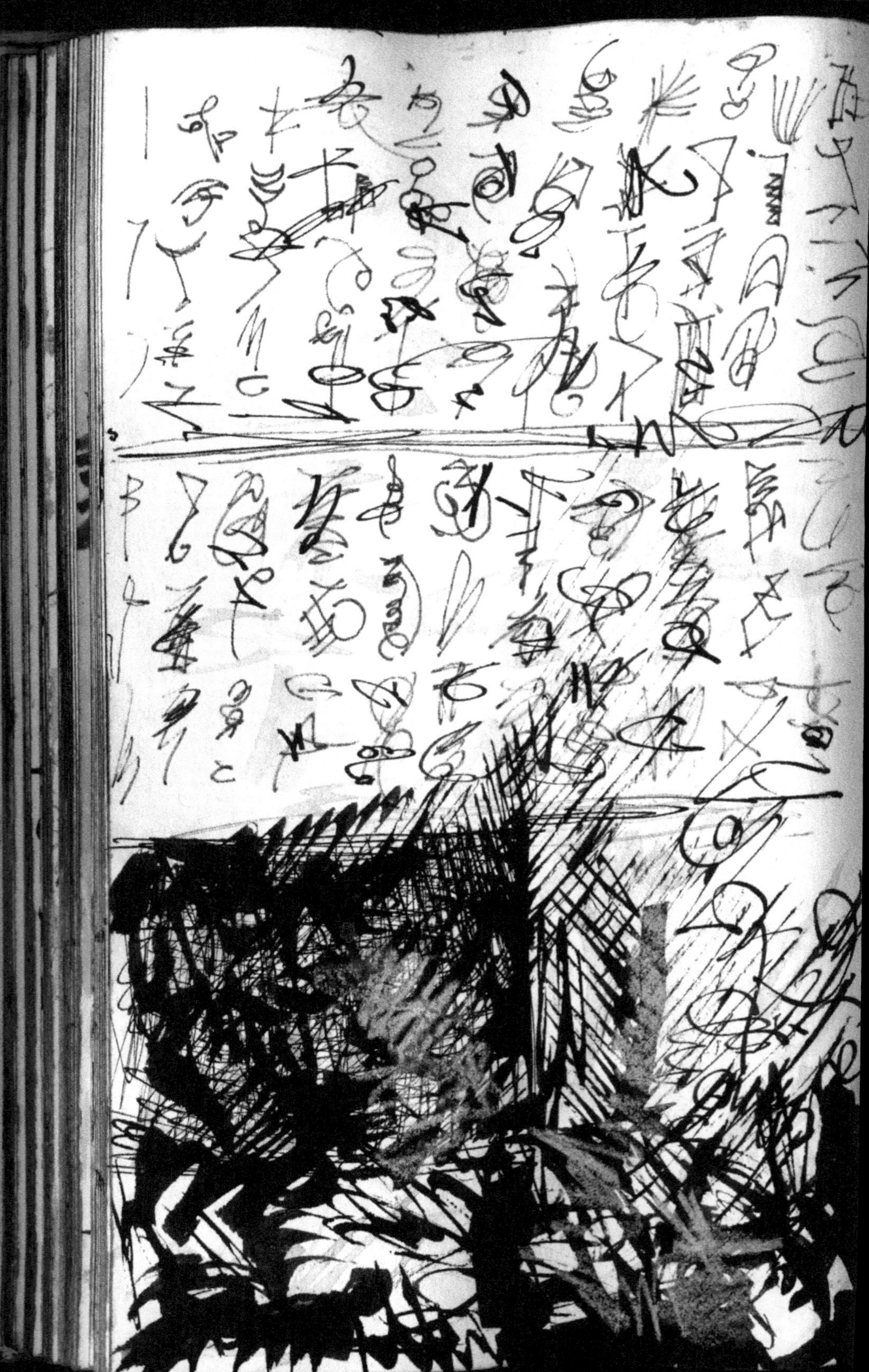

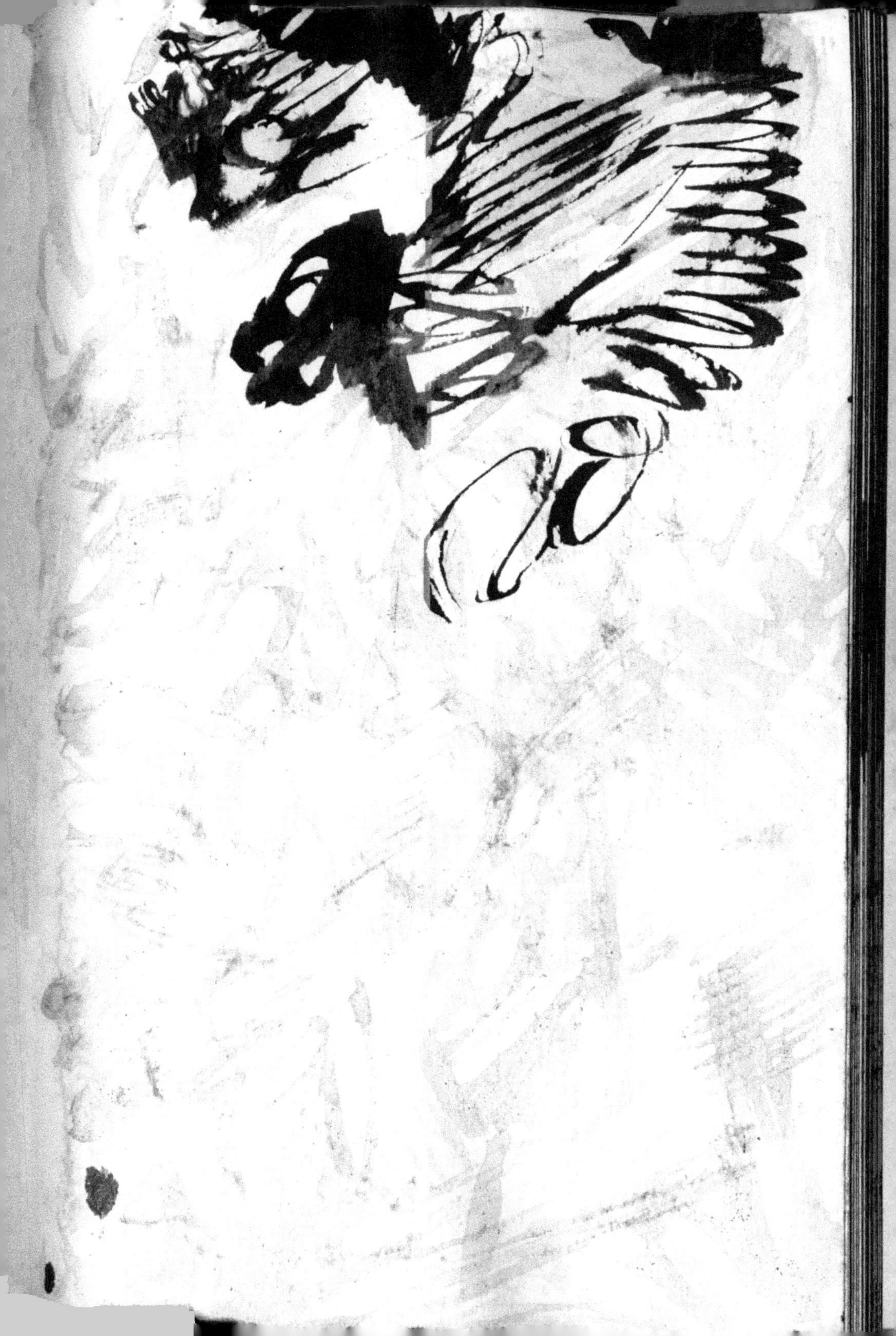

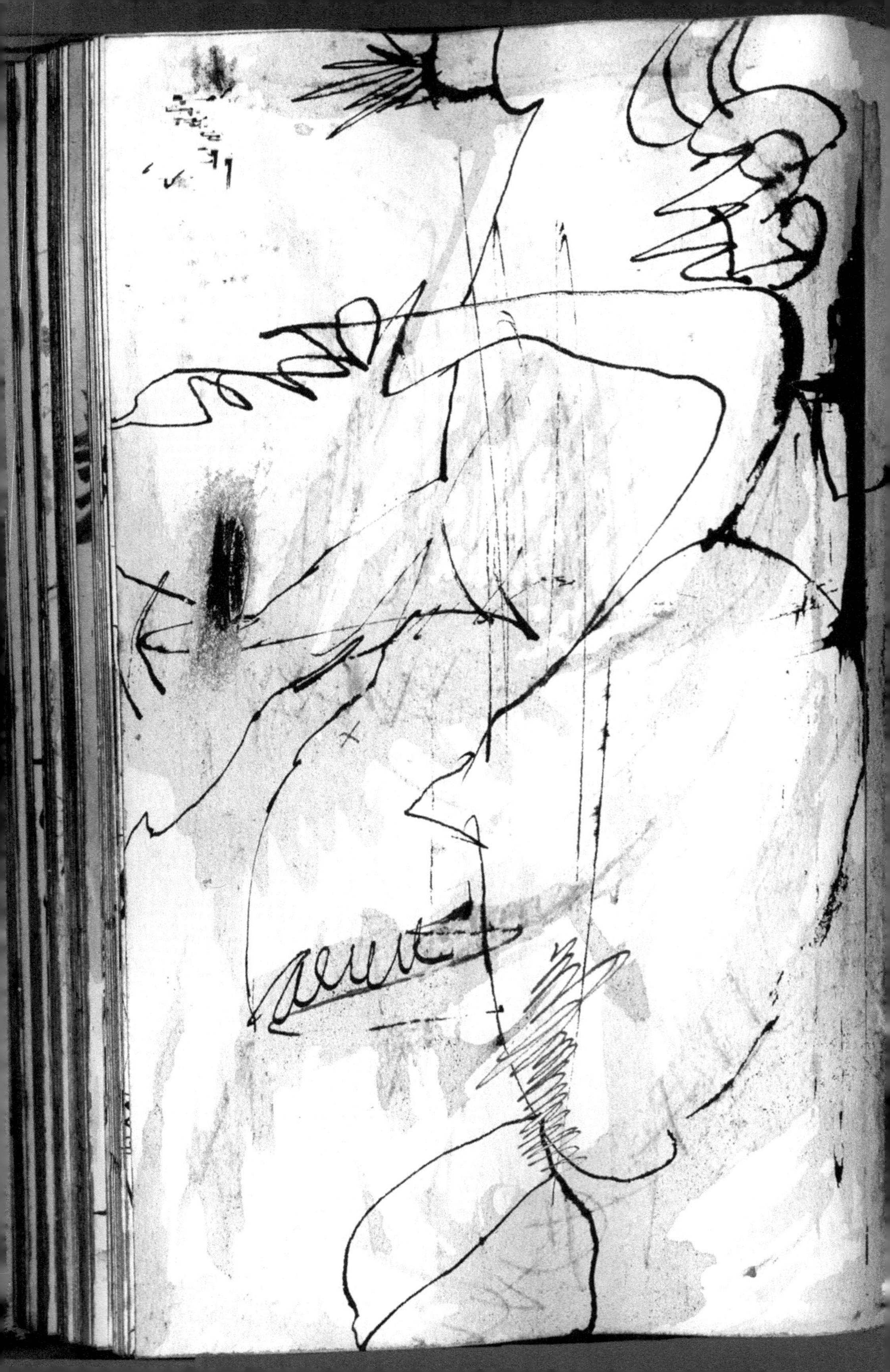

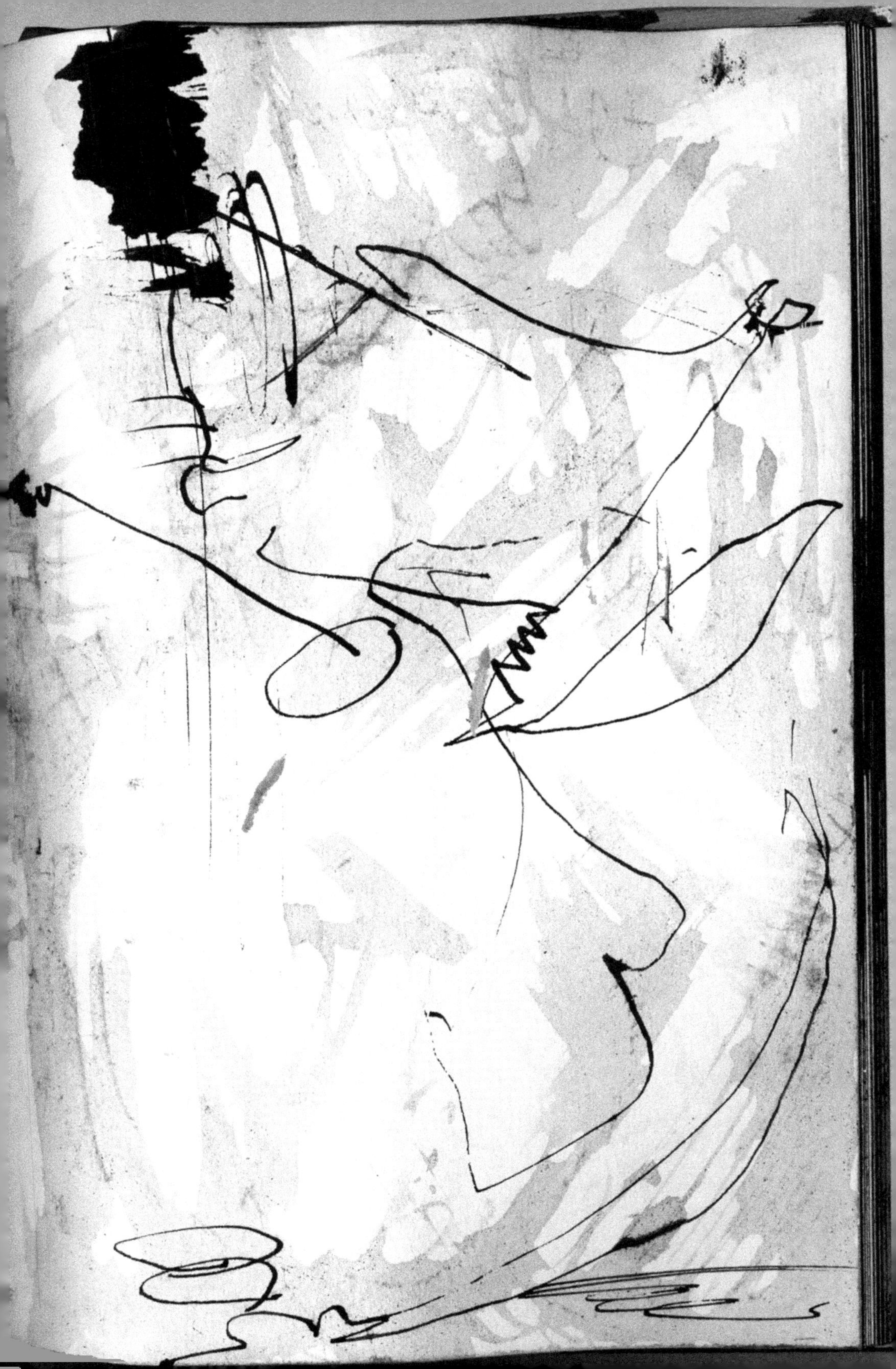

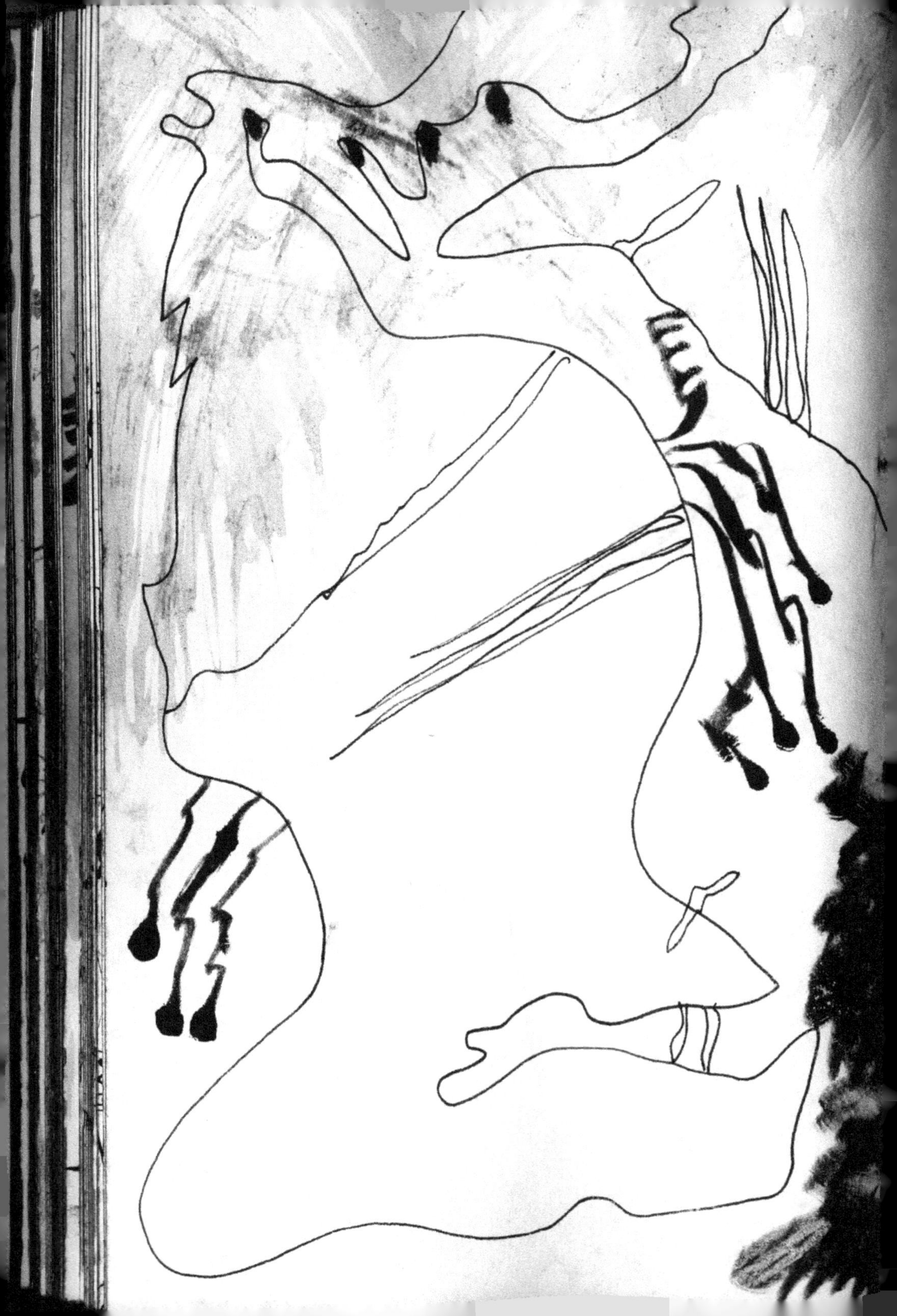

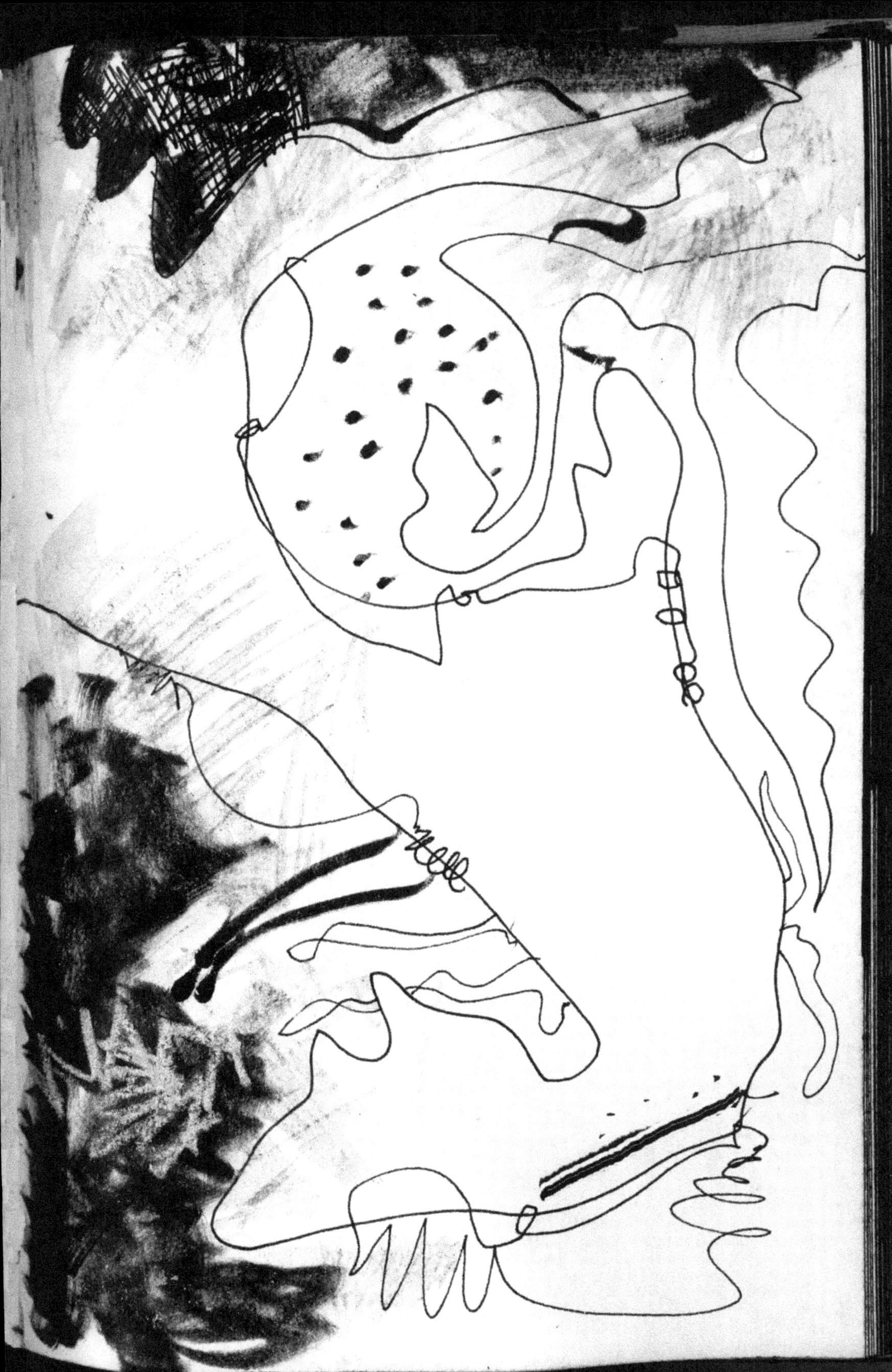

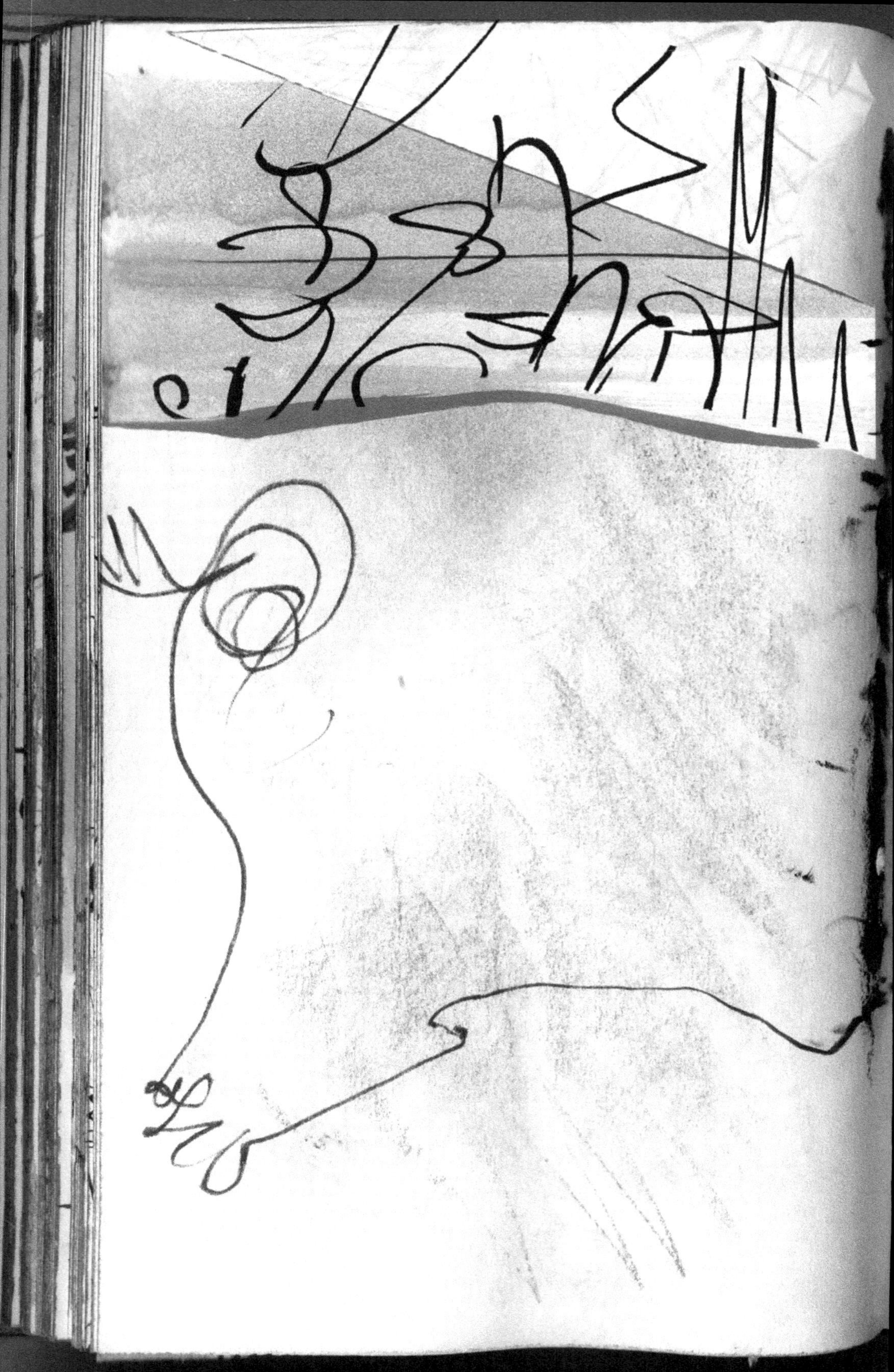

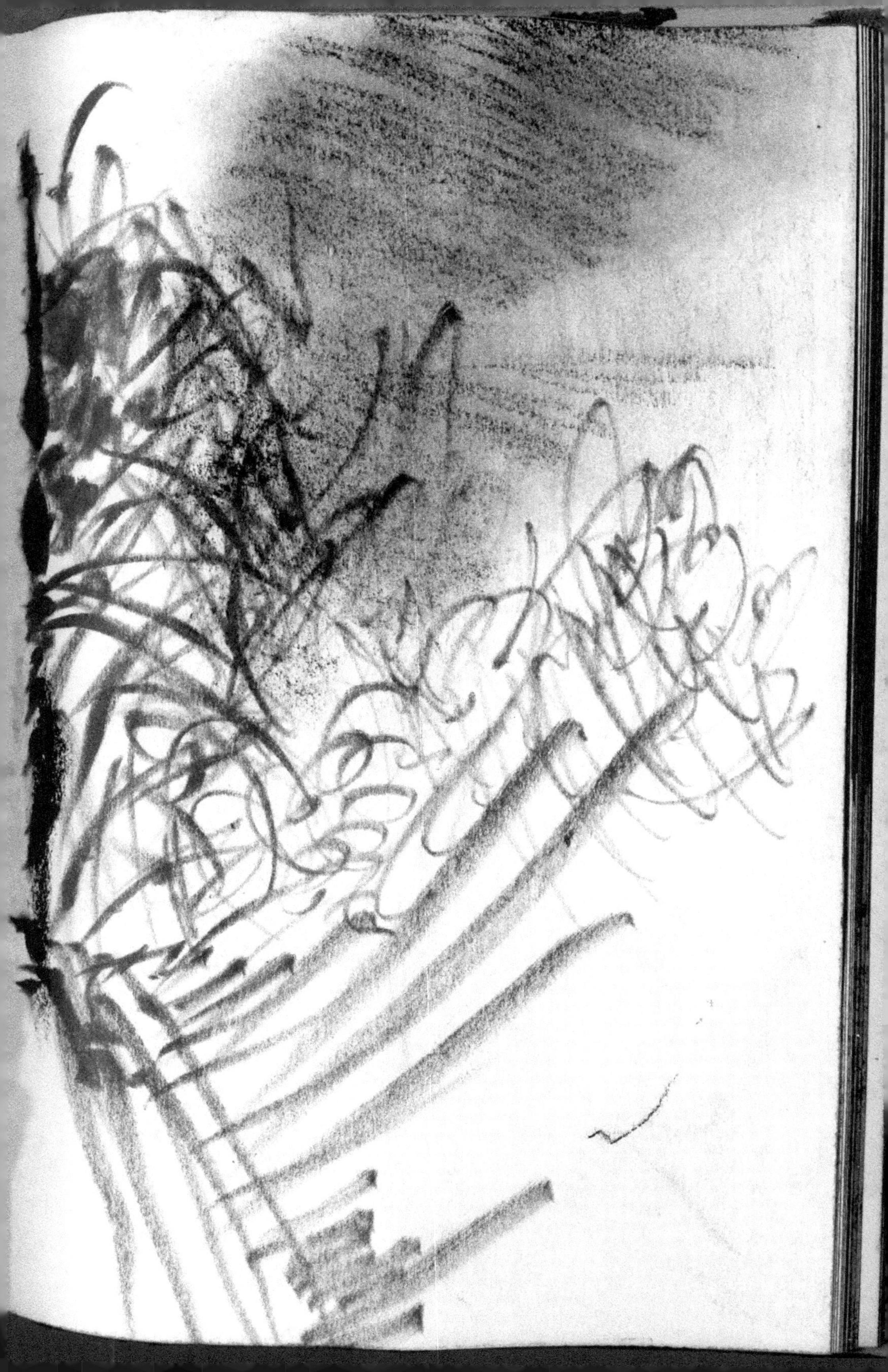

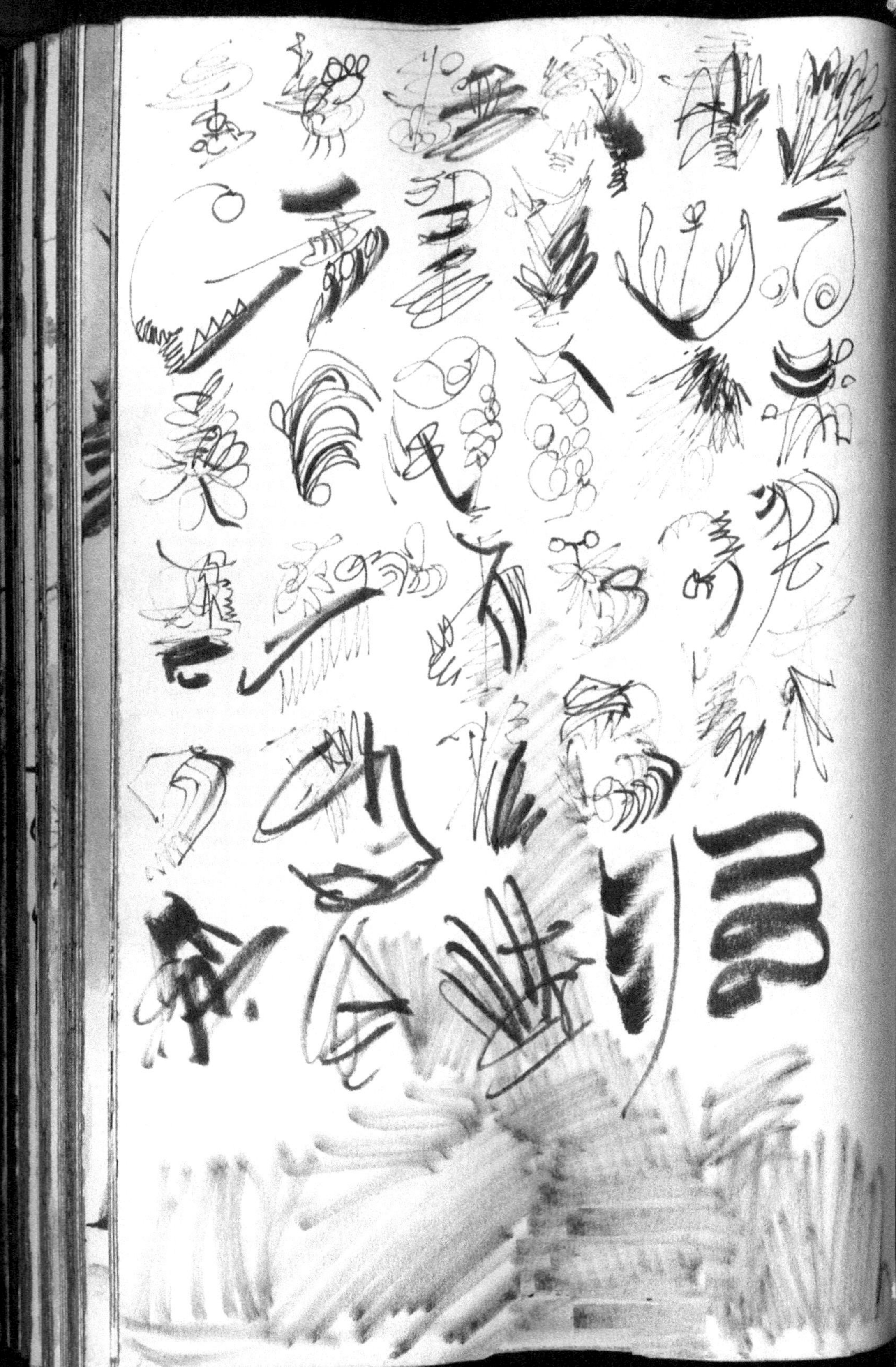

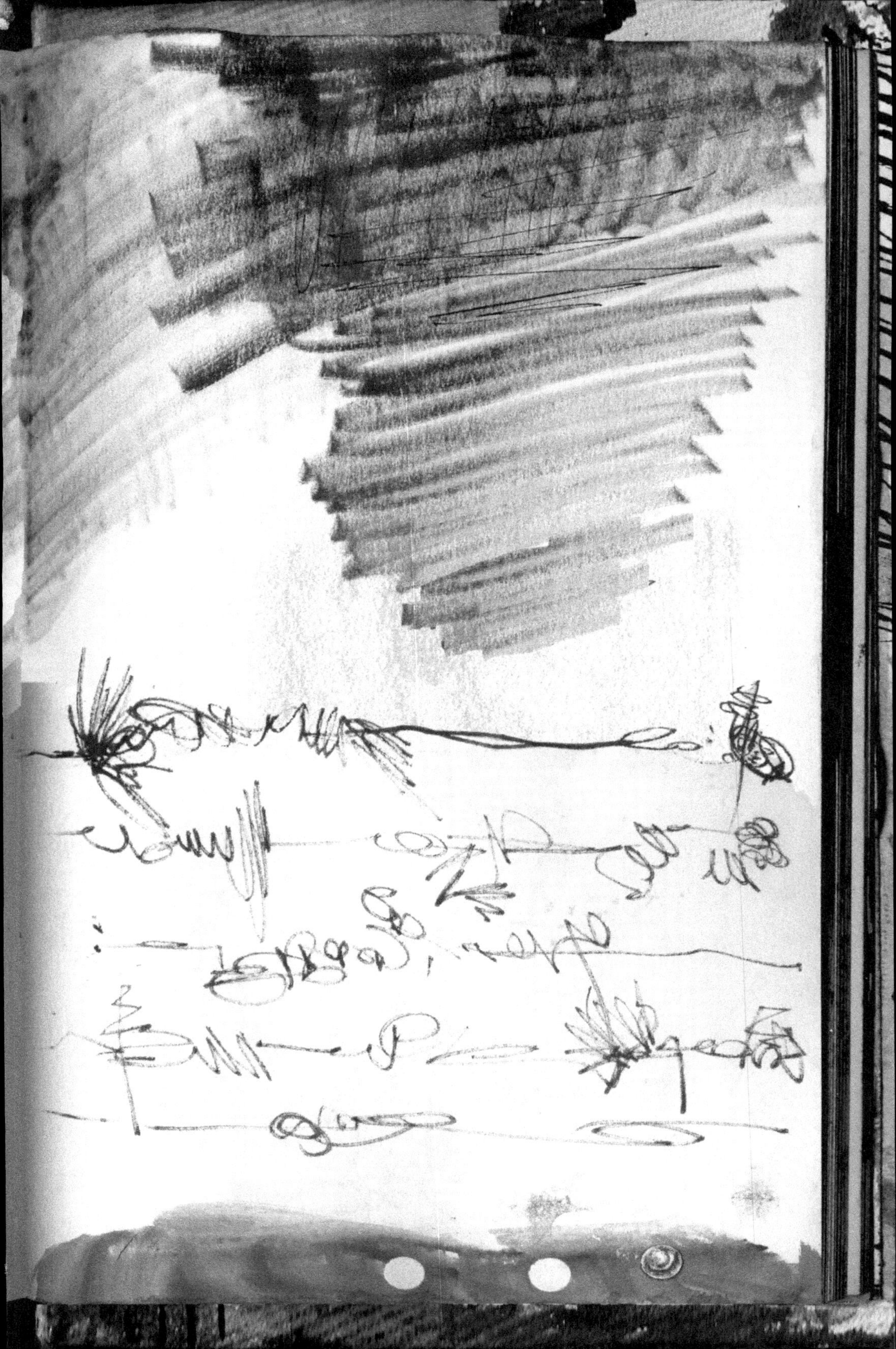

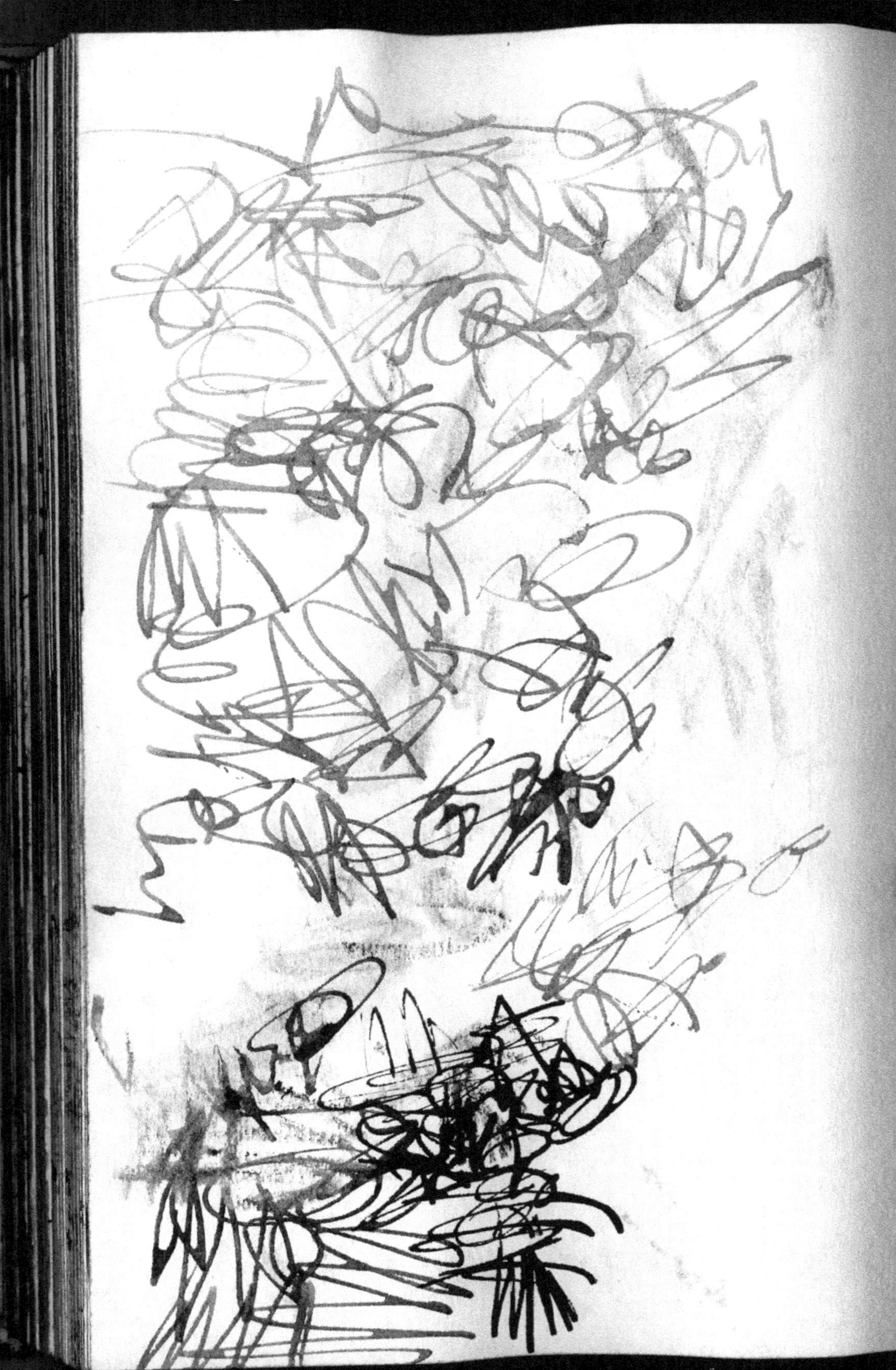

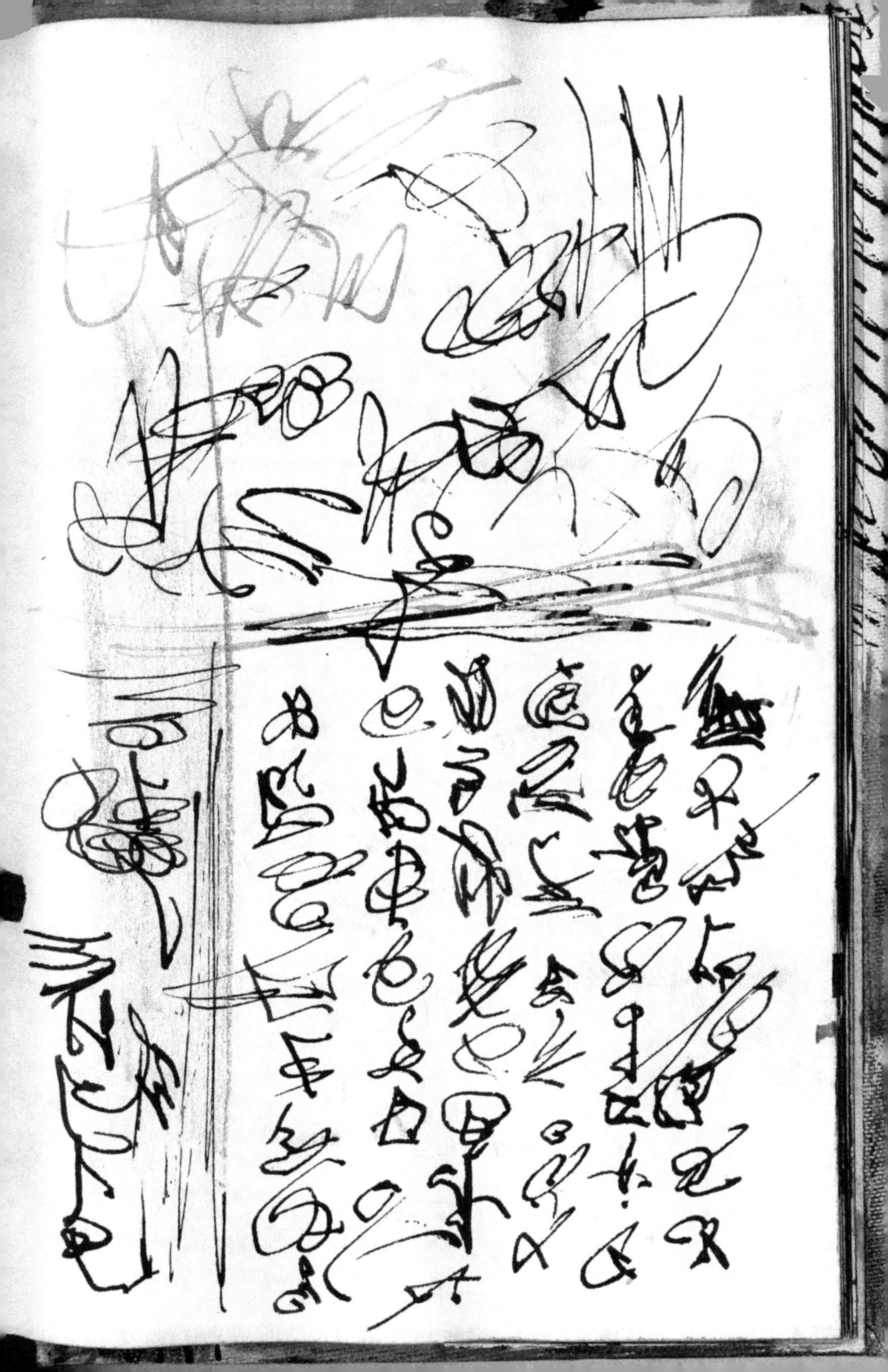

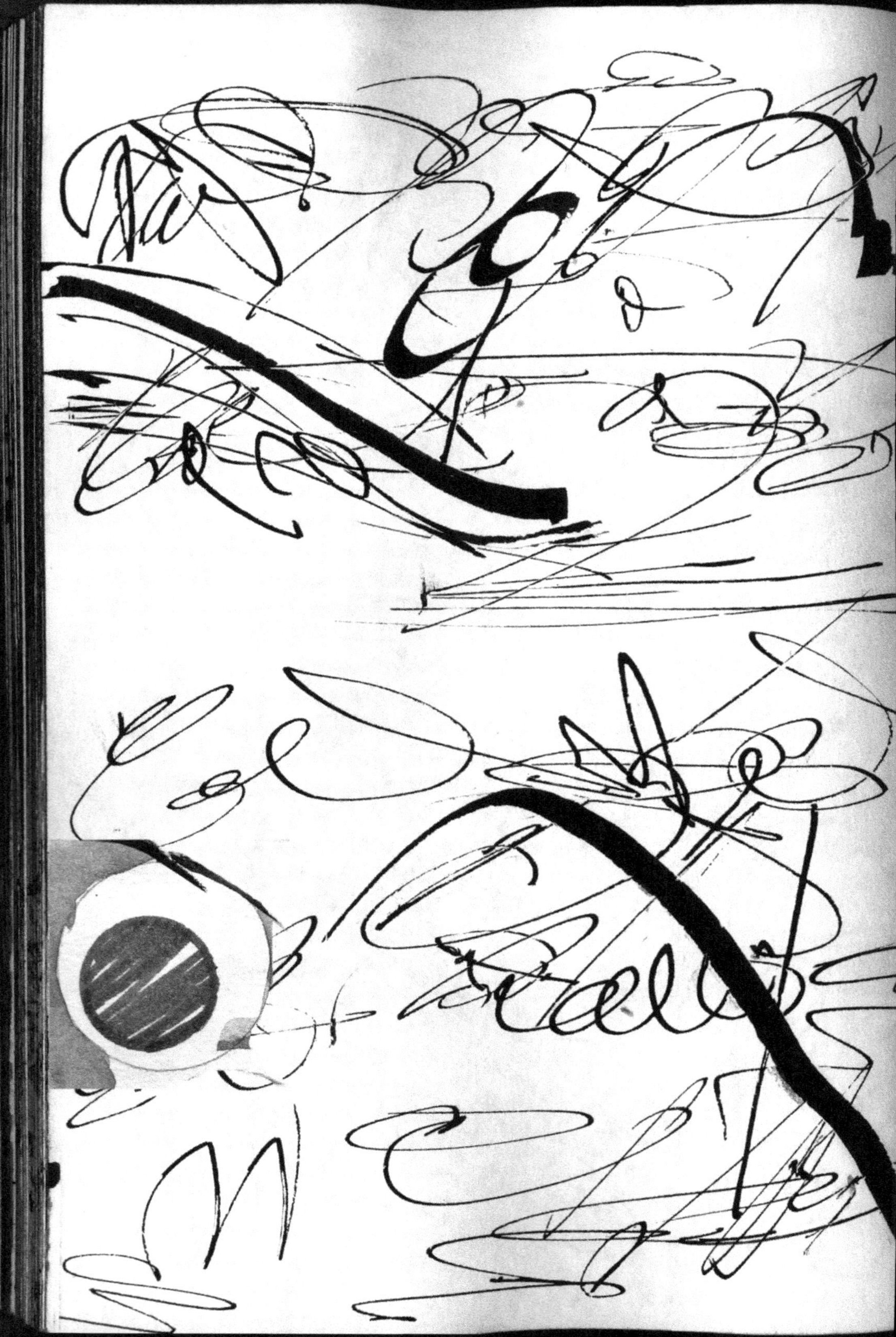

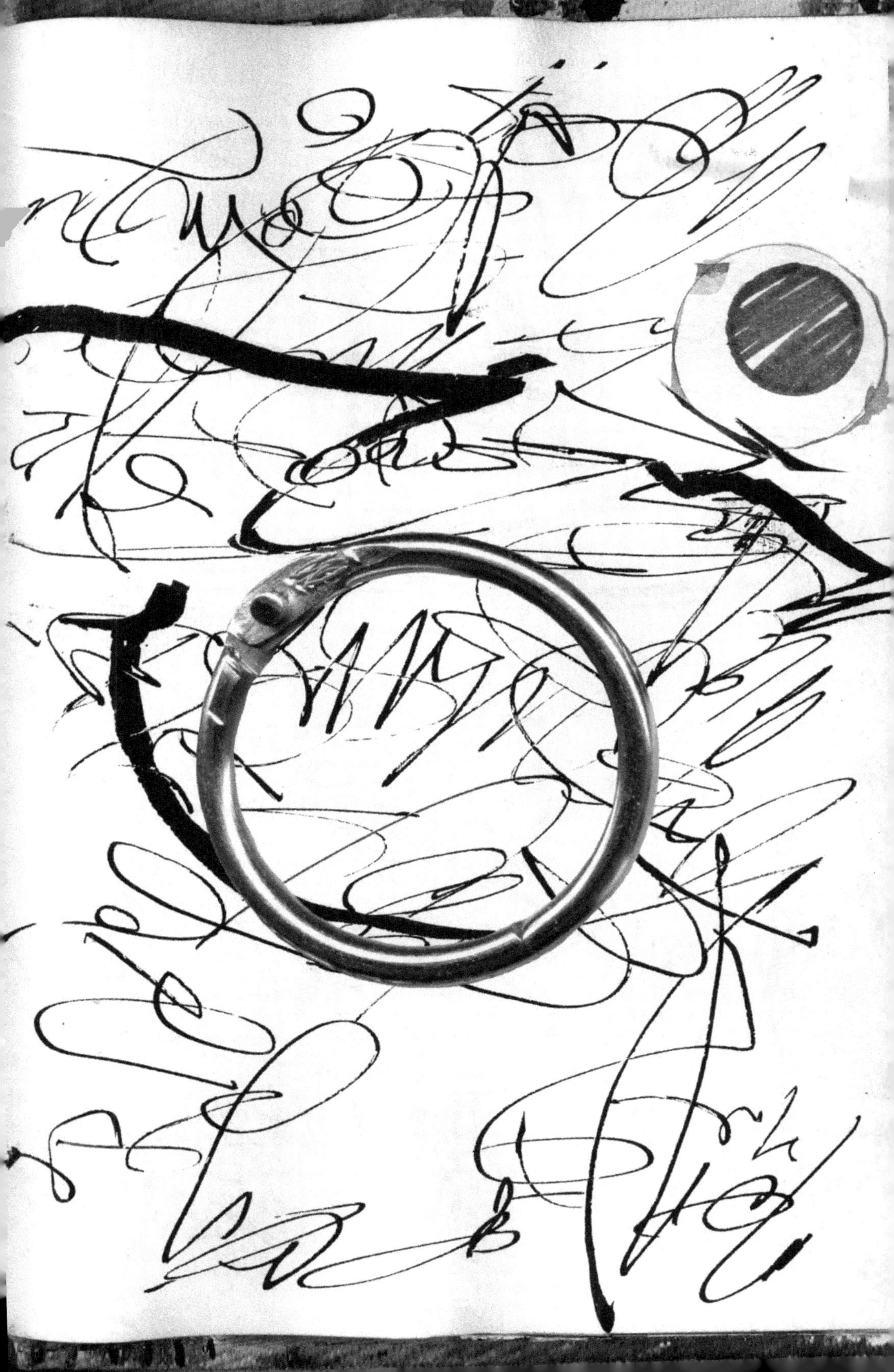

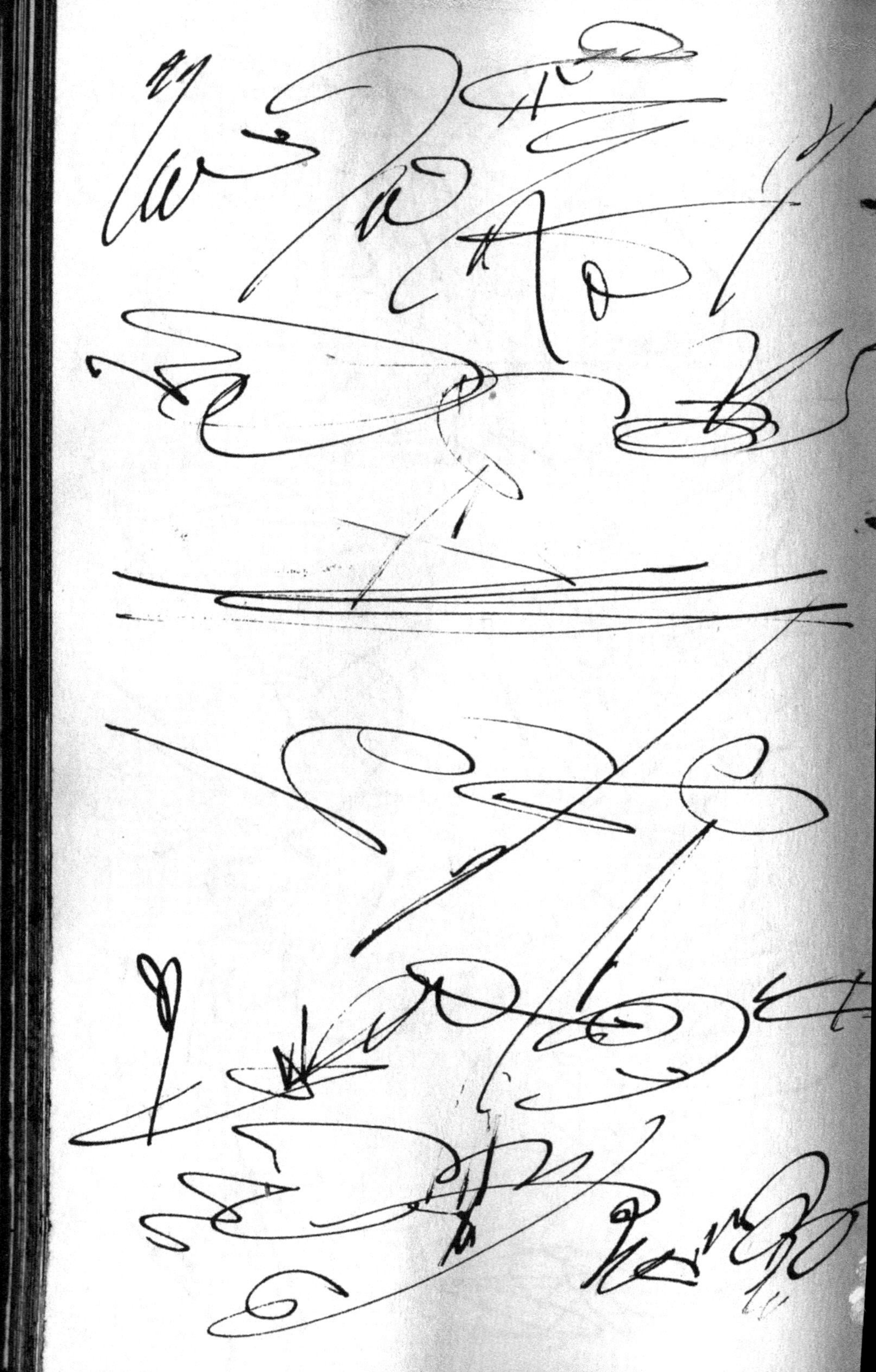

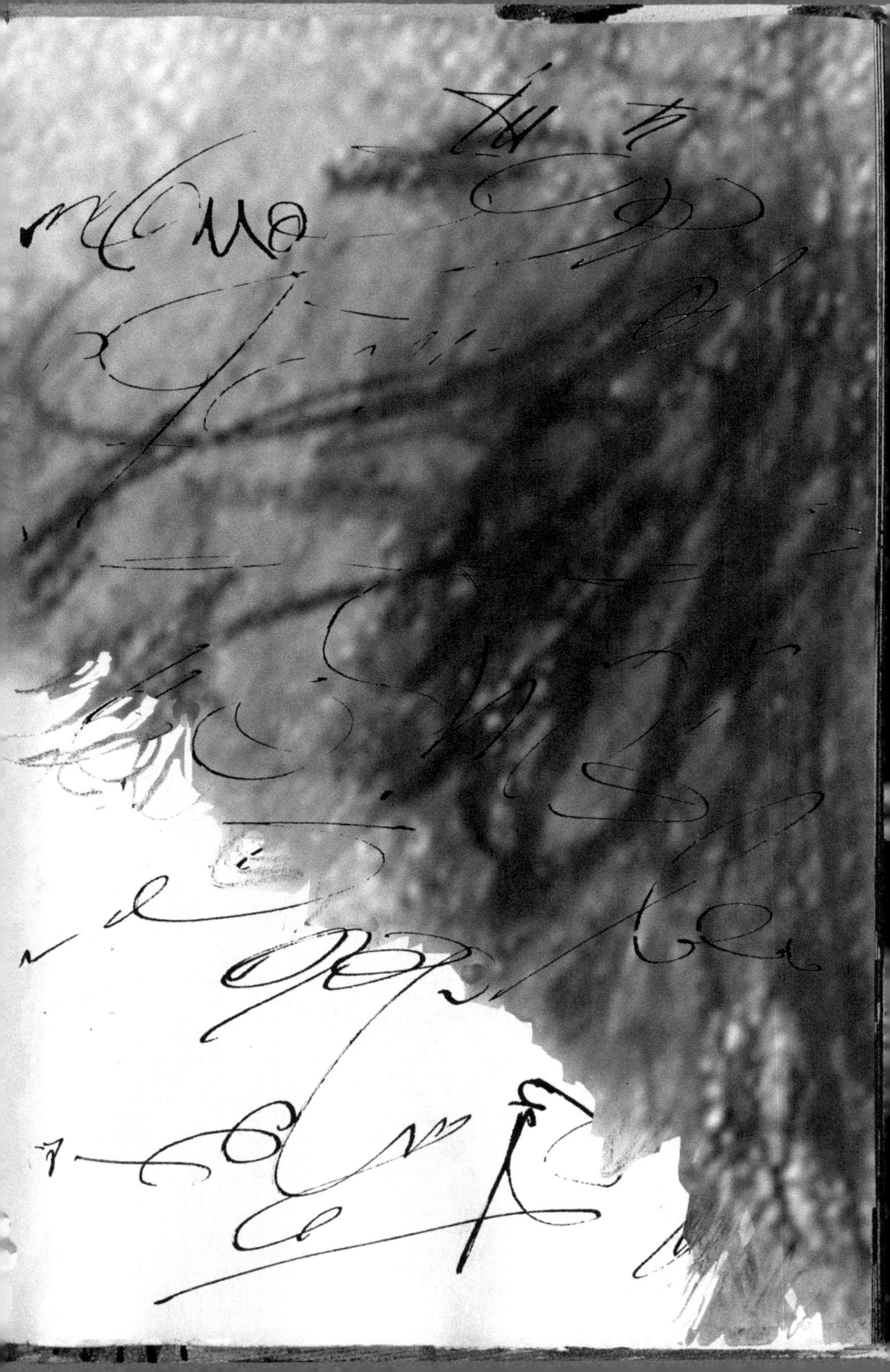

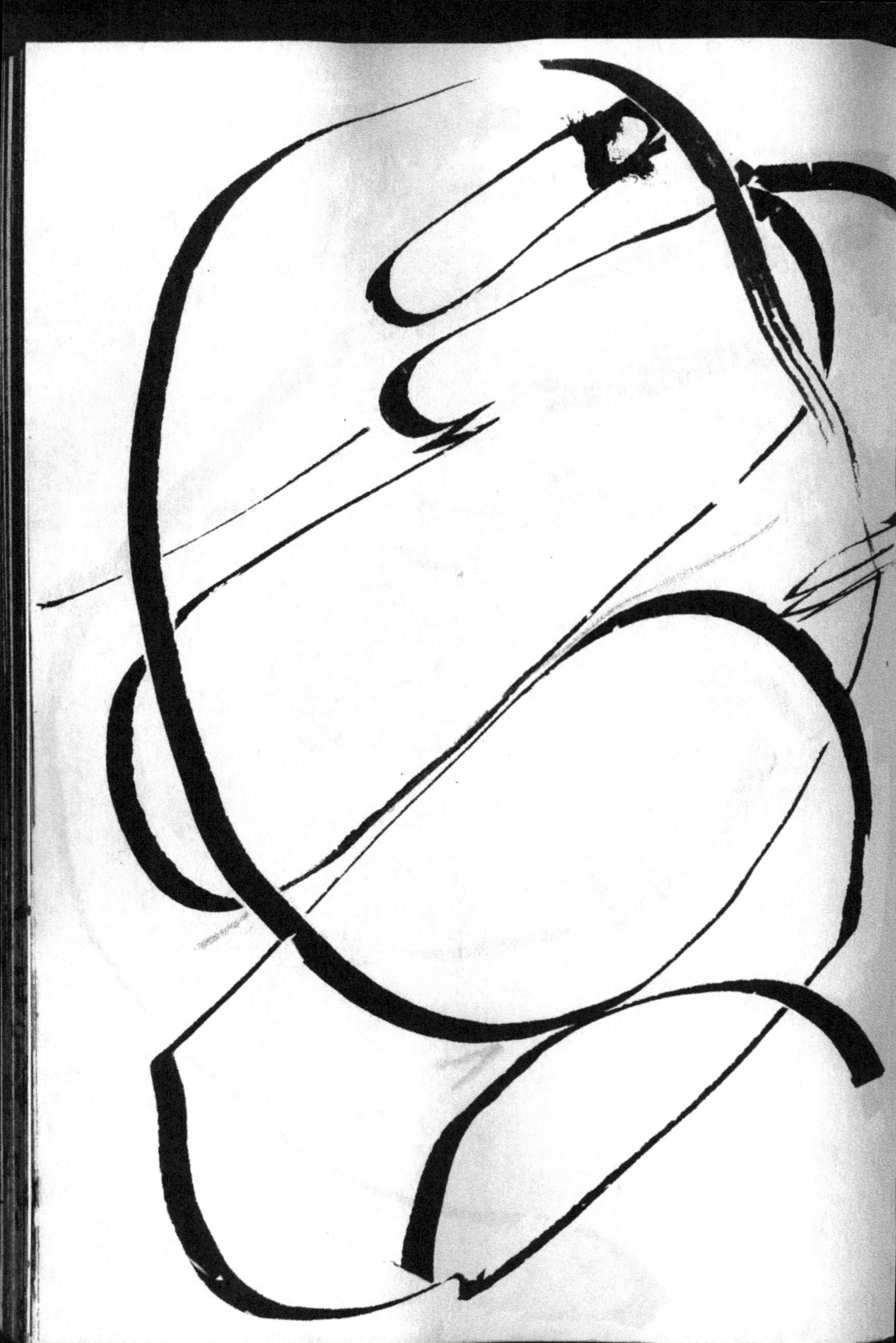

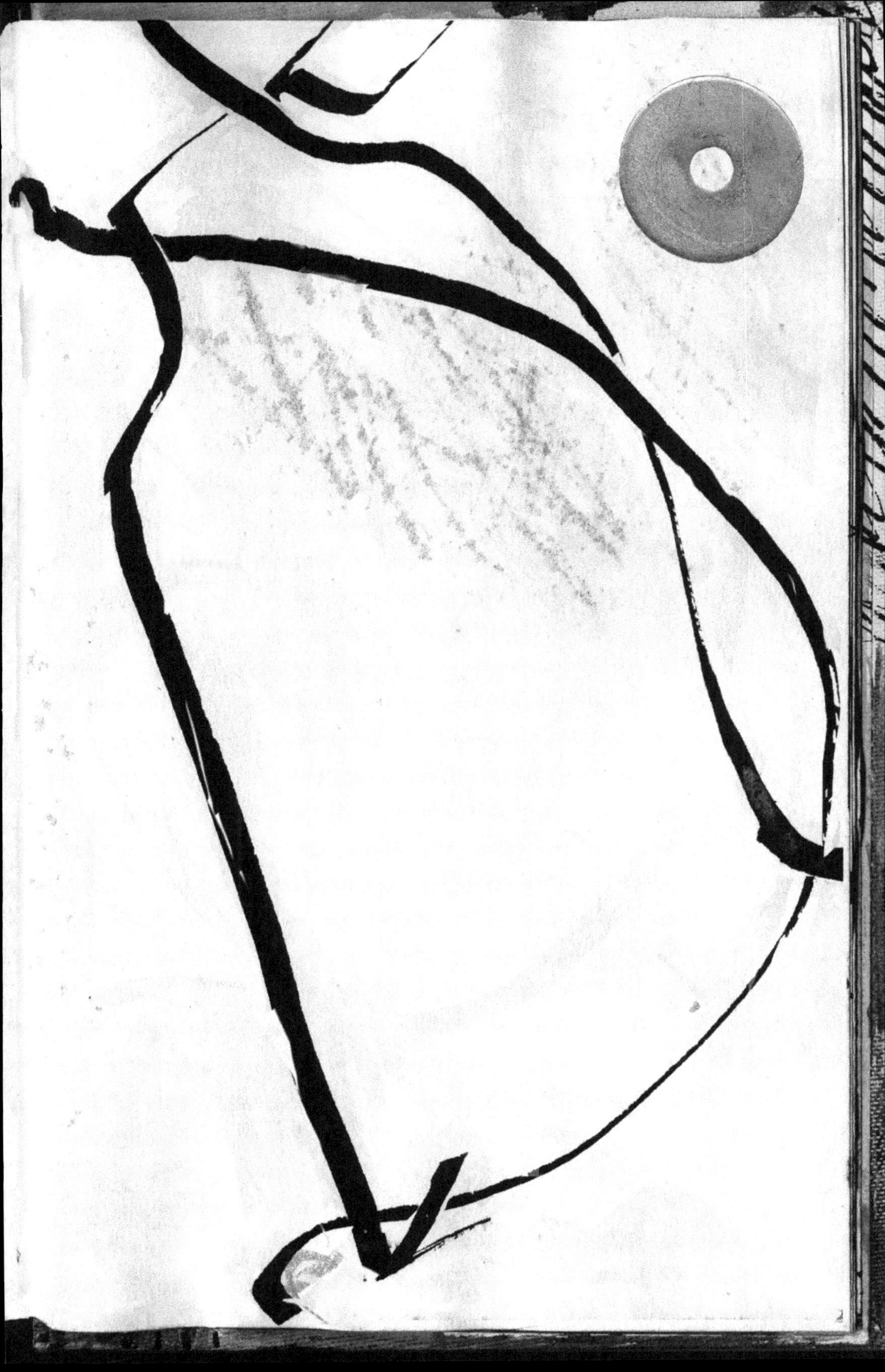

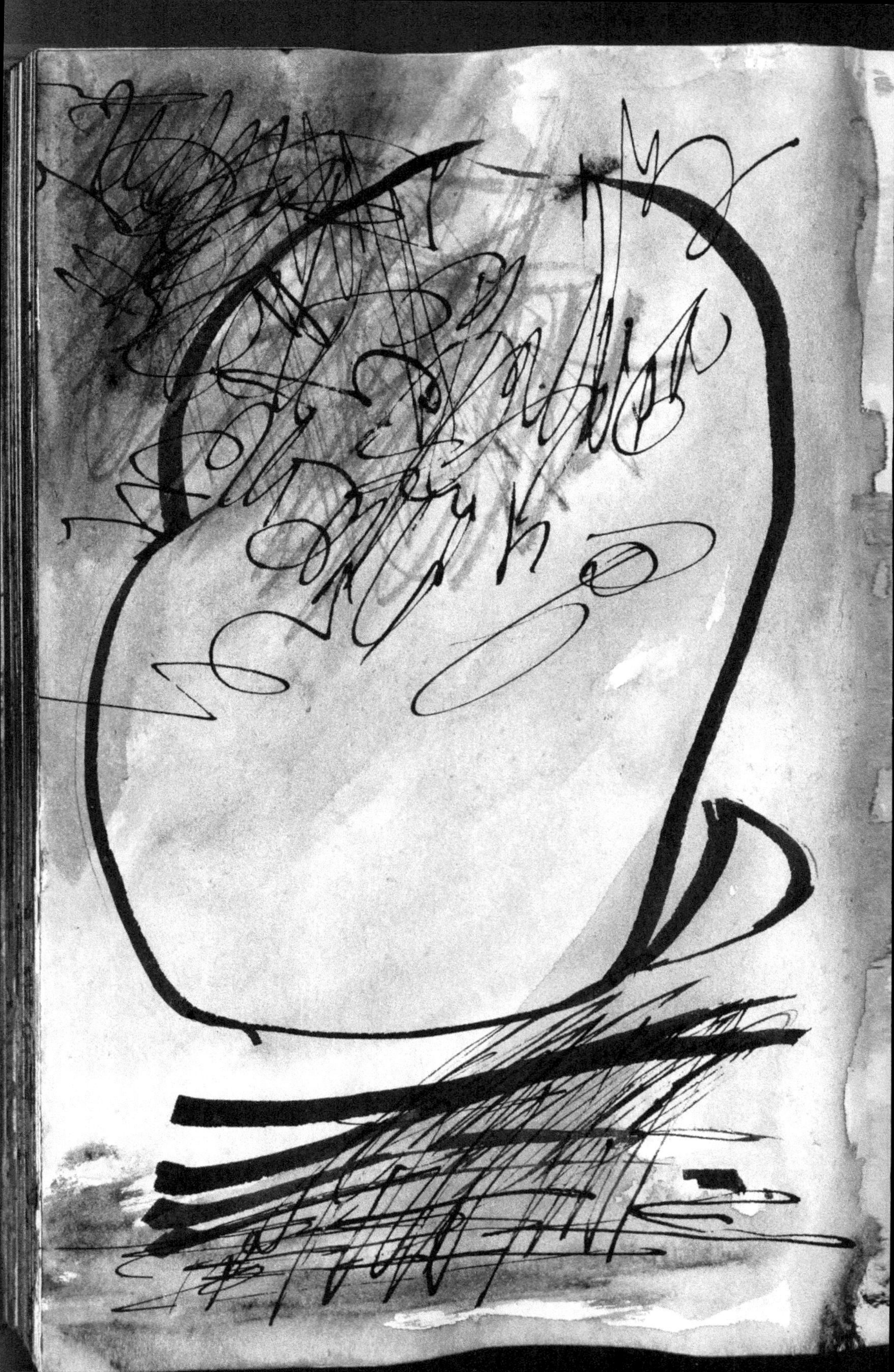

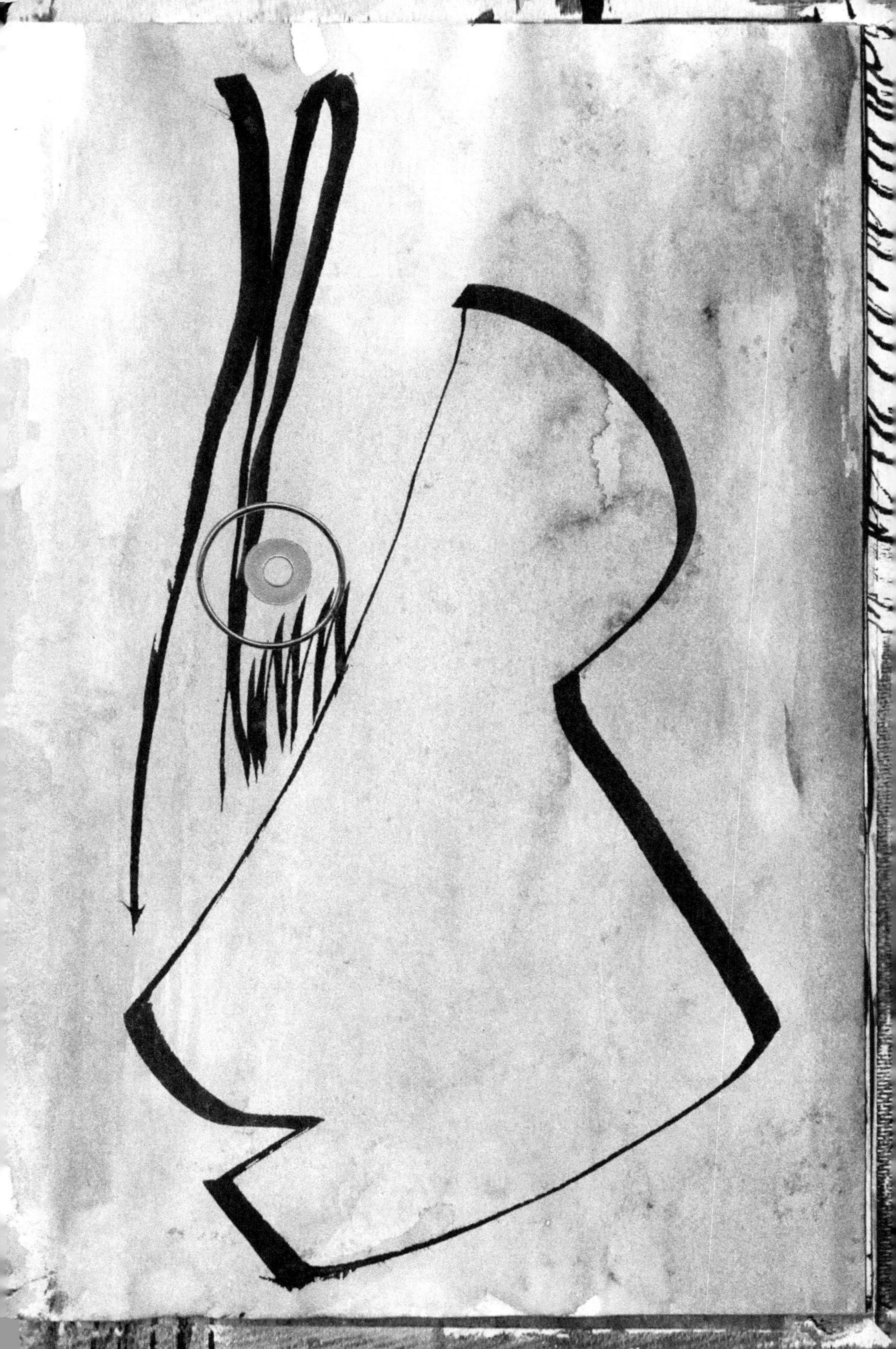

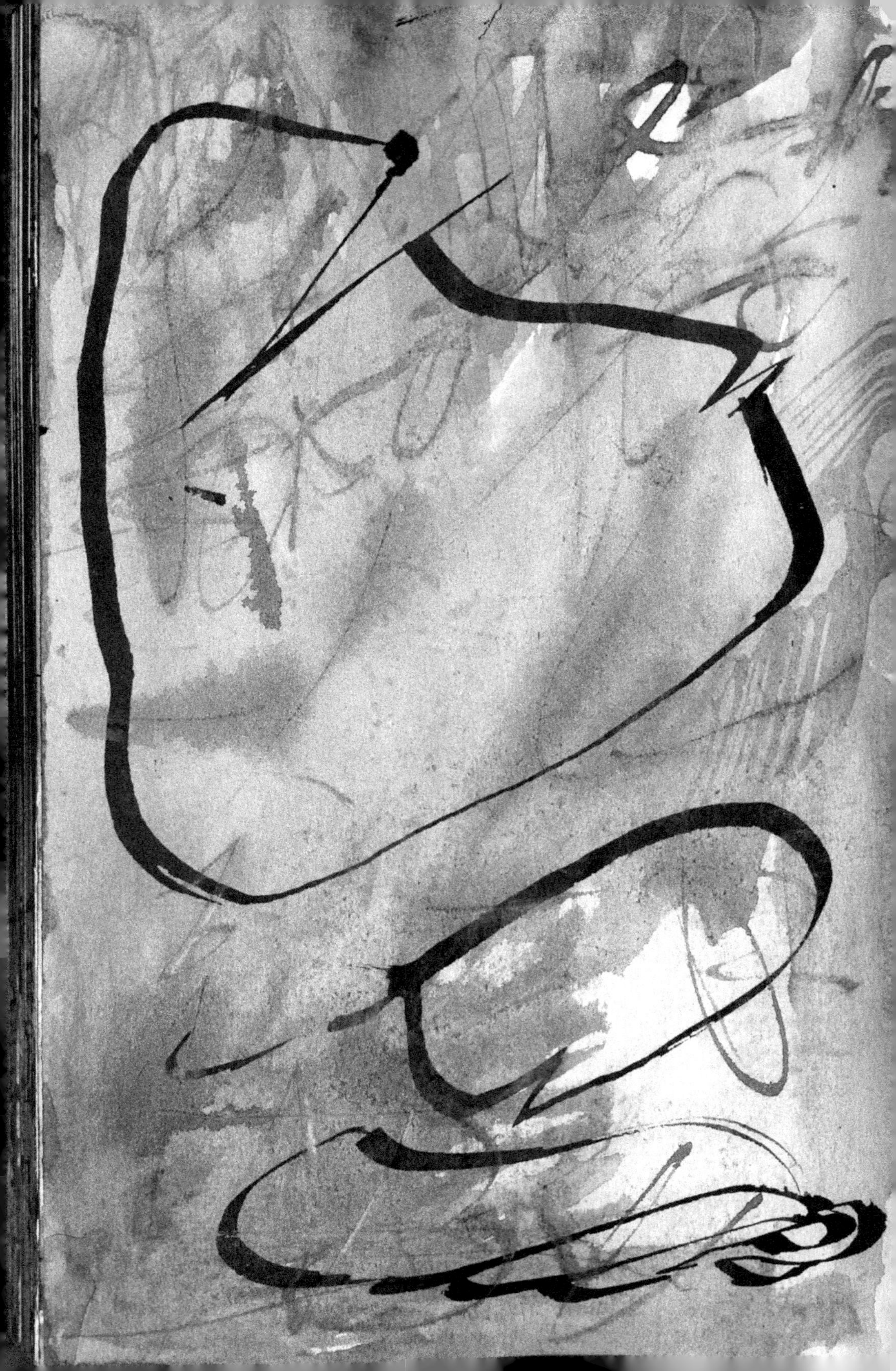

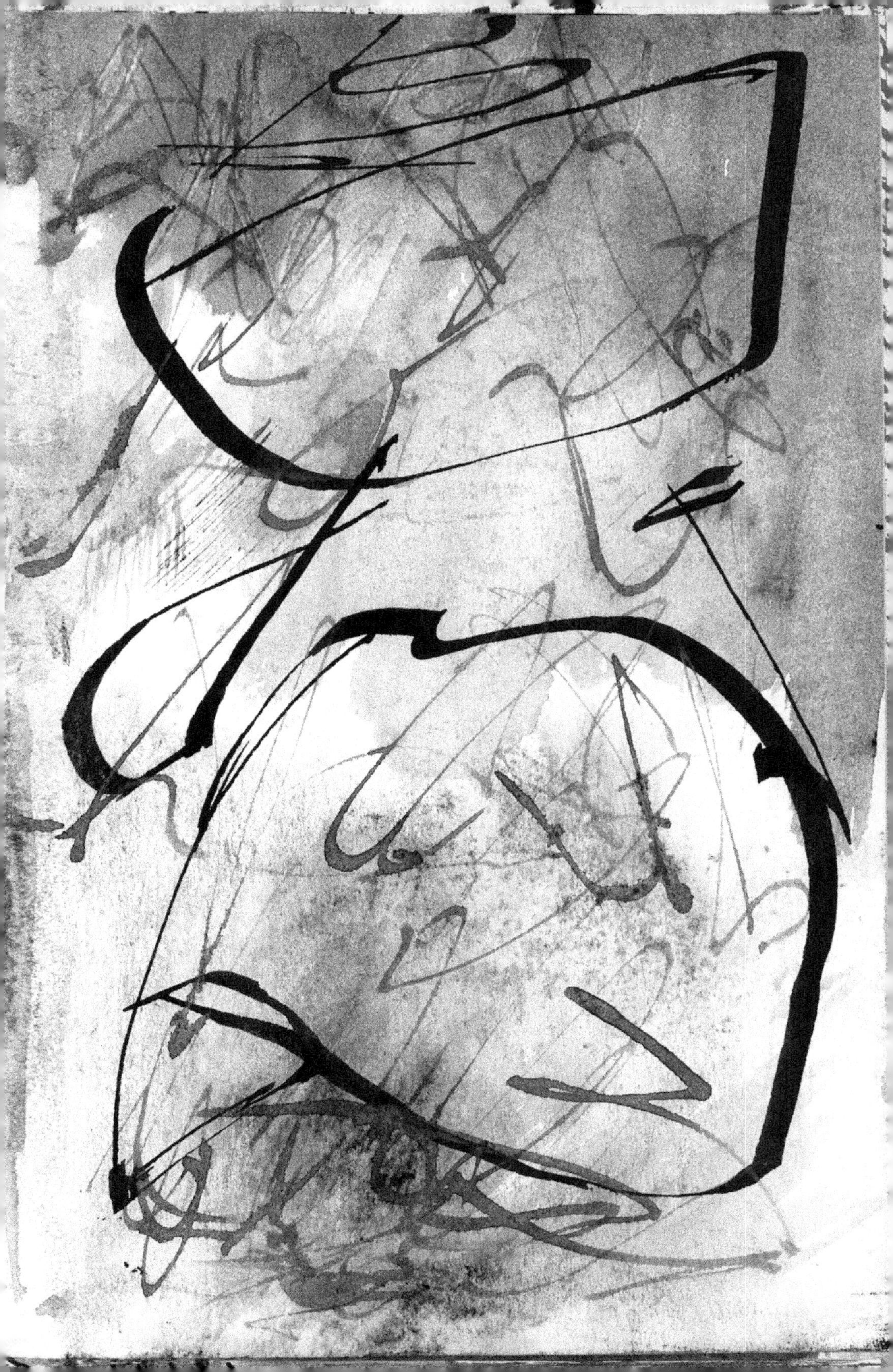

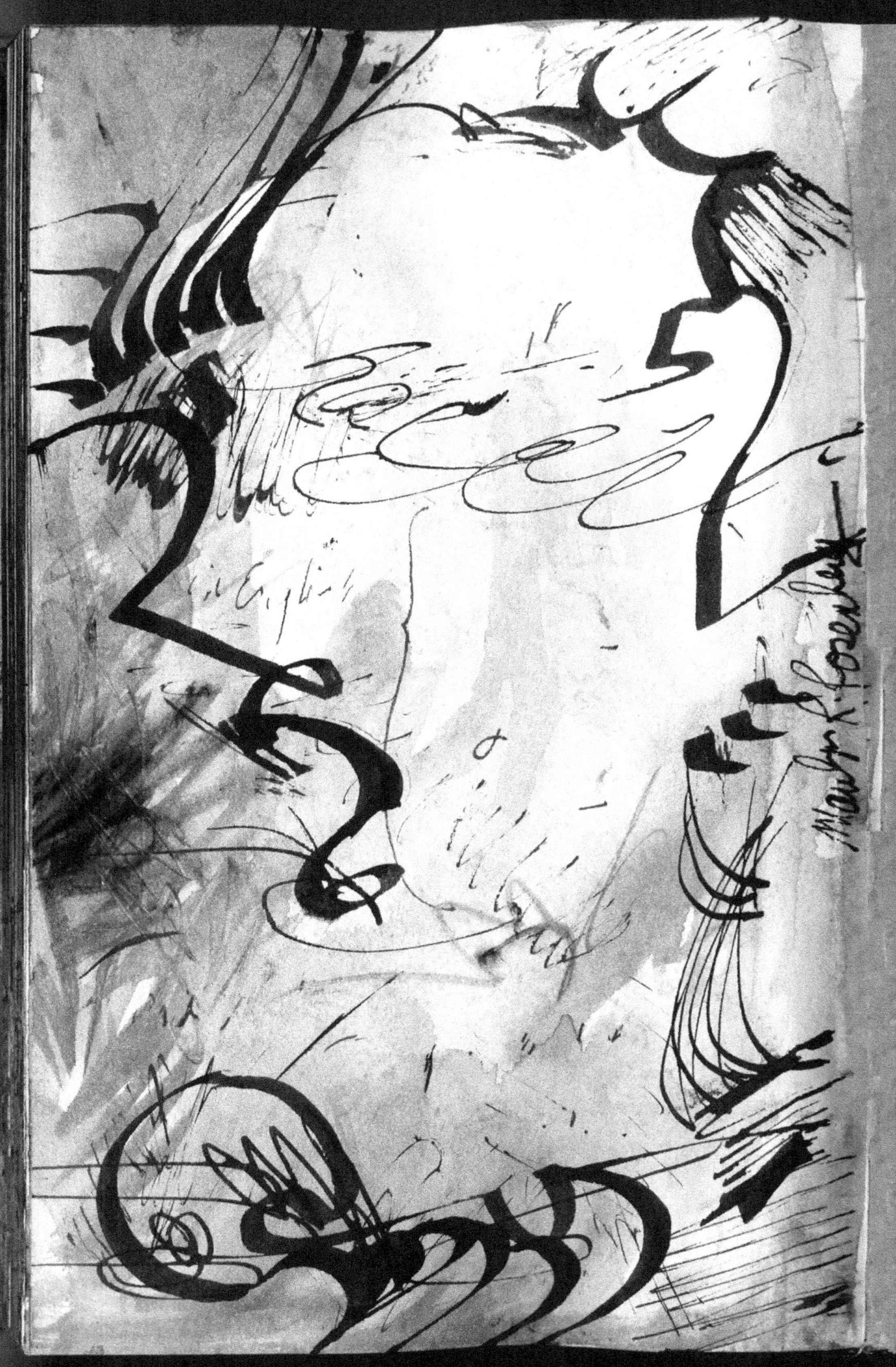

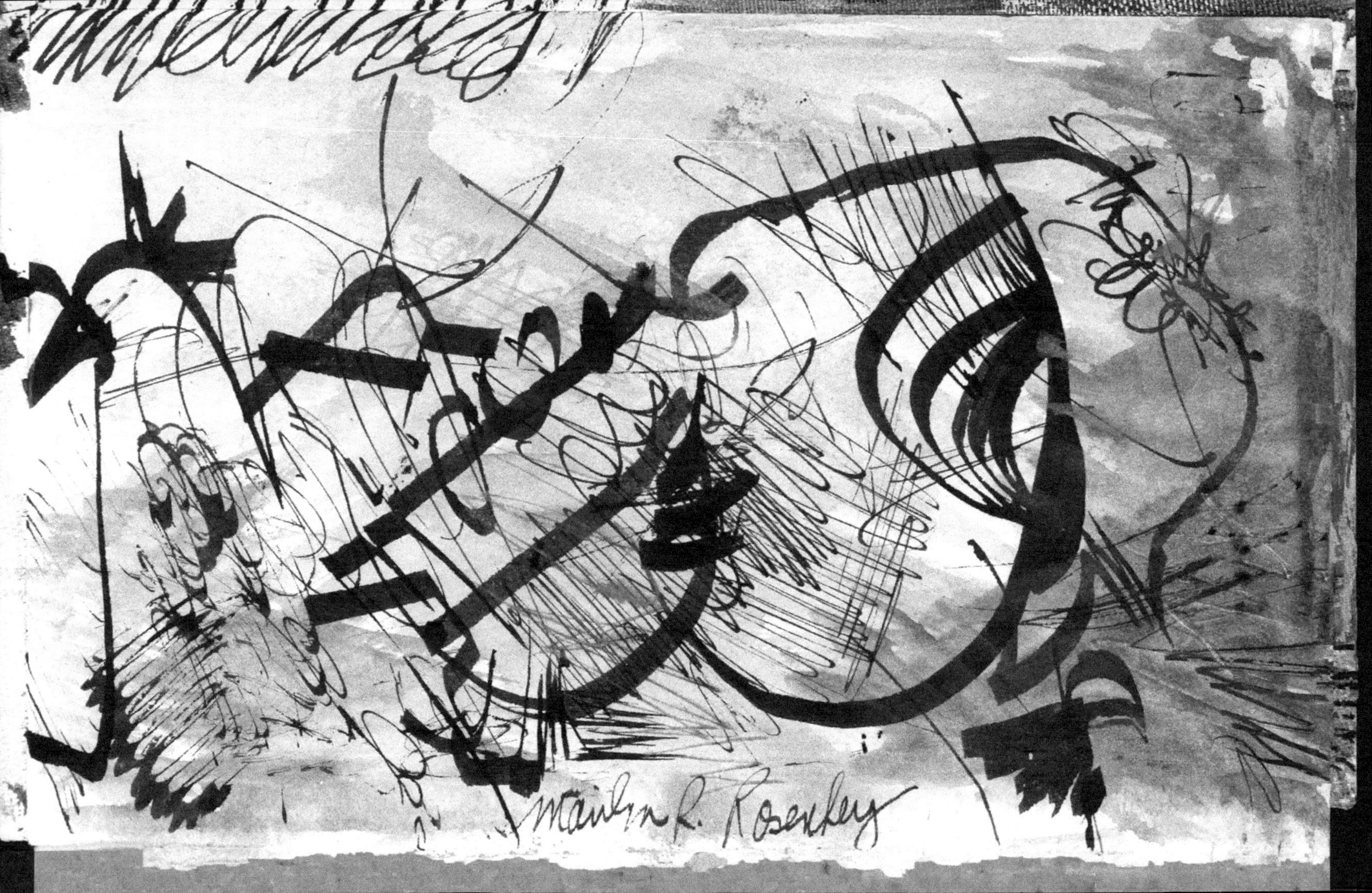
Marilyn R. Rosenberg

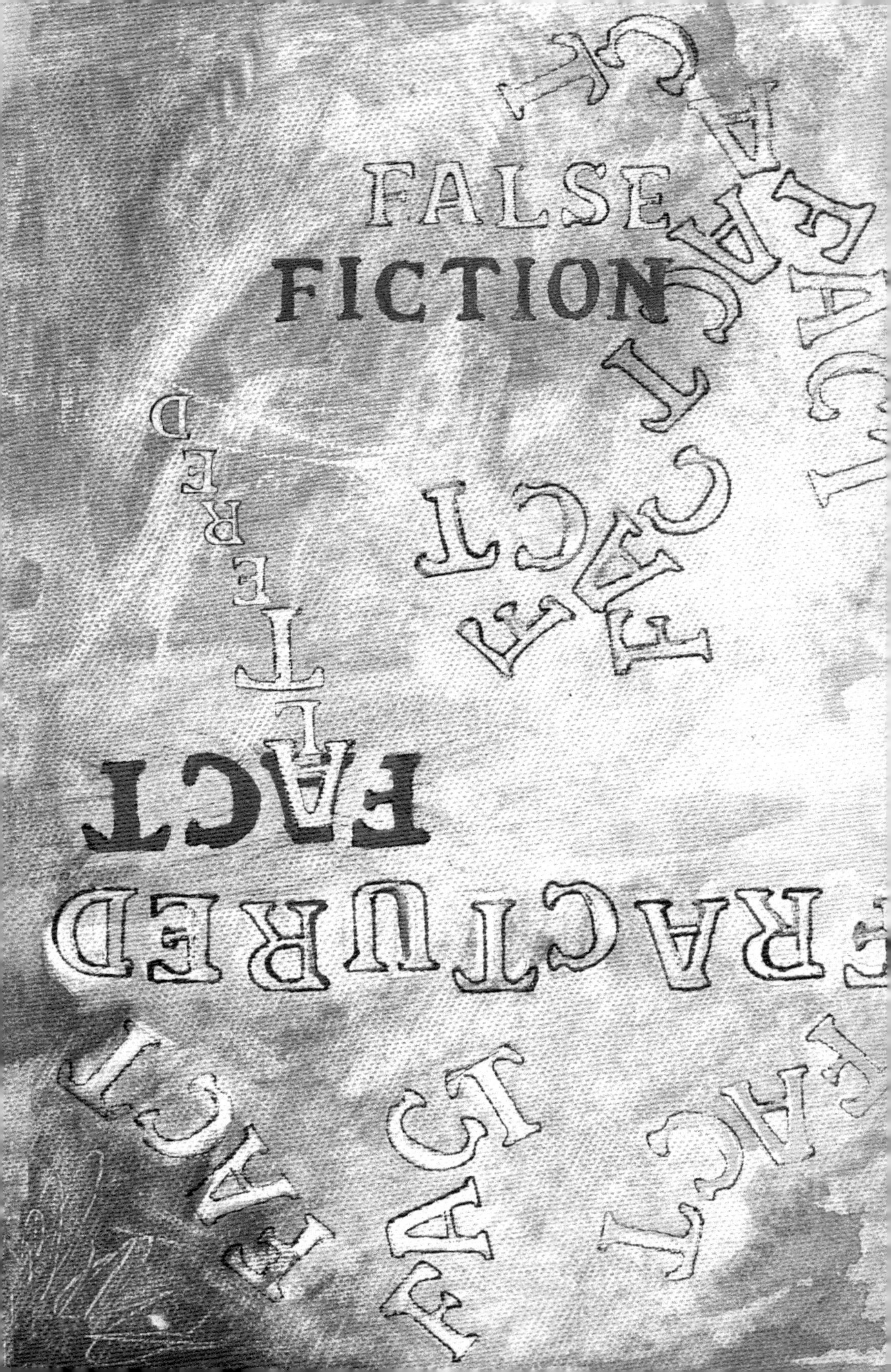
FALSE
FICTION
ALTERED
FACT
FRACTURED
FACT

Concept & Process:

The False Fiction Fractured Fact series started in 2001 with a diary/journal of 219 pages, worked on a blank bound purchased book, throughout pages both in and out of order. MRR often returned to pages to work on them again, as she still does in other new bookworks/artists' books. Related, are ***False Fiction Fractured Fact- THE OTHER SIDE***, in 2008, a visual/asemic poem published 2009, on Michael Jacobson's blog gallery ***The New Post-Literate: A Gallery of Asemic Writing***. She has also published ***False Fiction Fractured Fact: take it with you***, 2008 at ***Otoliths***. Other works include an asemic computer collage, ***False Fiction Fractured Fact: THE OTHER SIDE*** created in 2008 and published again on ***The New Post-Literate.***

The concept started here with a new irritation, a bite of memory, and a triggered reference as a glimpse, with a ghost of an old idea. ***FALSE FICTION FRACTURED FACT ALTERED*** can be read, continuing in both directions, and so has two beginnings and possibly no end, spiraling around, as do most of MRR's bookworks, and can be read in more than one direction. So seeing is both forward and backward, up, down and around. Broken unity, and hesitations in continuity, are so often concretely expressed by the fragmented circle. But, the complete circle does convey the absence of interruption, and many circles, whole and part circles are here. There are fish in various places, which for decades are the metaphors for groups, family or specific personalities. The name of a fish, the type of fish, gives the clue to its reason for being in the space it occupies. Calligraphic marks can recount one side of abstract conversations. Sometimes the open folio is one thought, but most often the facing pages are in dialogue, sometimes in heated contrast and possibly interacting or playing with the pages before and those pages ahead. Calligraphic drawing marks, indecipherable language, Ideogrammatic language, asemic poetry, is the language without known language, before written language, the language beyond any language. Varieties of Ideogram languages/ asemic narratives, tell abstract stories, of course. Interacting within themselves and with the viewer/reader, the pages do ask- are we filled with drawings or poems? Altered and added marks, layered, have hints of depth, space, and sometimes of darkness. Images of objects, and new marks together with those from this earlier series, develop new groups of visual and asemic poems/drawings. 2018 computer collages are 90, or so, pages in this edition artists' book - ***FALSE FICTION FRACTURED FACT ALTERED***. - Marilyn R. Rosenberg

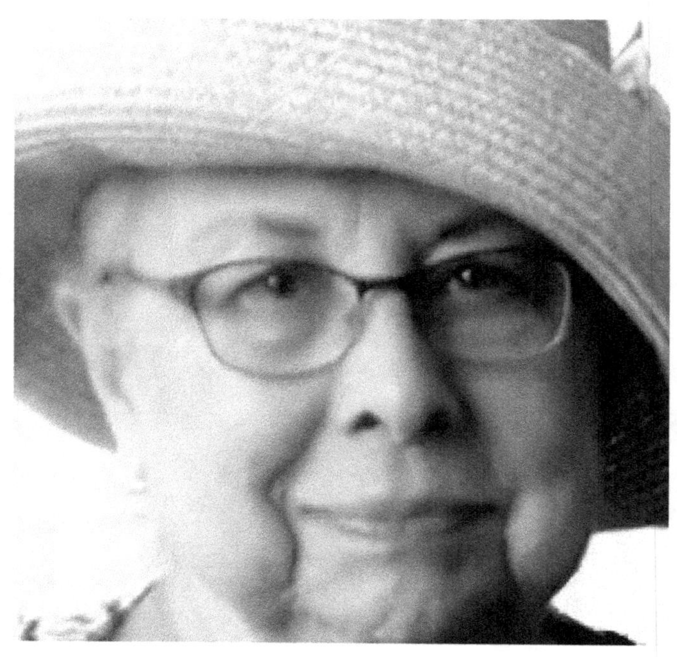

Born in Philadelphia PA, Marilyn R. Rosenberg is second generation in the USA and all of her family came from the Ukraine while it was under Russian rule. She and Bob have two daughters, 5 grandsons and one granddaughter. Through the years MRR has had a varied education, then in 1978, a Bachelor of Professional Studies in Studio Arts at Empire State College, State U of NY. In 1993 MRR graduated with a Master of Arts in Liberal Studies from the Graduate School of Arts and Science, New York University, NY, NY.

Marilyn R. Rosenberg, as usual, with actual and virtual collage, with pen and brush, stencils, ink, and gouache is making unique and edition images often in bookworks or artists' books. And using the mouse, the Mac, and scanner MRR makes marks, images and words. Since 1977 MRR has been in some one person exhibitions and very many international group exhibits. MRR's works are part of early mail art, and in current interactions. Ongoing MRR makes artists' stamps, bookmarks, artists' books, visual and asemic poetry. A small percentage are created with collaborators. Many unique sculptural bookworks, and published edition works, and works in catalogs, zines and anthologies can be found in university, college and museum library collections.